INTERSTELLAR GOTH PRINCESS BLUES

Lynn Ericson

ISBN-13: 978-1-956243-02-4

Library of Congress Control Number: 2022917062

LOST IN THE WOOD PRESS

www.lostinthewoodpress.com

Conway, Arkansas, U.S.A.

ACKNOWLEDGEMENTS

Cover Design by Peter O'Connor
https://bespokebookcovers.com

Copy Editing by Elise Williams Rikard
https://www.elisewilliamsrikard.com

Editorial Assistance provided by
Fellowship of Conway Literati

CHAPTER ONE

A PASSION FOR RESEARCH

"Get your head in the game!" Vanda whispered fiercely. "What are you even doing?!"

"What do you mean, what am I doing?" Lisette snapped, her jaw set. She stared back—defiant and unflinching—as they stood nose to nose, though she had to crane her neck back to meet the taller woman's gaze. "I'm diplomating! It's what we came for."

"You...are...flirting!" Vanda replied. "You know damn well you can't be flirting!"

"*I'm* flirting? *You're* flirting!" Lisette shot back.

"Yes!" Vanda managed to instill that single syllable from her dark-cherry lips with volumes of disdain. "I *do* that! *You* don't!"

They faced each other against the roiling red backdrop of a gas giant that dominated the bank of viewing ports behind them and the vast starscape beyond. The two women made such a striking visual contrast with each other it was hard not to believe the moment had been scripted. They did share a distant family resemblance in their long, dark hair and pale complexions—and both wore elegant, formal gowns—but there the similarities ended.

Vanda's hair hung straight and severe against a porcelain complexion ornately adorned with studs, and with an overt application of dark makeup. Her alluring, black gown hugged her figure suggestively.

The wavy curl of Lisette's hair, her flawlessly unblemished skin, and a restrained application of makeup that bordered on invisible, all worked in harmony to project a calculated air of youth and innocence. Her fitted ensemble of powder-blue lace spoke more of delicacy than sensuality, cementing that first impression of her in the process.

"Anyway, I'm not flirting," Lisette said, helpless to counter Vanda's logic. "I'm not flirting with anyone."

Vanda snorted. "Find yourself a mirror *fast*. Everyone can see it but you. The gossip's already buzzing behind your back. 'The Ice Princess is thawing!' The Ice Princess never thaws! The Ice Princess *can't* thaw!"

"I..." Lisette made to begin another retort but found her voice faltering.

"You were *smiling*," Vanda said with a snarl. "Smiling!"

"I...was?" Lisette could feel her own face falling.

"Oh yeah." Vanda gave a slow, accusatory nod. Vanda *excelled* at accusatory. Most of her predecessors had too, of course. Goth Princesses studied confrontation as part of the essential curriculum. Vanda, though, had achieved a special edge of her own that evoked the sharp menace of a primary school teacher pushed to the very brink of reason by a hopeless and arrogant student.

"Okay! Okay." Lisette's eyes fell guiltily. "Maybe I *was* flirting. I'll do better."

"You'll stay away from him is what you'll do," Vanda said firmly—if somewhat less harshly. "No more slip-ups."

"No more slip-ups," Lisette mumbled with a nod.

"Thank you." Vanda huffed out a long breath's worth of tension. "Take a few minutes. Pull yourself together. Go buy yourself a counselor, if that's what it takes. I've got to get back to the party."

Lisette bit her lip and fidgeted as she watched Vanda glide away down the curving outer corridor of the station, hair swaying like a metronome in an echo of her swaying hips. None of this was fair—not one bit of it. Lisette would have asked who'd died and made Vanda the Goth Princess, but that wasn't the real problem. The *real* problem was who had died and made Lisette the Ice Princess.

Lisette had found it kind of cool growing up knowing she was fourth in line for the title. That had been close enough to lend her some prestige and to buoy her childish dreams, but also far enough from the job that no one had really bothered training her up for it. Then adolescence had hit, and she'd become increasingly aware she'd dodged a bullet by not getting any closer to the responsibilities. Boys were cool. Men were awesome. And while the job didn't come with an actual vow of virginity, affecting a public air of disdain for the entire business of love, romance, and sex was non-negotiable. In a life almost devoid of privacy, that drained all the fun out of the game.

Lisette had been sixteen when the then-reigning Ice Princess had aged out of the job, leaving Lisette third in line. Then shortly after Lisette turned eighteen, the woman's successor managed to get herself killed in a tragic billiards accident, leaving Lisette second in line for the title. A year and a half later, cousin Cheela— whom Lisette had grown up with and quite liked—had stepped on her own train at a formal occasion and taken a tumble down an interminably long frozen staircase. The incident had left Cheela in a permanent vegetative coma and Lisette heir apparent to the Ice Princess crown. While that was going down, Cheela's rightful successor had been on interplanetary safari on the frozen tenth moon of Caryatis III, but she never returned—her entire party reportedly lost to an ambush by woolly tree frogs.

Lisette always secretly suspected the woman had eloped with her hunting partner, but she never dared voice the suspicion. Such a scandal could have torn apart an intricate web of diplomatic agreements shored up by little more than centuries of tradition.

Lisette might not have been properly prepared to plunge into the life of the Ice Princess, but she had always, always, *always* honored her responsibilities as a peer in the Xayarian Imperial House, and she cherished the peace it had achieved in its own small corner of the galaxy. Besides, she'd still be a youthful forty when she eventually passed on the crown and retreated into the ritual isolation of her retirement palace. There—she'd been quietly promised—no end of exciting debauchery awaited her, far from the prying eyes of the galaxy outside. It had seemed a fair deal at the time. Just now, though, she had to admit in her heart of hearts, that tantalizing life of self-indulgence felt so very, very far away. If she'd already been caught smiling in public, could she survive another seventeen years of this?

In silence, Lisette rested her hand on the transparent viewport wall that separated her from the endless void of space. She gazed longingly out past her own reflection at the swirling clouds of disorder that played across the surface of the planet below in all their brilliant shades of red, nearly red, and not-quite-so-red. *Such freedom in that chaos*, she noted wistfully. Yet, wasn't freedom just another word for nothing left to—

Her mind froze in mid-thought as a dark reflection suddenly loomed over her own. Involuntarily she yelped and spun, appalled at how completely she'd lost any pretense of detached stoicism as she felt herself throw her arms up to protect herself.

"My apologies, Your Highness. I hadn't meant to startle you." The Ivurnian ambassador loomed no less for that apology. The man had been custom-built for looming—perhaps literally. In the right light—or more to the point, the right lack of light—he might have passed for fully human. Even, then, though, he'd have been passing for a very shaggy human newly rescued from a shipwreck on some distant planet, who'd been loaned a fine suit to wear but had not yet been afforded the luxury of other personal grooming. He did keep his beard neatly braided, though.

"I, umm...yes. Of course," Lisette said, smoothing down the front of her dress, though it really didn't need any smoothing. "Apology accepted," she added coolly, happy to feel her mask falling back into place and her heart rate slowing as she schooled her expression back to one of unconcerned politeness. "I trust you will accept mine as well, Ambassador L'Roux, for my inappropriate slips of decorum this evening."

"Slips?" The ambassador arched a brow over one cat-like eye. It was a very green eye—deep, midnight green. "I'd thought you'd been delightful."

"The ambassador is most chivalrous," Lisette said serenely, "but I'm sure he is mistaken. I do not do delightful. For me there is only duty and cold, hard logic."

"Again, my apologies, Highness," the man said with a polite half-bow. "But in this instance, it is not 'the ambassador' who is mistaken."

Do not flirt. Do not flirt. Do not flirt. Yet for all her efforts at maintaining the mask, Lisette noticed she was biting the corner of her lip again. Through force of will, she relaxed her jaw back into a neutral position, then gave herself a good, mental slap. "Do not allow your chivalry to give way to impertinence," she scolded, turning her back on him again to stare out at the stars. When she glanced up, though, she could see his reflection meeting her gaze.

Beneath all of that unruly mane, Ambassador Yauhiri L'Roux was a handsome man. He was a devilishly handsome man—all six-feet-and-a-generous-amount-of-change of him. Lisette shivered under his gaze despite herself—and despite all her training. "You should go," she concluded quietly, breaking her gaze away from his.

"If you wish," Yauhiri replied evenly.

Lisette didn't hear him moving away, but when she looked up again he'd traveled halfway back to the door to the crowded banquet hall. Without turning around she continued to stare at his back until he'd covered half the remaining distance. "Ambassador?" She said it quietly, but he immediately stopped to glance back over his shoulder, cocking a bestial ear. "Where are you going?" Lisette heard herself ask.

"Her Highness asked me to leave," Yauhiri said flatly.

"And the ambassador said if I wished." Lisette's voice remained small, uncertain—a stranger to her own mouth. She glanced down again, only to be startled a moment later when a clawed hand slammed into the heavy window beside her face.

"Do not presume to play games with me, Highness," Yauhiri growled threateningly. "The geneticists may have left me looking like a simple beast, but never mistake me for one. I am welcome or I am not. I am here or I am gone. I am no one's lapdog to stand in the doorway, begging for permission."

"Forgive me again," she said, the penitence showing through her wavering mask, "but I do not want you to leave. It's not my place to want anything at all."

"That may be the single most pathetic thing I've ever heard," Yauhiri replied, though his voice softened and he withdrew his arm. "I'd been assured that Xayarians cut the beating heart out of their Ice Princess as part of her coronation, but I can hear yours pounding from a room away. They told me that they freeze the very blood in her veins, but I can feel the heat pouring off you like a blast furnace. There's not one iota of cold to you, Highness. You're one of the most alive creatures I've ever met."

"And don't you presume to play games with me!" Lisette rounded on Yauhiri in a rage, letting out three solid years of repression in a single burst. "Yes, I'm a fraud! Do you think I *like* living like this?! This thing is bigger than me or you or...or...any of this!" She gestured sweepingly, in an effort that could have been meant to take in the whole space station, but might as easily have been targeting the entire solar system and places beyond. "I might be the biggest fraud in the galaxy," Lisette snarled, "but I'm a fraud with responsibilities to honor. Then here you come reeking of barely contained power and lust, and do you turn it on the Goth Princess right in front of you?! No! You single out the one woman on the entire station who can't have you! The one woman who can't even admit to wanting you! What kind of insane—"

Then Yauhiri was kissing her, clawed hands locked tightly on her arms and pulling her to him. The next thing Lisette knew she was kissing him back, with hunger and urgency, every thought that she shouldn't be doing this banished from her—

"Wow," Sylvie chuckled. "How many times have you watched this episode?"

"What?" The non-sequitur snapped Lenore back to reality, breaking the spell. She could feel a flush rise on her cheeks as she emotionally disengaged from the actress she'd been watching. As she did, the object of their shared lust retreated back into the larger-than-life but distressingly flat private theater screen.

"You've been mouthing every line like you have it memorized," Sylvie said. "Or half the lines, anyway."

"Uh huh," Lenore grunted. She fumbled for the remote and froze the incipient lovers in their passionate embrace before powering down the screen. "Well, you know my memory. I can recite a nonsense ritual back verbatim after hearing it two or three times."

"How many times for *that* one?" the redhead grinned, nodding toward the dark screen.

"This makes...maybe twenty-three?" Lenore admitted sheepishly, while consciously choosing to not mention this was the first time she'd ever watched it without her mom in the room. She also breezed past any mention of all the times she'd read the novelization of the episode. She'd completely lost count of those, anyway, and could only have testified she'd worn the covers off the paperback.

Watching the show now had supposedly been combining research into the setting for their coven's next expedition with Lenore's personal research for her *Beauty and the Bestiary* blog. Her own interest in the *SJZ* universe largely began and ended with Ambassador L'Roux. Lenore much preferred a modern Gothic atmosphere to *SJZ's* space opera setting, despite a familial connection to the making of the show.

"You know, that guy looks a bit like—" Sylvie began.

"He does, doesn't he?" Lenore agreed without waiting for Sylvie to finish the sentence. There was no question that Sylvie had been going to say Alek Raine, the male lead of the best television show ever: *Dark Legacy*. The resemblance between the two actors was there. This guy wasn't him, though. Alek had never appeared in any episode of any incarnation of *SJZ*, and he'd been too young for this incarnation of *SJZ* when it was filmed back around the turn of the millennium.

It was likely no coincidence that Lenore's friends and family saw something of Alek in every guy she showed an interest in. Clearly, Alek was just her type, physically speaking. But whose type wouldn't he be?

"Speaking of which, you know I'm insanely jealous," Lenore said good-naturedly.

"Hey, I'm *not* sleeping with Alek Raine," Sylvie said, holding up her hands placatingly.

"No," Lenore agreed. "But you've slept with Diana Taylor *and* Felicity Ward—at the same time!—which is basically your version of the same thing."

"You know I never would have told you that story if we'd done anything *but* sleep, right?" Sylvie said, rolling her eyes. "Plus, they were on my 'to meet' list, never my 'to sleep with' list. I kinda think Alek is on your 'sleep' list. And you *have* met him."

"Casually, yeah," Lenore said. "Briefly. The point is Diana and Felicity are the stars of your favorite movies ever, and here you are now, practically besties. Don't even get me started about you meeting Lark and Holly."

"Yeah. Okay. Meeting Lark and Holly was a bit...over the top," Sylvie admitted.

Lenore snorted back a laugh. Lark Starling and Holly Marsh were fictional characters—the same fictional characters Diana Taylor and Felicity Ward had risen to stardom playing—yet in defiance of all sanity and logic, Sylvie had met both *characters* personally, in addition to the two actresses.

"You know what?" Sylvie said at last. "Go ahead and be jealous. It's fair."

"Thank you," Lenore replied with exaggerated graciousness.

"On the plus side, maybe you're about to meet Mister Ambassador there." Sylvie nodded toward the dark screen again.

"That would be most excellent," Lenore agreed, "but you know what I *really* want is to meet Scott and Cyn Legacy. That's the only thing that would make us even for you getting to meet Lark and Holly."

"Don't worry. I'm sure we'll get to visit *Dark Legacy* at some point," Sylvie said, "but this'll be your first time spending more than a few hours across a narrative bridge, and you know it's gotta be dangerous stepping into a monster-of-the-week show like that. *Not* the best place to start."

"I know. I know." Lenore sighed. "I still wanna."

"You wouldn't be Lenore if you didn't." Sylvie grinned.

"Darn straight," Lenore agreed.

"Anyway, have you finished your research?" Sylvie asked. "I came in because Brian's finished the paper that was hanging over his head, and he's more than ready for a mental break if you're still up for running a game."

CHAPTER TWO

STRANGER THAN FICTION

"The shaggy creature shakes off the effect of its fall into the old zoo enclosure and rolls over on its haunches," Lenore announced. "Now that it's out in the moonlight, you get your first good look at it. Its sheer bulk and muscle suggest some hybrid of grizzly bear and gorilla. The thing throws its head back and roars, revealing a mouthful of shark-like teeth—then the creature hurls itself up the wall of the enclosure toward you. Its powerful claws gouge their own holds out of the solid concrete."

"Well that's lovely," Sylvie said, her mouth twisting wryly. "Can I sense if the thing brought any backup?" Her dice clattered across the table in Lenore's cozy sitting room, and Sylvie recorded the willpower use on her character sheet.

"You let your mind slip outside the time stream," Lenore narrated. "Only seconds into the future you can see two more of the things leap from high windows in the wall of the reptile house behind you. In your vision, one of them lands right on top of Krista. Bones crack in her ribcage as its claws tear mercilessly at her flesh."

Sylvie turned to face Diana in the seat beside her before intoning, "'Behind you! There!'" in the slightly off voice she always used for speaking as her character.

"'Take them! This one's mine!'" declared Loki, the rosette-spotted house cat sitting beside Diana's elbow, before addressing Lenore directly. "I leap into the enclosure, trying to land on its face."

Diana—an elegant, dark-skinned woman somewhere in her late twenties, whose artfully unruly curls were familiar to anyone who'd ever seen a *Lovelace* movie—picked up a couple of dice and dropped them on the top of a miniature plastic castle tower in front of Loki. The cat proceeded to bat them into a hole in the middle of the tower's roof, where they rattled down a chute and out the door of the tower before bouncing to a stop.

"Yes!" Loki declared excitedly. "A plus seven! Take that, you ape-bear thing!"

Sometimes it amazed Lenore how quickly she'd become accustomed to the whole "talking cat" phenomenon, but mostly...well, she *had* become accustomed to it. Loki was just Loki.

"Take that indeed." Lenore grinned. "The creature gives out a shriek as a quarter-ton of tiger hits it square in the face. You both go plunging back down into the enclosure, and it hits its head hard on the concrete at the foot of the wall. What are you doing, Diana?"

"I spin and aim my shotgun for those windows," Diana said. It was her character, Krista, who'd been assaulted in the vision. "I'll shoot anything up there that moves, then dive for cover."

It was no less weird to Lenore, when she stopped to think of it, how quickly Diana Taylor had become just "Diana." The former actress had decided she was done with the industry life after the last of the *Lovelace* movies had wrapped, and walked out at the summit of a brief but meteoric career. She remained a legend among fantasy fans as the living embodiment of Lark

Starling, apprentice enchantress at the Lovelace Community College of Applied Magic.

Even weirder was thinking about how readily Diana sat down to act out imaginary adventures with them after everything she'd seen and done since retiring from acting. Diana had been the one who'd discovered magic was really real. She'd been the one to find an old, Victorian-era journal full of magic rituals and used it to form her own coven. She had been—and remained—the one to lead that coven into fantastical worlds everyone else could only dream of visiting. Yet for all her drive and all her experiences, Diana remained the same disarmingly charming woman who'd always seen herself as a fantasy-fan first and an actress second. To her, the line between imagination and actual magic had blurred into meaninglessness, and she reveled in both.

"What about you, Brian?" Lenore asked the last of her players for the evening—whom she suspected of having a hand on Sylvie's knee under the table. Brian was one more thing Lenore allowed herself to be jealous about. It wasn't Brian specifically she envied, though. She did like him, but she didn't *like* like him.

He was cute enough, certainly, and gave off just enough of a bad-boy vibe to make him interesting when—as now—he forgot to shave for a day or two. But what Lenore really envied Sylvie was the *concept* of Brian. The two hadn't openly announced themselves to be an item, but it was obvious to anyone with eyes that they were sleeping together. Lenore would have been thrilled to have her bed a little less to herself.

"I'll grab the zoologist by the arm," Brian said, "and drag her away from the action—literally, if I have to."

"She's too stunned by the sight of the beast to put up much of a fight against that even if she wanted to," Lenore announced. "You've nearly pulled her back as far as the entrance to the old aviary when you hear glass shattering, followed immediately by the blast of Krista's shotgun.

"And I think that," Lenore added, changing the cadence of her voice, "needs to be our cliffhanger for the evening. Some of us have a world to explore tomorrow—and unless I missed something, none of us has had dinner yet."

She hadn't missed anything. They ordered Thai, then wandered out together from Lenore's bungalow, across the dark studio grounds.

"I hate your cliffhangers, you know," Brian said.

"I do know." Lenore grinned. "And yet you keep coming back."

Formerly the abandoned Wintermotion Studios, the compound had been renamed and reimagined as Freyjur Studios, now under renovation to become the dedicated clubhouse of their little coven, the Freyjur. The name—which they pronounced "FRAY-ur"—had originated as a shortening of "The Sororital Order of the Freyjur," a secret, Victorian-era coven of high-born, hedonistic witches who'd assembled the spellbook Diana had discovered. And according to Diana, "freyjur" was the old Norse word for "ladies," with the singular version of the word—"freyja"—being identical to the name of Norse pantheon's equivalent of Aphrodite.

Brian and Loki weren't ladies, of course, but they weren't really part of the coven either. Brian had pronounced himself more than busy enough with law school to try learning magic on top of it just now, and the cat simply hadn't been built to execute human-developed rituals. The two called themselves the coven's "auxiliary," and that conveniently left the appropriateness of the name intact.

When Lenore had first moved out to Los Angeles as the newest member of the Freyjur, she'd crashed for a couple of weeks in Felicity's guest house. The second-most senior witch in the coven, Felicity had been Diana's co-star in the *Lovelace* movies. Unlike Diana, Felicity had continued to pursue an acting career and remained a fairly hot commodity in the business, so she maintained a nice little mansion a reasonable distance from the studios, and she bankrolled most of the coven's expenses as it pushed the frontiers of arcane knowledge. The previous weekend, though, Lenore had moved into the studio grounds where a private bungalow had been renovated for each of the six full members of the coven. Having lucked into her own rent-free place in L.A. was amazing. But—

"You okay in there?" Diana asked her.

"Hmmm? Yeah. Sorry," Lenore said, looking around at the odd mixture of bright, newly renovated buildings and sadly neglected old ones. "This place is just a bit gloomy still."

Diana nodded her understanding. "We'll have it cheery soon enough. They were still using the place for ghost tours when we bought it."

Lenore just nodded. As a girl, she'd visited the studio on one of those tours herself. Wintermotion Studios could boast a very storied history involving supposed curses, deaths, and ghostly encounters. The ghost tour company had intentionally left the lot a bit overgrown, and they'd done little or nothing to keep up the buildings. Whoever Felicity had contracted to fix up the old compound had clearly done more basic maintenance for it in a few weeks than had been done for it in the previous twenty years.

Gloom made an interesting place to visit, but Lenore had always hated living in it. That was why—to her parents' horror—she'd dyed her hair pink during her rebellious teen years and kept it that color ever since. Seeing some of the old buildings here repaired and repainted, and seeing all the grass trimmed up into something resembling manicured lawns was...nice. Still, it all came at a cost.

As the gloom of the studio faded, so did its sense of history—its melancholy. Melancholy could be cool. She already found herself missing it.

The little gaming group hung around chatting at the front gate until their late dinner arrived, then took it back to Diana's bungalow with its larger sitting room. There, the conversation continued for another hour, somehow covering anything, everything, and nothing at all. That, too, was nice. It was really nice. Lenore did feel just a little bit like a fifth wheel—with Sylvie snuggled up in Brian's arms on the couch and Loki curled up on Diana's lap while she stroked his ears—but mostly there was just an atmosphere of easy-going camaraderie and fun. It felt amazing...until it didn't.

By the end of that hour, Lenore found herself playing out emotionally—feeling fretful and nervous, and becoming increasingly silent. Nothing had overtly changed. It was only that—in Lenore's experience—friends had become semi-mythical creatures she bumped into every few months at a fantasy convention, or who simply lived on the other end of the Internet. She wasn't devoid of social skills, but the ones she possessed were very context-based. Being able to tell an engaging horror story at the gaming table didn't mean she wouldn't turn around later and start babbling inane fan trivia when she got nervous. It didn't mean she wouldn't get too clingy or too contrary or remain uncomfortably distant.

Lenore had found she could get by socially when she had a script to follow or could throw herself briefly into a role. She could also get by when she could stop and re-think each sentence before hitting "send." She could even get by just when people weren't forced to overdose on her individual quirks. But scripts ran out, roles became exhausting, and she couldn't "text in" her position with the coven. Sooner or later, someone here would overdose on her if they hadn't already. Everything would go downhill from there. It always did. She was simply a person best experienced in small vignettes. In the meantime, she'd try to prove she was valuable enough as a researcher that they might let her stay with a supporting role in the coven. Then she could keep the bungalow long enough for her to finish college and land a real job.

Eventually the post-dinner conversation had Lenore feeling awkward enough she chose to close her mouth completely before anyone could comment on how weird she was getting. The others had more than enough to talk about without her contributions anyway. She was working on her exit strategy when Diana offered an opening by asking her if she was all right.

"Tired," Lenore said, backing the assertion up with a wan smile. "I think I'd better crawl off to bed before I crash on your carpet."

"You're more than welcome to it." Diana grinned. "I could scrounge you up a pillow."

"Thanks. I think I can hold it together long enough for a five-minute walk," Lenore said, working to keep the tired smile up. "Good night, everyone."

"Thanks for the game," Sylvie said from where she remained cuddled up against Brian.

"Yeah. It was fun," Brian seconded. "Looking forward to finishing it."

"Looking forward to sidewalk-stomping more ape-bears," Loki added.

"Yeah. Good night, guys." Lenore got up and made her way back to her own bungalow. It didn't nearly take her a full five minutes.

Hold it together, girl. Nothing went wrong. Absolutely nothing.

But it was one thing to tell herself that and another entirely to convince her fight-or-flight instinct. Peopling was hard, plain and simple. Hanging out with them always devolved into going on high alert, trying to read everyone and every situation, trying not to look like an idiot. Always the let-down followed as ebbing adrenalin left her with the shakes and the doubts—so many doubts.

Lenore locked herself in for the night and made her rounds of the bungalow, making sure she was quite alone before stripping off her clothes and climbing into the shower—not that there was any chance anyone had broken into the studio unannounced. Perimeter security had been the top priority when renovation started, and the coven had bolstered electronic surveillance with magical wards. Lenore didn't particularly need to clean up right now, either. She just needed something to take the edge off her nerves before she'd be able to sleep.

She closed her eyes and leaned back into the strong, warm pulse of the shower, trying to relax while the voices in her head recited their litany of every misstep she'd made that day and all their dreadful expectations of how she'd muck up tomorrow. When she opened her eyes again, she let out a yelp, took an involuntary step back, and nearly lost her footing.

"Hey. Is it okay if I join you?"

Lenore sank down to the bottom of the tub and whimpered, ignoring the water pouring over her head as she clutched at the shin she'd just banged. "Do I have a choice?" she enunciated carefully and angrily as she stared up with blurred vision at the naked woman standing at the other end of the tub.

"Are you okay?" the woman asked with concern.

"No, I am *not* okay!" Lenore snapped. "I slammed my effing shin into the edge of the tub. I thought we'd settled this!"

"Sorry! Sorry," the woman said apologetically. "You know I hate to shower alone. I still can't shake that new Hitchcock film. You've seen it, haven't you? I wouldn't want to ruin it for you."

"Yes, I've seen it!" Lenore snapped. No child of her mother's could have made it through adolescence without being exposed to the entire Hitchcock library. "But it doesn't give you the right to barge into my shower!"

"*Our* shower," the woman insisted, "until the studio gets this mess sorted out. I still can't believe they did this to us. My contract clearly states that I get a space to myself, but momma didn't raise me to be some self-obsessed fool. I'm not going to throw you out. We'll figure out how to make this work. And in the meantime, I don't have to shower alone! Thank you so much for that."

Lenore let out a tortured sigh and just sat glowering at the woman while she waited for the worst of the pain to pass, berating herself the whole time for getting into this mess. All she'd wanted was to prove for once that she belonged somewhere—that her best was finally good enough.

She'd been invited into the coven based on her supposed natural gift for rituals, and trying her hand at the "willing spirit" ritual the others hadn't managed to get results from seemed like the natural place for her to start. They'd left the ritual out of her beginner's spellbook, but Diana sometimes enlisted Lenore into helping with spells she was having problems with, and Lenore had made a point of committing that one to memory for herself when she'd discovered it. She'd run a phonetic comparison on the chant with the rituals in the beginner's book and tried tweaking a few of the syllables that might have been transcribed badly. She'd also ignored the very bland and generic list of spell components and had tried adding a personal touch for the spirit she'd tried to contact. In the end, she finally did get results, albeit imperfect ones. This wasn't how the spell was supposed to behave.

Lenore had managed to contact the raven-haired '50s bombshell Denise Drake, who'd tragically died on the grounds back in 1961. That part had gone as expected. Rather than returning to whence she'd come after they'd finished a nice chat, though, Denise had made herself at home and decided she and Lenore were not merely roommates, but that they were roommates with absolutely no sense of boundaries.

Mercifully, that hadn't turned Denise into a constant presence. Lenore hadn't seen the dead woman at all for a couple of days, and had let herself start hoping Denise had finally gone. But when the woman was present, she was *very* present.

"My life is so weird," Lenore muttered as she watched Denise reach past her to grab for the soap.

CHAPTER THREE

BLITHE SPIRIT

One of the upsides of having Denise for a roommate was she seemed to have a memory like a sieve. That made meaningful communication difficult, yes, but while Lenore could hardly move the needle of Denise's comprehension for the better, it had proved every bit as hard for her to move it for the worse. Every slight or disagreement slipped out of Denise's mind within five minutes, and then she'd return to her usual, cheerful self as if nothing had ever happened, whether Lenore apologized or not.

Hardly anything that had occurred after Denise's death seemed to stick with her for long. At most she'd hold onto it until she vanished for what might have passed for a good night's sleep, then she'd return with the information completely re-framed to fit a narrative in which time had stopped back in 1961. The overall effect left Denise seeming like some sort of advanced chat bot who could hold very lucid conversations, up until the moment you realized she'd completely lost the context of what you'd been talking about ten minutes ago. Mercifully, when things were going well, that seemed to make it easier for Lenore to relax around Denise than to relax around most of the living. Lenore felt like she was dealing with a pet that alternated between exasperating and adorable. Denise was never going to judge her unless she did something deeply, overtly wicked.

When Lenore eventually emerged from the bathroom, wrapped in a fluffy pink towel from the set she'd bought to match her hair, she found Denise there, also wrapped in a towel, albeit one Lenore had never seen before. Denise glanced back from sorting through the wardrobe to flash Lenore a smile. "Thanks for indulging my sillies," she said. "And break a leg tomorrow."

"Thanks. You too," Lenore said, before muttering, "Not that I'm an actress or anything."

"Hey now! Some folk look down on television acting, but not me," Denise said with deep sincerity. "A paycheck's a paycheck." She pulled out an elegant nightgown of satin and lace from the wardrobe and proceeded to unselfconsciously trade out her towel for it.

Like the towel, Lenore had never seen that particular nightgown before. She certainly hadn't placed it in the wardrobe, and the wardrobe had been empty when Lenore had moved in. Whatever else might be true about the afterlife, it appeared to have a well-managed props department.

"Umm...You know there's only one bed?" Lenore pointed out, eyeing the nightgown with some trepidation. This marked the first time Denise had visibly prepared to settle in for the night. When Lenore had considered the pleasures of a less lonely bed, this wasn't at all what she'd had in mind.

"In the theater they used to look down on us movie actors the way movie people look down on television today," Denise said, perching on the corner of that lone bed. "Everything new is bad, right? Cheap and inferior? It's a phase the public will get over? Me, I think television's here to stay, but what do I know? I'm just some brainless set of measurements that's really good at filling out a dress. The world will forget me before I turn thirty-five."

"You do good work," Lenore said, her instinct to provide comfort overcoming her annoyance with the ghost. "I really like your films. It's not your fault they never made better parts for you." She dug around in a drawer until she found one of the oversized t-shirts she used as a night dress.

"Hardly matters *why* I don't get better parts, does it?" Denise said. "I'll still wind up forgotten, and I'll be out of a career before that, so it's all about the paycheck, right? Get it while you can and marry well while you're still a commodity.

"Sorry," Denise added after a pause. "Not meaning to play the wet blanket. My point is just that we're *both* getting paid. Hooray for us!" She grinned.

Lenore—who had ducked back into the bathroom while Denise was talking—re-emerged in a well-worn, pink t-shirt bearing the caption, "I'm not a vampire. My reflection is just on strike."

"So you start filming on this Star Jockey thing tomorrow?" Denise asked.

"I...Yeah," Lenore said. "Space Jockey. It's *Space Jockey Zero*." Had she mentioned anything about the *SJZ* project around Denise? She couldn't remember doing it. Of course, just because she couldn't see the ghost at any given moment didn't mean the ghost wasn't there. The dead were notorious for that.

"Oh, right: like the Raymond Carr serial. I saw those in the theater when I was a kid. So who's your character?" Denise asked. "Is it a big part?"

"The Ice Princess, Lisette Winquist," Lenore said, offering up the first thought that would keep this conversation sounding like a conversation. Things could get unnerving around Denise when she was given too many unexpected responses to deal with. "It's not a star role, but I'll get to be a love interest for a while."

"Ooh. Fun. Who gets to melt you?" Denise asked with a playful wink. "Anybody I know?"

"Probably not. Look, I really need some sleep, so could you—" Before she could finish the sentence, Lenore realized with a start that Denise had abruptly vanished. She'd been left talking to herself.

"Ummm...Denise? Hello?" Lenore waited—listening through several heartbeats, then several more. After that she kept listening for most of a minute, finally spun around scanning the room visually a few times, then gave up and crawled into bed with some relief. "Thanks?" she ventured, in case the disappearance had happened in response to her aborted request.

Still, she tossed and turned for a while, all planned benefits of the shower undone by her unannounced visitor. In the end, she turned on the decadently large television that had come pre-installed on the wall of her bedroom and streamed an episode of *Dark Legacy* to fall asleep to. No matter how cordial Denise had always been, there was something inherently nerve-wracking about the knowledge a dead woman might intrude on her privacy again at any moment. Alone in this otherwise private space, silence left nothing else in her head to push out that thought.

When sleep still eluded Lenore, she considered tracking down the scene from *SJZ* that Sylvie had interrupted earlier, with the thought of maybe sinking even deeper into the fantasy and releasing some tensions, but the potential for Denise reappearing randomly, and with even more embarrassing timing than in the shower, quickly killed that idea. Lenore resigned herself to letting the familiar dialog of Cyn and Scott Legacy at least lull her into a sort of numb detachment if not true sleep.

She had finally just entered a comfortable half-dream state when the warm sensation of an arm draping itself across her shoulder cut persistently through the mental haze and refused to be dispelled. Lenore tried to mumble discouragements to Denise, but must have fallen fully asleep at some point before that, because her body remained locked in paralysis.

An actual dream, then, and not a ghost? Probably. And that was the last coherent thought she had for the night.

Lenore woke with the background buzz of generalized anxiety still plaguing her. It wasn't Denise's fault. It wasn't anyone's fault. That was just the price she paid for having a social life. Basking in the warmth for a while always ended with her doing time in an emotional dungeon. Lenore wondered for the thousandth time whether she needed meds or a therapist or something.

At least she'd ridden out the initial letdown in the night. Social disaster felt like a less impending doom than it had when she'd fallen asleep, and she still had the morning to herself. There would be time to put her game face back on before the big adventure began.

Lenore wandered through the bungalow checking for ghosts again. She'd never seen much of Denise during daylight hours—morning least of all—but any time Lenore could start a visitation on her own terms seemed to be a win. When she was actively looking for Denise, Lenore could drop into game master mode on sight and take charge of the situation. Even better, if she could be the first one to speak, she'd found she could "set the scene" for Denise, suggesting the shape their chat would be taking. If Denise had been nearly as good at stepping into her role in life as she was in death, she must have been a director's dream.

Once Lenore was as satisfied as she could be that she was alone, she treated herself to another shower and emerged feeling human enough to actually enjoy her morning coffee, half of a leftover donut, and a few more minutes of her favorite SJZ episode before she heard the sound of the front door opening. Since every living soul in the compound would have had the decency to knock—and since Lenore had made sure the front door was still locked and bolted when she did her morning rounds—that could only mean one thing.

A moment later, Denise came breezing into the sitting room, dropping her handbag and shedding her once-fashionable coat as she came. Both objects vanished within moments of leaving her hands.

"Silly me," Denise laughed. "I got all the way to the sound stage, and no one was there. Completely forgot we weren't shooting today. I should go to the zoo or something like real people do with a day off. You want to come?"

The question actually came out sounding a little desperate—like Denise really didn't know what to do with down time and was hoping for a tour guide to show her how it worked—and Lenore couldn't escape an uncomfortable pang of guilt for turning her down. "I have to be on set right after lunch. Sorry."

"Oh." Denise chewed on her lip for a moment before rallying with a smile. "Well, that's nifty. I thought you weren't starting until tomorrow."

Lenore shrugged, not sure what to say to that. There wasn't exactly anything to be gained by pointing out Denise had also thought she'd be starting tomorrow back when tomorrow was today. "It got moved up," she said finally.

"That's great," Denise said. "Hey, would it bother you if I sweet talk my way in to watch? My nephew loves space operas. I need to start collecting autographs for him—starting with yours."

"Why not." Lenore shrugged again. If Denise couldn't be trusted to keep quiet and out from underfoot when she thought the cameras were rolling on someone else's set, when could she be trusted? Lenore really didn't expect to see Denise that afternoon at all, though, based on her habits to date.

"He'd be over the moon if I can get hold of a prop ray gun or something like that for him," Denise said. "Any idea who I'd need to flirt with to make that happen?"

"I...don't know. No," Lenore admitted. "Would it help if I can get you one? Is that like, you know...unfinished business for you?"

Denise laughed brightly. "I wouldn't be asking if it was finished! But it's not a big deal if it would be awkward. I love Charlie to bits, but he can live without a television prop."

"You're sure?"

"Pretty sure. Yeah." Denise didn't have much success stifling her laughter, but Lenore gave her credit for trying. "Hey! You were going to tell me who's your make-out partner!"

"No one you'd know." It was a pretty safe bet Lenore could kiss everyone she encountered on this upcoming expedition and not one of them would have been anyone Denise remembered. The version of the show she was expecting to visit had been made closer to now than to the end of Denise's abbreviated life.

"Raymond's not doing the show, is he?" Denise asked. "If he was playing your guy I'd have to steal the part from you."

"I'm sure they couldn't afford him," Lenore said.

Denise sighed. "You're a hopeless gossip."

"I am? What did I say?" Lenore asked.

"Pretty much nothing," Denis huffed. "Like I said: hopeless. Do you know how long it's been since I've had time for a date? Feed my fantasies already. By authority vested in me as Hollywood royalty, I'm sending you on a quest to bring me sordid gossip. Name me some names. Paint me a scandalously fun picture about someone, even if it's second- or third-hand news. Make it all up if you have to! What's the point of even having a roommate if you can't stay up all night together drinking things you shouldn't and talking about things you shouldn't?"

"Make it up?"

"If you have to." Denise threw up her hands. "Oh, never mind. You're right. What's the use?"

"You've, ummm…You've lost me," Lenore said.

"Yeah." Denise gave a resigned sigh. "Sounds about right." Suddenly she was wearing the coat again and clutching her handbag with both hands. "Anyway, I just had an amazing idea.

I'll bet I can get Charlie to play hooky and go to the zoo with me. His mom already thinks I'm a bad influence. Might as well prove her right."

"I...can make up gossip," Lenore said, feeling suddenly, unaccountably miserable. And she absolutely could make up gossip—that was just basic game mastering—but Denise had already left the room, and a moment later Lenore heard the front door open and close. If she went and checked, she knew she'd still find it locked and bolted. It had been every time she'd checked before.

"I didn't deserve that," Lenore told the remaining half of her donut. "I totally didn't." The donut didn't argue with her. It did, however, seem to stare at her reproachfully. She tossed it down onto the coffee table in disgust. Then she went to fetch paper and a sharpie, wrote out, "Debug that damned spell already!" in big, blocky letters, and taped it to the bathroom mirror. She wouldn't be able to concentrate properly on the problem right now even if there'd been time. It would have to wait until she got back.

CHAPTER FOUR

COVEN BUSINESS

"I am so tired," Felicity said. With a heavy sigh, the angel-faced blond woman sank into her favorite reclining chaise in the coven's informal conference room. They'd set it up in an old prop warehouse that had been completely restored on the outside and completely refurbished on the inside to serve as the heart of the coven's operation. They'd expanded the original office space in one corner of the warehouse, adding a few essential rooms. The entire second floor of it had been given over to this space that resembled Lenore's decadent imaginings of a working lounge in some booming Silicon Valley startup back in the giddy early years of the World Wide Web. They'd all gathered there now—the six active members of the coven and their two-member auxiliary—for final preparation on the new expedition.

The seven humans in attendance had decked themselves out in the height of *SJZ* cosplay couture courtesy of Margaret Caverly, the actual costume designer from the *SJZ: Electricity* incarnation of the series. Surprisingly, that hadn't been arranged through Felicity's studio connections—or even through Diana's—but through Lenore's. Lenore hadn't watched that one particular episode of *SJZ* so many times *just* because she had a bit of a fangirl thing for Ambassador Yauhiri L'Roux. And her mother hadn't grown up as just any Goth girl: she'd been a *professional* Goth girl. More specifically, Lenore's mother had been—and still attended fan conventions as—Amelina Mallory.

Amelina's acting career hadn't been long, and it hadn't been particularly noteworthy to anyone but *SJZ* fans. But to them she would always be Vanda Malette, *the* Xayarian Goth Princess. The family resemblance between Lenore and Vanda didn't immediately jump out at most people. That was partly because Lenore took more after her father, but mostly it was because Amelina Mallory would rather have eaten shards of glass than be seen with pink hair. All that aside, the story told within the family was that Amelina had been so stunned with the Goth Princess costume Margaret had made for her, she wept tears of joy the first time she saw herself in it. Thus began a life-long friendship that had endured long after Amelina gave up the lights of Hollywood for the lights of Vegas. That's how Lenore had grown up with an "Auntie Margaret" who'd made all her Halloween costumes as a kid and whom she still saw at least two or three times a year.

Auntie Margaret never disappointed when it came to any kind of cosplay, but she'd outdone herself this time; not surprising, considering making costumes for the coven had been a high-budget, paying gig for her, and she remained the ultimate authority on turn-of-the-millennium *SJZ* costuming. As a personal favor, she'd even made Lenore's tunic-dress costume in her favorite shade of pink. No pink version of that costume had ever appeared on film, but one *had* been worn by a one-shot character in a comic book once, so when the others had given her a good-natured hard time about it, Lenore had been ready to defend the outfit as canon—to the death, if necessary. Some might consider that a strange hill to die on, but it was *her* hill— and it was a pink hill.

"I'm tired of people being cruel," Felicity finally added after a long pause. "I'm tired of people being greedy. I'm tired of people being selfish and petty and foolish. Mostly I'm tired of people dying. I'm sick of it. I'm sick of feeling like I'm drowning every time I look at my phone. I'm ready for it to all stop."

She tugged at an opal ring on her finger—twisting until it came off—and held it up demonstratively. "And one of the worst parts? We've got these lovely, lovely little trinkets, but even with our resources we have to ration them. Not one of us has had a single day sick since we put these on. I want soooo much to hand them out like candy, but they are *insanely* expensive to make. I cannot say this enough: do not, do not, do *not* lose yours." She twisted the ring back onto her finger as a hush fell over the room.

"So...it's bad?" Diana finally asked quietly.

"Inoperable," Felicity muttered, staring at her feet. "Advanced. I gave Val a ring—told her it was for luck, asked her not to take it off—but I don't expect it to help. Long shot at best, from what we know about how they work."

"Her kid sister," Diana explained to the questioning eyes. "I'm so sorry, Fel. I assume this is why you bumped *SJZ* to the top of our list though?"

"Yeah. I've never told Val—told *any* of my family—about all this," Felicity said, "but she's about to find out. She's a total *SJZ* freak, so worst-case scenario this is...one of those wish...thingies. But it also opens up options. In *SJZ*, it's canon that they've *beat* cancer. What's *not* canon is what form the cure takes. No telling once we find it if we can bring it to her or if we'll have to bring her to it.

"Whichever it turns out to be, we're going to make it happen. I know magic is too unpredictable for me to promise her anything. But if it works, we're not just going to save her, we're going to be able to save countless other lives. I intend to do that even if it means shooting people with tranquilizer darts, kidnapping them, and dumping them off in some random hospital bed once they're cured."

"Well, *that's* going to start a conspiracy theory," Manami said. Nami belonged to the younger generation of the coven, along with Sylvie and Lenore, and had been Sylvie's roommate when the three of them had lived in Las Vegas. Japanese by birth but raised in America, Nami still considered herself a Vegas girl through and through. She would have made a much better roommate for Denise, too. When Nami wasn't practicing witchcraft, she was busy making her mark in burlesque, and she treated the whole world as her personal locker room. She'd welcome the ghost into the shower with her without batting an eye.

"Like anyone's going to notice or care about one more conspiracy theory floating around right now." Felicity waved a hand dismissively. "Anyway, we're going to go ahead and start this project without waiting for Val. She dropped everything and headed out on a bucket list tour, but it's supposed to bring her to L.A. next week to see me. By the time she gets here, we're going to have all the specifics nailed down and be ready for her. I figure even with the usual distractions *la química* throws at us there will be plenty of time to do our research and find a medical facility."

By "usual distractions," Felicity meant "considerable distractions," of course. *La química* was the name they'd given to the odd twist that waited for them on any world the narrative bridge ritual might open to them—a twist that had so far left Lenore feeling like the designated driver at a bachelorette party.

As an integral part of the ritual, the coven had to feed it some work of fiction—nearly any work of fiction seemed to do—and the spell would search for an alternate universe among all of the infinite possible realities, looking for a ringer that would match the underlying world in the fiction. The thing was, what the spell ultimately found and opened a door to was *never* really an identical match. It was a near match that seemed to get ninety-nine percent of the details dead-on. The other one percent—a very important and prominent one percent—always differed in some way that made them intoxicatingly more attractive. That was not simply to say that they became more pleasing to the eye. They became more sensually, sexually seductive, like the entire alternate reality existed just to seduce its visitors.

Actually, that wasn't a fair observation. For all intents and purposes, it *did* exist to seduce its visitors—or at least the spell had chosen it specifically because it *would* seduce its visitors. Lingering across a bridge for any amount of time was an open invitation to a very personalized sort of sexual adventure. To the Victorian-era coven who'd written the spellbook they were now working from, that had been the entire point of the ritual. The high-born ladies of the Sororital Order of the Freyjur had been completely fed up with having to endure middle-class morality, and had been deadly serious about their worldly fun. They'd clearly spent insane fortunes in refining ways to enjoy their illicit pleasures with little-to-no risk of consequence. If they'd ever dreamed of exploiting the resulting power in the way the modern coven was trying to, no hint of those dreams had made it into the book they'd left behind.

"All right then: Everyone's on board with that mission?" Diana asked.

A chorus of unqualified agreement washed through the room. Even Lenore in her inexperience didn't mistake the question for a question. It was a courtesy. Anyone heartless enough not to go all in on this mission would find herself in the express lane out of the coven, to say nothing of the fact she could be turning down a place in history.

Lenore had known from the outset Felicity had loftier goals for the coven than just larking about in their favorite fantasies, but this was *big*. It was too big to get her mind around, really—because if they could pull off what Felicity was proposing, what *couldn't* they accomplish? Beating cancer wouldn't be the end of it. It would barely count as a beginning.

"All right, then," Diana said. "Let's review what we're getting into." She tapped the tablet on her lap and a screen on the wall lit up. On it, the still image of a retro-future rocketship hung against what would have passed for a field of stars in a low-budget television show circa the dawn of commercial television. The words "Space Jockey Zero" splashed across the image in a blocky, comic-book-worthy font.

"Everyone remotely interested in science fiction at least knows *SJZ* by reputation," Diana said, "but nobody really knows everything there is to know about it. There's even some argument over its origins. What we generally accept as the debut of *Space Jockey Zero* was a serial short released to movie theaters in the early 1950s, starring Raymond Carr as Lieutenant Noah Ramsey. A later legal dispute claimed the story had been stolen from an earlier comic book, *Confederacies of the Asteroid Belt*. That dispute was settled out of court, but it muddies the waters for us. We can only guess where the facts of this fiction actually start. From there, things just get murkier.

"The last theatrical episode was released in 1953. Filming resumed in 1954 as a low-budget television production. Mostly it clung to existence as an executive's pet project for his son, who'd loved the serials. Almost no footage survives from those early television years."

She tapped the pad again and the still image changed to a mildly less clunky black-and-white opening credits sequence that silently stepped through introducing the cast of a light-hearted space-opera. "The trail picks back up in 1959, when the show got reinvented as a science fiction sitcom."

Another tap brought up a new credits sequence, this one in color and with a noticeably younger cast. "During the sixties it got a spin-off sitcom specifically targeting teenagers."

With the next tap, a still image replaced the credits sequence. It featured a pulp-style, science-fiction novel cover that declared itself "The Mutineers" and "A *Space Jockey Zero* novel!"

"For a few years in the early seventies," Diana went on, "*SJZ* existed only as a series of novels and a monthly comic book before getting re-branded and relaunched as a science-fiction soap opera for young housewives who'd grown up on the sitcom. That's when a growing science-fiction fandom latched onto the show and transformed it from a modest niche success story into the cult classic that we know as *SJZ*, with its insane catalog of incarnations and spin-offs across all forms of media."

A final tap from Diana set off a slideshow that began stepping through a parade of books, merchandise, and film paraphernalia. She left it running in the background.

"This journey will be unusual for us in a lot of ways," she said. "So far we've mostly visited fantasy worlds, not science fiction, and the genre might throw us some curves. Also, we've never entered a world with anything remotely like the jungle of canon source material available for *SJZ*.

"For this 'narrative bridge' ritual, we've picked an episode from the turn-of-the-millennium television re-launch as our focal point, hoping it will connect us to the timeline somewhere during that incarnation of the show. We're also hoping the bridge will lead to eCity, the space station where most of that incarnation took place, but honestly, we could end up anywhere and anywhen in all that sprawling universe.

"Wherever we do find ourselves, if your gut tells you it's dangerous, listen to it and speak up. Some incarnations of the show were played for laughs, but just as many were deadly serious—emphasis on 'deadly.' We can expect some narrative protection from the spell early on, but *never* take it for granted." Diana didn't re-tell the story of the friend and *Lovelace* co-star who'd died on one of these expeditions. She didn't have to. Everyone in the room had either heard it or lived it.

"Any one of us is authorized to pull the plug on the entire operation based on nothing more than a bad feeling. There are other universes out there with cancer cures. We can abort to any of them. Job number one has to be keeping all of us alive. We're not going to trade a life for a life here. We don't need to."

Lenore nodded her understanding along with the others.

"Once we find a medical facility," Kassia, the last of the coven's veteran members jumped in, "we bring back any medical tech and documentation we can legit get our hands on, not just a cancer cure. Don't overreach by doing anything illegal or immoral to get it, but we've got a backer who's been lobbying for us to do something like this for a while now. She's promised a research team to try to record and reverse-engineer everything we can bring them before it evaporates. For all we know, any *SJZ* miracles could turn into total garbage on our side of the bridge, but it's time to try."

CHAPTER FIVE
CLOSED SET

It still struck Lenore as odd to think about the coven having outside financial backers, but one of the first things she'd learned about magic on being inducted was that magic was a rich woman's game. *Some* rituals came cheap and relatively easy, but many of the more interesting and potent rituals could easily consume tens of thousands of dollars' worth of rare minerals and other esoterica. If Felicity was stressed about the price tag on their rings; each must have cost in the high six figures to make, if not seven figures. And it suddenly dawned on Lenore: if her everyday jewelry looked anywhere near as valuable as it actually was, she wouldn't dare leave the house without at least one bodyguard.

"And remember," Diana was saying, "it's okay—maybe even essential—to have some fun even though this is easily the most serious job we've ever assigned ourselves. Like Felicity said, we've got a pretty big window of opportunity, and it's becoming clear we can accomplish more by working *with* the narrative and with *la química* than when we're fighting them."

"Well, that's the first sensible thing anyone's said—to have fun, I mean."

Lenore jerked in alarm at the sound of Denise's voice in her ear. Her insubstantial roommate had settled unnoticed into the empty seat at her elbow.

"Something wrong?" Diana asked, looking to Lenore with concern.

Manami answered before Lenore could recompose herself. "She just grew up thinking 'fun' was a curse word. Have you met her parents?"

"Yeah. No. I'm fine," Lenore mumbled. No one else showed any sign of seeing or hearing the ghost, of course. "Just a muscle spasm." If she ever admitted she'd mucked up the ritual that had conjured Denise, it was not going to be in a full coven meeting where life-or-death matters were being discussed.

"That's what we need on the lot!" Diana exclaimed, lightly slapping her forehead. "Remind me after we've got Val on the mend to hire us a licensed massage therapist."

"We can do that?!" Manami asked excitedly.

"Maybe just on Tuesdays or something? That's in the budget, isn't it, Fel?" Diana prompted.

"Hey, if you guys want it and we can pull off this miracle for my sister, I'll make it happen no matter *where* the money comes from."

"All right," Diana announced, climbing to her feet. "Let's go build a narrative bridge."

Lenore found herself filing out of the room last, with Denise haunting her steps.

"Wow," Denise murmured. "You didn't tell me you were working for Ida Lupino!"

"What?" Lenore whispered.

"The director. That *is* Ida, isn't it? Maybe this job *will* turn out to be more than a paycheck for you."

"Oh, umm. Yeah. Maybe." Lenore felt sure she'd heard that name before, but couldn't say it meant anything to her. Apparently Ida had been a director, though. Lenore had to wonder whether anyone in the coven really bore a physical resemblance to Ida, or if something else had sparked this particular ghostly delusion.

They stepped out of the door to the conference room and onto a narrow but ornate spiral staircase that wound down to the floor of the vaulted central chamber in the great library at the Lovelace Community College of Applied Magic. Even as they did, the arcane imagery covering its cathedral-style ceiling melted away to be replaced by a whole new mural. Marble statues, exquisite oil paintings, gilded fixtures, and furnishings of lustrous, elegantly carved mahogany filled the room with baroque splendor. The coven had the central chamber all to itself, but beyond that students and faculty could be glimpsed wandering in and out of sight among the labyrinthine corridors and alcoves of the library's stacks.

The first time Lenore had come here she'd mistakenly thought she'd just stepped through a portal created by the narrative bridge ritual, but the whole thing had turned out to be an illusion—and not even a magical one. Most of the central chamber and its furnishings were real enough, even if the statues weren't genuine marble, but the illusion had been achieved by paneling the walls and ceiling with video screens, creating what amounted to a full-room virtual-reality immersion experience. When you knew what to look for you could see the actual boundaries of the room from the designs on the carpeting.

Kassia, as the coven's resident tech guru, had planned the whole thing and seen to its execution. The team she'd had in doing the work had thought they were putting together a state-of-the-art sound stage, not a magicians' clubhouse, and technically it could be used for one. Was it more expensive to build and maintain than a green-screen studio would have been? Considerably, but of course that wasn't the point. Did all those screens and the associated computing power burn through a decadent amount of energy? Also yes, but power from the

California sun was being harnessed every day to power them by means of the solar tiles on the roof. Eventually the plan was to run the entire compound entirely on some combination of solar and magically generated energy, but the magical power source plan remained a theoretical dream to be pursued at an unspecified time in the future. The coven had so far developed only a handful of its own, original rituals, after all, and inherited the rest from a time before there was even a grid to get off of.

Diana led the way toward one of the illusionary aisles between shelves, which shimmered to a ghostly, monochrome blue as she stepped within arm's reach of the screen. Then she paused and—with a sigh—asked, "Kassia, have you changed the password yet?"

"Umm, no. Sorry."

Diana sighed again, resignedly, before announcing, "Open sopapilla!" The ghostly image faded to black, and the screen slid slowly, silently upward, revealing what amounted to a walk-in closet beyond with a door at the far end.

Lenore hadn't seen them all, but purportedly the old warehouse had nearly fifty of these nearly identical little rooms secreted behind the video screens. That was the whole point in using the converted warehouse for the heart of their operation: a place to store doors, all safely tucked away together for security and easy access.

"Coming through!" Felicity announced as she wheeled a small table with a pentacle etched into its glass top past the crew and into the closet. Five lightly used candles also adorned the table, nestled in the permanent, inset, silver candle holders that had been built into the table at each point of the pentacle. "Sylvie, you're odd girl out today. Just hang with our handsome auxiliaries and warm up your wand."

Lenore felt pleased to be recognized on this important occasion as a more reliable ritual caster than Sylvie despite being the newest member of the coven, while at the same time feeling envious at the mention of Sylvie's wand. Sylvie might be the least accomplished ritualist in the coven, but that was largely because of how much time she'd spent practicing with that wand. She hadn't worked out many tricks with it yet, but the tricks she *had* worked out were really cool. Thanks to that wand and the patient tutelage of her own cinematic idol, the infamous enchantress Lark Starling, Sylvie could boast being the only member of the coven who'd learned to employ spontaneous magic. For that matter, since Lark had gone home to the real Lovelace Community College, Sylvie might possibly be the only person on Earth who had ever performed spontaneous magic.

For all the other Freyjur, spellcasting remained a drawn-out matter of magic symbols, focal objects, laboriously brewed potions, exotic reagents, and intricate, finicky chants. Nothing in the writings of the original Sororital Order of the Freyjur hinted at the existence of spontaneous magic either. Until Lark took Sylvie under her wing, none of them had considered the possibility they *could* learn that sort of magic.

With the outer wall lowered back into place for the sake of quiet and concentration, the five women huddled around the little table. Diana took down an old, boxed DVD set of *SJZ: Electricity*, season two, from a small shelf by the inner door and set it in the middle of the table. The candles were lit. Five large crystal vials were pulled off a shelf and passed around the table until each woman had opened hers and settled it into the cup holder hanging off the edge of the table beside her.

While that was going on, Lenore looked around a bit nervously for any sign of Denise and let out a relieved breath to find none. Hopefully she'd counted herself among the auxiliaries and gracefully remained behind, accepting this little room had been declared a "closed set." If the ghost had followed her in here and shown the least inclination to break Lenore's concentration, Lenore would have had to confess immediately to what she'd done rather than risk botching this expensive ritual.

Diana glanced around, making eye contact to confirm they were all ready, then cast her gaze upward and carefully intoned the name of the pagan goddess the coven's own name honored: "Freyja!"

"Yes?" a feminine voice chimed in answer from speakers mounted on the walls.

"Let's open a narrative bridge," Diana said.

"Executing narrative bridge protocol," the voice chimed again.

The little room's overhead light dimmed and went out. Soft, instrumental music with a meditative Asian sound began to float out of wall-mounted speakers. Long seconds passed wordlessly while incense smoke began to float up from a floor vent.

Diana reached out her hands for Felicity and Kassia beside her, and the gesture rippled out around the table until the five women had all linked hands in a circle. Then Diana took the leading and most complex part in their intricate, five-part chant. The words of the chant weren't English. They weren't Greek or Aramaic. They weren't Latin or even faux-Latin. For all Lenore could tell, they weren't really words at all. The entire thing seemed to be nothing more than a two-minute-long collection of nonsense syllables the original coven had written out phonetically.

With the narrative bridge being considered the Freyjur's most important and most mentally demanding ritual, each member had been required to commit two of the five parts to memory, and to be able to recite those parts flawlessly without any sort of visual aid. All told, the effort had taken nearly an hour and a half, but only because she'd taken the time to memorize all five parts of the chant. The secret for her was to listen to the parts, not read them. Her memory wasn't exactly eidetic, but it was close enough that after spending most of that hour listening to Sylvie and Manami running through the parts a few times, the sounds had burned themselves into her head so thoroughly they might as well have been a digital audio file she could play back inside her head at will. For her, this was the easy bit.

The final intonation of the chant trailed off into silence. Almost imperceptibly at first, the flickering orange flame of the candle in front of Diana began to slowly fade through yellow on its way to green. Green shifted gradually into blue, blue to purple, then purple to red. About that time, the flame in front of Felicity was shifting slowly to yellow. The color of the first began to tail the second, following in perfect synchronicity even as the speed of the transitions began to edge upward.

One by one, the other candles around the table fell in step, evenly spacing out the distance of their hues around the color wheel as they did. Then each woman picked up her vial and tipped it gently over the flame in front of her. Shimmering white sand flecked with motes from every color of the rainbow began cascading down into the candle flames, where they would instantly dissipate into a growing, swirling cloud of chromatic smoke. The clouds merged with the incense to form a colorful, aromatic mass that began to lazily swirl counter-clockwise, chasing the still-shifting colors of the flames.

The lazy spin became a steady one. The steady one became an eddying breeze. The breeze began building toward a miniature cyclone. Abruptly—as the wind began to howl, tossing their hair around like a blustering autumn wind—Diana broke the circle of hands, pushed back from the table, and stepped quickly to the inner door of the closet. She turned the knob. She shoved the door open, revealing nothing at all but a blank, empty, tiny, square room barely deeper than the door was wide. A heartbeat later, the cyclone leapt off the table and straight through the open door in a brilliant arc of rainbow light so bright they all had to shield their eyes.

When the light faded, the candles went out and the whirlwind had gone, leaving not a displaced hair on anyone's head to hint the wind had ever been there. The tiny inner closet had vanished as well. Through the still-open door where it had been now lay the futuristic steel-blue wall of some sort of access corridor.

"Ladies," Diana announced, gesturing through the door with a triumphant grin, "welcome to the penultimate frontier."

CHAPTER SIX

SPACE CRUISERS

"Well, *this* isn't perfect," Felicity observed wryly as she, Sylvie, Lenore, and Kassia walked the corridors of the *Queen Ilo*—an interstellar luxury cruise ship—falling well short of blending in. "Not that it's ever been, really."

It could have been worse, but this was a civilian ship—and the costumes they'd chosen were all governmental uniforms, so the four of them stood out from both the crew and the passengers. Also, the tech and architecture looked wrong here. This was not some retro-future television starship from the turn of the millennium. Whatever era they'd landed in, all the design sensibilities here seemed closer to present-day science fiction television—or maybe to motion-picture science fiction from ten years ago.

At least no one had challenged their right to be there yet. It probably helped that Felicity and Kassia were taking it all in stride, walking around like they owned the place. By now, Lenore knew, both of them were well used to this sort of thing. Knowing which fictional universe your destination would resemble was a far cry from knowing where and when you'd wind up in that universe. The first visit always involved a certain amount of scouting around simply to determine what passed for the local version of "normal."

In this case, not one of them could remember seeing or hearing of such a thing as an "interstellar luxury cruise ship" in *SJZ*, much less the *Queen Ilo* specifically. Between that and whatever amount of in-universe time they'd missed their temporal target by, the chances of them getting their costuming on the nose hadn't been noticeably more than zero. At least everyone they'd passed was speaking English, which meant the coven had matched the costumes to the culture if not to the specific time and place.

"You should have let me keep trying to figure out that information terminal," Kassia said. "This place is huge. It'll take forever to find anything."

Felicity waved a hand dismissively. "We're fine. You just keep doing whatever you're doing to make sure we can find our way back out."

"Wait," Kassia said. "Was I supposed to be keeping track of that?" She threw up her hands defensively and backpedaled a couple of steps from the weight of Felicity's glare. "Kidding, *chica*! Of course I know where home is."

Felicity rolled her eyes at Kassia, then turned her attention back to the business of watching where she was going just in time to dance back and avoid walking into a fully loaded luggage cart as it emerged from a side-corridor. While they watched, the unattended machine slid silently past them, floating several inches above the deck. "Now there's another thing we could use back home," Felicity chuckled. "Maybe we can try reverse-engineering anti-grave tech next if this—"

"Linty! No!" A woman shouted from nearby as a fluffy, white, mastiff-sized, rabbit-like creature with six legs and a pelt covered in lavender leopard-spots barreled out of that same side corridor and collided with Felicity. Before any of them knew what was happening, it had slammed her to the deck, pinned her there under its considerable weight, and begun vigorously licking her face with a long, sinuous tongue.

"Oh, Linty! What have you done?" The woman moaned apologetically as she wrestled a leash onto the thing's collar and dragged it off of Felicity with great effort. "I'm so sorry. She just rushed out when I opened my cabin. I'll bet she smelled your perfume." The woman braced herself with one foot against a support sticking out from the bulkhead and her whole weight thrown back to keep the over-friendly beast under control. "Are you all right?"

"I, uh...Maybe?" Felicity gasped, trying to regain her breath as Kassia and Sylvie helped her back to her feet.

They all stared at the woman, who wasn't—in a strict sense—human. If Lenore had her *SJZ* lore straight, the woman was a Nidruni. Like most alien races that have ever appeared on television, that meant she appeared mostly human with a bit of quirky cosmetic work. For the Nidruni, that involved ivory skin accented with crystal-blue freckles and a set of four ram-like, sapphire-blue horns curling back from her temples. Her steel-blue hair hung down in a pair of long, elegant braids, and an expensive-looking, double-slit dress the color of her horns hugged the woman's enviable figure.

Although Felicity still clutched protectively at her right arm where it had slammed into the deck, an irrepressible grin began to spread slowly across her face. "I mean, I should probably see a doctor. To be sure."

"But I am a doctor." The woman smiled a dazzling smile.

"Are you?" Felicity asked, wide-eyed. It was *not* her best job of acting.

"That's what it says on my license." The woman laughed brightly and gave a self-deprecating shrug. I'm Elovna. Come on. Let me get this naughty little fluff monster locked back away and I'll have a look at you." Elovna dragged the creature back the way they'd come with much grunting, many chastisements, and some rapid clicking of her tongue.

"All right," Felicity said quietly, shrugging off the helping hands. "Leave finding medical to me. You three just learn everything you can about where we are and how we can come back better prepared next time."

"Is it my imagination, or does she recognize that woman?" Lenore asked after Felicity had disappeared down the side corridor and through a cabin door.

"You mean Doctor Elovna Agra?" Kassia shrugged. "Probably. She's a recurring character on *SJZ:Escapade*. And I *did* walk in on Felicity making out with an Elovna cosplayer last year."

Sylvie laughed. "I *do* like this spell."

"Anyway, that does take some of the pressure off," Kassia said. "Let's go find that information terminal again and see if I can pull up a deck plan for us."

"Why was Felicity even worried about getting lost here?" Lenore asked as Kassia led them back the way they came. "The homing ritual is free and hard to mess up, and even one person can do it by herself."

"She thinks it's a hassle." Kassia sighed. "Hard to mess up, but it still takes a good twenty minutes—and she says it makes her teeth hurt."

"It does?" Lenore asked.

Kassia shrugged. "I think it's better to say the homing ritual is easy to mess up, but hard to mess up badly. Sometimes spells have side effects."

"Speaking of spells going wrong, can we get out of sight somewhere so I can try out my wand?" Sylvie asked. "It was acting up in the last world we visited. I'd like to know if I can rely on it here before we get in too deep."

"Good point," Kassia admitted. "We should try a ritual or two while we're at it."

"Where *is* your wand, Sylvie?" Lenore asked. "I thought you'd had like a 'sword-cane' made for it. 'A wand cane?'"

"Eh. I did," Sylvie said. "Wasn't working for me. Too costume-y to be inconspicuous most places. And it protected the wand, but didn't really do anything to free up my hands. So…" She held up her arm to display the intricate, decorative blue-and-silver vambrace that sheathed it from wrist to elbow. The vambrace had matched the rest of her outfit well enough that Lenore had taken it as just a cool costuming touch. Now, though, as Sylvie's fingertips traced a straight line down the back of her arm, Lenore could see the slender outline of the wand embedded in the metal. "Don't tell the others, okay? I want to see their faces when I just point my arm and fire off a spell." Sylvie grinned.

Kassia rolled her eyes. "*Et tu*, Sylvie. I'm surrounded by actresses, a stripper, a storyteller, and an acrobat—"

"I'm not sure I'm properly an acrobat," Sylvie broke in. "It's just parkour. And Nami prefers—"

"And an *acrobat*," Kassia went on firmly. "And Nami doesn't care."

"She doesn't," Lenore confirmed helpfully.

"Okay, *I* prefer," Sylvie admitted. "My parents might freak out a bit less if I ever had to tell them I'd been rooming with a 'lady of burlesque.'"

"Would they?" Lenore asked.

"Probably not, no." Sylvie sighed. "But that's what I always told myself. Anyway, is that a restroom over there? That could be a good place to experiment."

"It *might* be a restroom," Lenore said uncertainly. For all she knew, *SJZ* didn't *have* restrooms. Certainly she'd never seen one on screen. The architecture surrounding the door did remind her of a public restroom back home, but the door lacked both readable labels and recognizable icons.

"No worries," Kassia said, heading straight for it. "This early in our visit, *la química* will be working overtime. If we barge into the wrong room right now, it's going to be wrong in a fun way." She cast a smirk over her shoulder as the door slid accommodatingly open for her, then she disappeared inside.

"She's not wrong," Sylvie said with a shrug. "Watch our backs while we tinker with a few light spells? Don't want anyone barging in unannounced."

"Sure," Lenore said, deciding if anything *very* fun happened beyond that door she'd hear about it soon enough.

"Soon enough" turned out to be less than thirty seconds later, when the two came scurrying back out, laughing and liberally spattered with something white that resembled whipped cream.

"What?" Lenore demanded.

"Well, it wasn't a restroom," Kassia managed. She wiped a handful of the cream from her cheek, licked it cautiously, and made a face of mild disappointment.

"I'm not sure *what* it was," Sylvie admitted. "Some sort of cosplay laser-tag food fight arena? It was weird."

"I think we went in a service entrance," Kassia added. She looked down at herself as she shook the white glop off her hand. "Now we *really* need that restroom."

"I'll bet there's one back near that information terminal." Lenore let out a quiet laugh and shook her head ruefully.

"Probably right," Kassia agreed. "And if not, we'll be that much closer to home."

They attracted even more attention now, walking the ship's corridors in such a state. One cluster of Xayarian Goths—in their traditional formal wear of black lace, leather, spikes, and silver piercings—studied the trio with particularly sour, disapproving faces as they passed.

"It's okay!" Sylvie reassured them cheerfully. "We're professionals." It didn't soften the glares.

"Professional *what*?" Kassia asked quietly as they rounded the next corner, leaving their somber audience behind.

"I've been a professional stunt woman for two whole weeks now," Sylvie said with affected primness, "and if that wasn't a professional stunt, I'm sure I don't know what is."

"One you get paid for?" Lenore suggested.

"Yeah, well, there's that," Sylvie admitted.

"At least the Xayarians are a good sign," Kassia said. "We can't be *too* far off from the hub of galactic civilization if they're hanging about on a cruise ship with us."

They found the information terminal again before they found a restroom.

"*¡Excelente!*" Kassia exclaimed with a fist pump as the holographic display sprang to life. "They're giving us a refund!"

The others laughed as they read the prominent announcement—that actually promised travel credit rather than a cash refund—to anyone who had been headed to the Chimera Sector. Apparently a leg of the *Queen Ilo*'s journey had been canceled due to incursions by the "A.I.M war machine."

"Sounds like foreshadowing to me." Sylvie smirked. "What *is* an A.I.M. war machine?"

"No clue," Lenore admitted.

"Well, one's going to pop up if we're here long enough," Sylvie said. "Mark my words."

"A.I.M. is one of *SJZ*'s heavy-hitting cybernetic threats," Kassia said, while her fingers danced across the holographic controls in a series of what would have been taps and swipes on a physical surface. "Fairly modern addition to the universe. Let's all remember the Chimera Sector is a place to skip out on if we can. I'll try to find out where we are and when the ship's scheduled to get close. We should probably head home before risking it."

"Let's pretend that thing will be in any sector that touches Chimera too," Lenore said. "I've never seen a published game adventure where that wouldn't be true: tell the players a threat was seen someplace, and it means the threat will be showing up someplace else nearby."

Sylvie nodded her agreement. "Sound thinking."

"*De acuerdo.* I'll bet the *Ilo*'s still planning to skirt Chimera," Kassia said. "I'll find out how long we've got before it enters one of those sectors. We should be safe until then. First, though..." With a bit more prodding, she coaxed some decent holographic schematics of the ship's public spaces out of the terminal—along with the location of the nearest restroom.

"Oh, look," Lenore said, studying the hologram, "we're right next to...is that a park?"

"Looks like," Kassia agreed. "They put the outside on the inside." The public spaces did appear to have been built around some sort of vast, multi-deck green space that took up a third of the ship's width, with plenty of space for a small lake and what looked like an associated water park in addition to the gardens.

"And there's a door to it right over there." Lenore pointed. "I'm going to go have a look while you two get cleaned up. Just meet me there. I'll stay in sight of the door."

"Fair enough," Kassia said. "Even a *novata* like you can't get in too much trouble on a vacation liner like this."

Sylvie swatted Kassia's shoulder familiarly and glared at her. "Tell me you did *not* just say that."

"What?!" Kassia asked.

"You *know* what happens in a movie after someone says something like that," Sylvie said crossly.

"Yeah. Okay." Kassia opened her hands in surrender. "Better stick close, Lenore. Sorry."

It was Lenore's turn to glare. "No. If it could go wrong out there it can go wrong right here or even if I'm standing right beside you. And like you said before, if we get in trouble now it's still pretty much guaranteed to be fun trouble. As long as we don't overstay our welcome, I'll be fine. I'll keep an eye out, I'll listen to my instincts, but I'm not going to be coddled just because I'm the new girl. I signed on for adventure just like the rest of you."

"It's not because you're new," Sylvie said apologetically. "I've barely been here longer than you. But I'd be freaked out for myself if—"

"I know story tropes at least as well as you do," Lenore said testily. "Especially the awful ones. I'm a *game master*. I grew up watching slasher flicks when you were watching cartoons about funny animals. Just..." She sighed, letting the anger out in a long breath. "Just go get cleaned up. I'll be fine."

They went. She watched them go until the restroom door slid closed behind them, then she turned and headed for the green space, chastising herself all the way for being so touchy.

Lenore hadn't really seen "the narrative" in action yet, but apparently it was another thing like *la química* going on behind the scenes of the bridge ritual. Or maybe those two things were different faces of the same phenomenon. Either way, the senior members of the coven hadn't picked up on it until Sylvie had noticed and more-or-less proven every world they stepped into would be following story tropes.

The observation had briefly renewed debate over whether those worlds had been created by the ritual or the ritual had simply gone searching through infinite existing realities to find the one that best suited its purposes. Ultimately, though, that was more philosophy than any of them wanted to deal with. Whether created or located, a world remained persistent from that point forward, and the more time any one person spent in any one world, the less it behaved like a story for them. Whatever was going on, they'd probably never know, they could probably never change it, they weren't going to stop making it happen, and believing the worlds were being discovered rather than created simplified all the related philosophical questions.

Anyway, in a setting where tropes served as an actual force of nature, Lenore stood by her assertion that no one in the coven was better equipped to survive than she was. If anything, she and Sylvie should be protecting everyone else.

The door slid open, and Lenore stepped out onto a balcony three stories up, overlooking a sprawling botanical garden much larger than any earthly sporting arena. Ahead of her, a walkway led out into the canopy of the treetops. Looking down she could see people of all ages, both alien and human, walking and playing out on the lawns and in the shallows of the little lake. Looking up she could...make her head swim, staring up through the transparent dome at some enormous artificial construct that was hanging as if upside down in front of a field of stars and a colorful, hazy nebula. From what she could see, Lenore could only guess whether she was looking at a tiny portion of some colossal megastructure that might circle an entire star, or just seeing a significant chunk of a *really* big space station.

Either way, the sheer scale of it brought home the reality of where she was and what she was doing here harder than everything else put together. Up until that moment, it had still felt like a lark—like she was attending a science fiction convention where everyone was in cosplay and in character, walking the corridors of what amounted to a high-tech hotel. But this eclipsed the spectacle of the illusionary library Kassia had created in their clubhouse and upped the game by several magnitudes.

Lenore suddenly felt as if that skewed, deep-space cityscape was trying to capture her in its gravity, sending her plummeting straight up through the dome toward it. She sat down hard on the deck, then crawled over to grab the balcony railing—just in case the feeling wasn't illusory.

"Oh. There you are. Is everything all right?"

It took Lenore a moment to reconcile the words with the voice delivering them. After her slightly addled brain had parsed them for meaning, it had to go around and do it again to be sure she hadn't misheard. The person saying those words to her should have been Sylvie or Kassia, or in a pinch maybe Felicity, but they hadn't been delivered by a woman at all. The fell on her ear in rich, masculine tones that could never have been mistaken even for Brian. Or Loki, for that matter. Heck, she wasn't sure she'd met anyone at all with that sort of voice. It *screamed* romantic lead. Whoever that voice belonged to, *la química* had sent him. Or the narrative had. Maybe both.

She put off acknowledging the words for a heartbeat longer, going through a quick, mental safety checklist that included touching *both* her coven-issued rings to be sure they were there: the opal that ensured she couldn't contract or pass on any illness, and the black pearl that insured against...other sexual consequences. If *la química* was involved in this "chance" meeting, it would be her first real trial-by-fire in dealing with the effect. And after going off on the others about how she could take care of herself, now was not the moment to get overconfident about how she'd react to *anything*. The least display of pridefulness at this moment would be *begging* the narrative to knock her feet out from under her.

Lenore pushed through the mental inertia of the disorientation and schooled her emotions. She put on her game master face. She was in charge now. Everything would be fine. "Yeah. I'm good. Everything's fine," she said, pulling herself up on the railing. "It was just a little 'mental exercise' thing—walking myself through a train of thought, you know? It helps sometimes. Sorry. I thought I was alone."

She turned to flash what she hoped was a radiant smile at the speaker, and to get her first look at him. Yes, this guy was definitely *la química*'s handiwork, even if the introduction wasn't. She'd seen less buff and chiseled men bare-chested on the covers of romance novels. Not that he was technically bare-chested himself, but the sleeveless thing he wore—not quite a vest, not quite a shirt—left her feeling plenty well-informed about his physique for making that comparison. A few distinguished dark locks streaked his otherwise strikingly blond hair, and his dark eyes literally sparkled with star-like flecks. All in all, the man was no Alek Raine, but aside from his failing that test, she couldn't claim he wasn't easy on the eyes.

"You're not seriously trying to lose me already?" He chuckled. It was a good chuckle—the sort that sent shivers down her spine.

Lenore dropped her gaze, closed her eyes, and waved her hands dismissively in front of her face. With luck, it would pass for denial, but to be honest the gesture was a physical manifestation of her efforts to cut through the mental fog of *la química*. There could be no pretending now it hadn't come for her. Oh, sure, the moment felt giddily pleasant, but if the phenomenon thought she was about to let her guard down here and now of all moments, it was in for a huge disappointment.

"Of course I'm not trying to lose you," she said as she looked back up to meet his gaze. "But what was your name again?" Lenore cocked her head disarmingly and turned on her best impish grin in attempt to pass the question off as flirtation.

"Ow! Well, *that's* going to leave a permanent scar," he declared while clutching at his heart. He did laugh as she'd hoped, but he didn't take the bait and "re-introduce" himself. "I love the new outfit. It's sooo...not you. Still pretty sexy, though. I guess you've been out shopping?"

"Yeah," Lenore agreed, willing Sylvie to come and extract her from this conversation. The clear case of mistaken identity didn't shock her, though. Lenore had met Lark Starling herself before the enchantress had returned to her home in the *Lovelace* universe, and the woman had been an absolute dead ringer for Diana, who'd played her in the movies. Lenore had met Felicity's character too—Holly Marsh—and Holly had looked no less a clone. Running into doppelgangers seemed to be an occupational hazard in the coven. Only—

"Wait. Hold on. Time out. No." Lenore waved her arms in front of her in a sweeping gesture, like a referee calling a foul. "This is a trope too far. I'm not buying it."

"Uh...What?" the man asked, his face a sudden mask of confusion.

"I don't have a twin here. I *can't* have a twin here. It doesn't make sense. I'm not an actress. I've never been an actress. Well, yeah, there's the role-playing—even a bit of LARPing—but that doesn't count. I've never played an *SJZ* game in my life! You can't just throw my evil twin in here and not expect to break my suspension of disbelief. You didn't even foreshadow her, for God's sake!"

"This is like a Goth thing, right?" the man asked uncertainly. "You're on some sort of drug?"

"I don't have time for this," Lenore said disgustedly. "I need to go cure cancer." She turned away and stepped back into the corridor without sparing him another glance. If he made any move to follow her, she didn't hear it. "Shoddy, stupid, space-opera storytelling," she muttered darkly. "The sooner we get this done and get out of here the better."

A commotion ahead greeted Lenore as she approached the information terminal, and she hurried forward to find one of the Goth women she'd seen earlier standing wide-eyed with her back to the closed restroom door while Sylvie and Kassia could be heard pounding at it and yelling from the other side.

"Oh, for..." Her friends hadn't settled for cleaning up. They'd tried out their spells. They'd tried out their spells without her standing guard like they'd asked, and someone had walked in on them. She *knew* they'd be the ones to get into trouble.

"I'm coming!" Lenore yelled, rushing up to try pushing her way past the woman in black.

"You don't want to go in there," the woman cautioned Lenore nervously, refusing to budge. "Just come away with me. It's for the best."

"What?" Lenore demanded in her best disgruntled-game-master voice. "You've never seen stage magic before? Don't make me call security."

"Please?!" the woman begged urgently. She remained wedged where she was, her arms braced against the door frame. "This has to stop. *You've got to come with me.*"

"I've got this!" Lenore shouted to be heard through the door and over the commotion. "Just settle down. It'll be a minute!" The pounding and shouting ceased.

"Look," Lenore said, fixing the woman with a challenging gaze. "I'm not going anywhere with you. Not gonna happen. Whatever techno voodoo you used to lock that door, you're going to use to unlock it. Then you're going to quietly walk away, we'll all pretend none of this ever happened, and *you* won't get thrown off the ship. Not even a little bit. Okay?"

"Yeah," another woman spoke up from behind Lenore. "That doesn't work for me."

Lenore spun around to find another Goth, tall and angular, pointing some sort of derringer-sized futuristic firearm at her chest. Lenore had only a moment to stare in blank uncertainty before the woman pulled the trigger, and a blinding blue flash of light hit Lenore like a ton of marshmallows.

CHAPTER SEVEN

GILDED CAGE

Lenore drifted slowly up out of a warm, comfortable sleep to the sound of Denise's cheerful voice. "Wake up, kiddo. Morning's wasting. Are we still on for going to the zoo today?" Lenore replied with an incoherent mumble she vaguely hoped would convince Denise to let her be. Comfortable or not, Lenore couldn't remember the last time she'd felt this exhausted. She'd been having a really nice dream about Alek Raine, too. *Really* nice.

"That was an interesting shoot yesterday," Denise persisted. "I just *love* the way Ida works. I don't know where she got a budget like that for a television space opera, but your girl's got some sort of clout. I say you've really lucked into something."

Lenore offered another ineffectual grunt of protest, but the damage had been done. She could feel her brain begin to stir and set about the job of sorting out dreams from reality. That business with Alek had already been tucked neatly away on a shelf with all those other dreams she'd hoped to revisit someday but probably never would.

Memories of the gun being pointed at her bubbled up, along with memories of the flash of light. She felt no pain, though, just fatigue. Whatever had happened, she was okay. She'd probably just been shot with a standard-issue space-opera stun gun, then the others had reached her and dragged her home to—to someone's bed. This wasn't her bed. It was too soft.

She dozed again, drifting through jumbled dreams. She felt herself sinking into the bed; sinking into a cloud; then suddenly was sitting bolt upright in a near panic. If she wasn't in her bed, maybe she hadn't been able to hear the ghost because they'd taken her back home. Maybe she'd heard the ghost because she *hadn't* survived.

But...no. She wasn't dead—or at least this wasn't one of those heavenly clouds with its oppressive, never-ending boredom her parents had occasionally threatened her with. Then, more doubts hit her as she realized this place looked amazingly like her parents' idea of an actual paradise.

She found the unfamiliar bed she'd been curled up in to be larger than any bedroom she'd ever lived in, and to be clothed all in blood-red velvet and satin, while she herself seemed to be clothed in nothing at all. Mercifully, the only other person in the cabin appeared to be Denise, perched at the foot of the bed—and of course, Denise had already seen everything. Still, Lenore pulled the top sheet protectively over her chest as she continued to take in her surroundings. She *knew* this room. Or...again, no. She'd seen one very much like it in *SJZ* episodes. With all its decadent and dangerous-looking black-and-red decor, this cabin had to be the personal quarters of an important Xayarian Goth noble. So Lenore had been taken prisoner, and mercilessly forced to...get a long, comfortable, and badly needed rest?

Had this been more of that "mistaken identity" nonsense? She felt disinclined to find out, but if she knew anything about space-opera tropes, this would be one of those gilded-cage scenarios. Well, one obstacle at a time.

"So...zoo?" Denise asked brightly.

"Denise, what are you doing here? I thought you couldn't leave the lot."

"It sure feels like it sometimes. Studio contracts are awful." She rolled her eyes and sighed. "But even I get a day off, and no one can claim time at the zoo with my girlfriend isn't innocent and wholesome enough for my image."

"Give it a few decades," Lenore said dryly. "Anyway, we'll shock everyone if I walk out the front door in a bed sheet. Did you see where my clothes landed?"

"Did you go drinking last night and not invite me?" Denise asked with exaggerated hurt in her voice.

"I'm just really, really tired," Lenore said. "I was out before my head hit the pillow. Anyway, that wouldn't be wholesome, would it?"

"Depends on who you're seen drinking with, and how much, right? I don't see your clothes, though. Or the dresser." Denise showed an uncharacteristic moment of genuine surprise, but quickly shrugged it off and went back to taking everything in stride. "I guess they all got moved into the closet. Small price to pay to have someone else clean your room, though, right?"

Lenore started to ask Denise where this closet was then, but stopped herself, deciding better of it. Simpler to just get up and look. It wasn't like there were that many doors in the cabin—or as if anything Denise thought she knew could be relied on. She also started to ask again about how Denise had even gotten here, but thought better of that too. Denise couldn't possibly know.

Anyway, Occam's Razor—which stated the simplest explanation for anything would be the most likely—would say Lenore had simply been wrong in her assumptions. She'd grown up on so many stories about ghosts being anchored to some place or other, she'd just assumed Denise would be tied to the movie lot where she'd died. Perhaps instead of being bound to a place, Denise's spirit had been bound to the person who'd summoned her back into mortal realms. It would certainly explain some things, starting with why the ghost had been right here waiting for Lenore when she woke up.

One more incentive to put figuring this whole thing out at the top of her to-do list. Yes, Denise was sweet in her delusional way. She might have been an ideal roommate for someone who hated being alone—but Lenore would never be that person. If she didn't figure out how to regain control of her personal space, it would be only a matter of time before she cracked.

Wrapping the sheet around herself in her best imitation of a toga, Lenore slid out of the bed and headed for the door that looked most likely to be a closet. However she'd wound up without her clothes, she felt safe concluding it had been a relatively innocuous series of events. By all accounts, *la química* had some very strict ideas about consent. During the early stages of the visit, when its influence remained strongest, she'd be safer here than she'd ever been back home. For obvious reasons, the coven had done no experimenting to find out just how long they could count on that sort of protection, but they'd only known it to fail once. That whole trip had turned into a disaster on many levels for Diana and her original coven. One of them never made it home. Things hadn't started to go bad at all until they'd been in that world for over a week, though. Lenore would be out of here long before then.

"Ah. Your Highness is up."

Lenore stopped in mid stride on the way toward what she'd hoped was the closet, and wound up taking a stumbling step forward before catching herself. She turned to find the tall, angular woman—the one who'd been the last thing she'd seen before blacking out—standing in a doorway that had slid silently open for her.

"You shot me!" Lenore heard herself snap before even realizing she was going to open her mouth.

"Pardon?" the woman blinked. "Her Highness surely had a bad dream." She dropped to one knee and spread her arms open respectfully. "I remain ever your loyal bodyguard, and would never, ever shoot you. Not unless Your Highness was behaving a royal brat and putting countless lives in needless danger, which of course you would never do. Ergo, I could not possibly have shot you."

"Oh, for...I *don't* have a doppelganger here!" Lenore said abruptly. "You've got me mixed up with my mom. *She's* the Goth Princess."

"Ah: the mistaken identity game again, but with a new twist. Her Highness is most droll. I can barely contain my mirth. Sadly, though, there is no time for jocularity. Your Highness's schedule is quite packed. In just one hour you'll be taking tea with the Pudding Princess."

"There's no such thing as the Pudding Princess...is there?" Lenore had started the protest strong, but realized she knew precious little about the larger *SJZ* universe.

"If so, she will be most aggrieved to hear it," the woman said sadly. "Should I send someone to tell her that?"

"What? No! Look, just to save time: no matter how oddly I behave or how much I protest, you're going to insist I'm the Goth Princess, right?"

"Of course, Your Highness."

"Fine. That's a weight off." It meant she really didn't have to work at keeping up an act. She could be as clumsy or awkward as she liked, and the narrative would smooth things over for her. All she really had to do was play along and work on her exit strategy. She'd seen the schematics. The ship was enormous, but it wasn't so big she'd have trouble getting back to the narrative bridge and out. Like Diana had said, it was easier to work *with* the narrative than to fight it. "I guess I should be getting dressed then."

"I totally agree. Her Highness remains as insightful as ever."

"What's your name, though?" Lenore asked. "I'll humor you if you humor me."

"As Your Highness wishes." The woman rose gracefully, once again standing most of a head over Lenore. "My name is Chlodina, and I am pleased to make your acquaintance once again."

Even with the worst of the pressure off, Lenore was *not* looking forward to this narrative thread. She knew exactly how a Xayarian Goth Princess was supposed to behave. All she had to do was channel her mother. Amelina Mallory had landed that role as the Goth Princess because her natural inclinations lent themselves so beautifully to it. The trouble was, Lenore had *rejected* being her mother years ago. This whole experience promised to be draining at best, and probably painful as well.

"And I presume I have some sort of body servant?" Lenore pressed.

"Her Highness means Jalissa, I'm sure," Chlodina answered primly.

"And do I normally just yell for her, or how should I do this?"

Chlodina let out a long-suffering sigh. "How long are we going to play this game, Highness?"

"Only as long as it takes to find my mother and get this mess properly straightened out," Lenore assured her. "Oh, and my own name is Vanda, right?"

"Of course not, Your Highness. That *would* be your mother. Your Highness is Princess Diva."

"It would?" Lenore raised an eyebrow. "Well, that doesn't make a lot of sense. I don't look *that* much like my mother, and it's not like my dad was ever here, so it's not like I've got a full sister you could be taking me for. How blind are you to mistake me for my *half*-sister, then?"

"Very blind, I'm sure," Chlodina said. "Now if it pleases Your Highness, I would consider it a personal kindness to find that this entire conversation was over."

"Yeah. Sure," Lenore said with a dismissive wave of her hand. "Go...do whatever you'd be doing if it wasn't this."

With a curt nod of acknowledgment, Chlodina spun on her heels and left the room, and Lenore slumped into the ensuing silence like a child collapsing into a bean bag chair. As always, it would take her a minute to ground herself from being the object of a stranger's attention. Recovering from the attention of a friend could be hard enough, but putting on any sort of face for strangers always meant her body and mind were on high alert, pumping out adrenalin. Afterward, simply recalling what she'd been doing and what her priorities should be now always came as a challenge.

Before she could get that sorted out, she found her comforting silence broken by a quiet and polite—but enthusiastic—applause. "Oh, wow! That was a great scene!" Denise said excitedly.

And so much for being off-stage. Lenore offered Denise a wan smile and a sheepish, "Thanks," before returning to the bed and collapsing into it face down. After a few seconds of wallowing in the pillow, Lenore reluctantly turned her head to the side and spat out a mouthful of hair. "Jalissa?" she addressed the air in a normal voice. Some other person might have instantly forgotten that unfamiliar name uttered once during the stress of a tense exchange, but only because that person wouldn't have been Lenore.

Several seconds ticked by before a chime sounded and a ghostly, holographic projection of the Goth woman who'd barricaded the restroom door shimmered into existence in the middle of the room. "Yes, Your Highness?" The woman was nearly as short as Chlodina was tall. She'd barely come up to Lenore's nose when they'd been struggling. Her dark purple hair hung down one side of her head in an intricate braid, and the small tattoo in the middle of her forehead might have been meant as a stylized spider.

"Look, I already know you're not going to believe this," Lenore said tiredly, "but I'm going to tell you anyway. I'm going to tell you because the truth is destined to come out at some point, and when it does, I do *not* want the grief of you claiming I lied to you. I am *not* Princess Diva. My name is Lenore. I just want to get back to my friends. Oh, and I want my own, pink clothes back. I hate black. But I know that's not happening just yet, so please just keep them safe so I can have them when this all makes some sort of sense. 'Kay?"

Jalissa shuffled her feet awkwardly for a moment, but then rallied and straightened up, adopting the more confident air Lenore would have expected from a Xayarian Goth. "Of course, Your Highness."

"Also, do get in here and find me whatever clothes you *do* consider appropriate for my schedule. I somehow doubt it would be fitting for me to take tea with the 'Pudding Princess' while wrapped in a bed sheet."

"Your Highness is not wrong," Jalissa answered agreeably.

"So my name's Diva. I'm the Goth Princess. What else do I need to know about me?" Lenore asked while Jalissa rifled through the contents of the suite's walk-in closet. "And you can stop making those faces you don't think I know you're making in there. I was straight with you. If you want me to play this game your way, you'll have to work with me."

"Just so Your Highness is quite clear in understanding that any faces I might have been making were only expressions of respect and reverence," Jalissa said.

"Of course they were. So answer the question."

"Your Highness has me at a loss," Jalissa said, pulling a long, black dress worthy of a late-night horror-movie hostess off the rack and holding it up for Lenore's approval. "How could I presume to know even where to begin?"

"No!" Lenore snapped, startling herself a little at how easily that moment of channeling her mother came. "Absolutely not. I do *not* wear black. Do I have *anything* pink in there?"

"Certainly not, Highness," Jalissa gasped. "Would blood red be acceptable?"

"Fine," Lenore muttered. "Find me something red. And for where to begin, you can tell me where we are. I only know I saw a very large structure outside the ship. No idea what it was or where it was. Are we even in a star system?"

"The Electra system, Your Highness."

"Oh! Well, that's nice," Lenore said, surprised to hear something had gone according to plan. They'd come very nearly to the place they'd meant to, if not the time. "So that was eCity I saw?" As the hub of galactic civilization in *SJZ*, ElectriCity would have all the latest in medical technology. If there was any possible way to find a cure for Val in this universe, they could find it on eCity. "Are we still docked there?"

"What?" Jalissa paused in holding up a long red dress made half of lace.

"Isn't that more sort of a wine red?" Lenore asked.

Jalissa shrugged helplessly. "Is there a difference?"

Lenore waved her mother's dismissive hand. "It'll do. Are we still docked?"

"We're *on* eCity, Highness," Jalissa said. "Chlodina helped you back to your residence here after...your little mishap."

Lenore blinked. "Wait. What?"

"You're on the space station, Your Highness," Jalissa said patiently. "That's where you're needed right now."

"But the ship? The *Queen Ilo*? It's still docked here, right?"

"I...don't know, Highness," Jalissa replied. "It's possible, but I never learned the ship's itinerary. Please don't worry, though. I personally cleaned out your cabin, inspected every nook and cranny for personal effects, and left a message with your regrets for the young man. He will understand that duty had to come before your little adventure, I guarantee it."

Lenore managed to make it back to perch on the bed before her unsteady legs buckled out from under her. "Well *find out*," she demanded, putting the impression of her mother on autopilot while she retreated into her own mind to grapple with what she was hearing. "If it's still here, get it...impounded or something so it can't leave. If it's left, either chase it down and bring it back or take me to it. Make it happen, or I don't care if all of civilization hangs in the balance, I will throw a tantrum like you have *never* seen and blow up any diplomatic agreements I'm here to salvage. Don't think I won't. You can't *begin* to comprehend the price I will pay if the *Queen Ilo* gets away before I'm done with her, and anyone who allows it to happen will take the fall with me. *Do you understand*?"

When the *Queen Ilo* left, Lenore's bridge home would leave with it. She'd seen the effects getting stranded on the wrong side of a bridge could have on the mind. Without protective magics—and she *was* without protective magics—she'd be certifiable within months, and presumably dead within a couple of years. Even without being abandoned by the agenda of the narrative bridge when it disappeared, her only hope would be a rescue party—and she had no idea if the coven would even know she'd left the ship.

"Yes, Your Highness," Jalissa said coolly. "Quite understood. I will see to it at once." She finished laying out Lenore's clothes for her and retreated from the room.

Lenore went back to wallowing face-down in the pillow. "They both hate me already," she moaned aloud to Denise. "My life depends on both of them, and they both hate me. I can't believe what a brat I was to them."

"It's just a role," Denise offered helpfully. "They know that."

"No, they don't," Lenore said into the pillow. "That's whole problem."

"An actress has to be able to let it slide off her and get back to reality," Denise said. "That's the job. They'll be fine. *You'll* be fine. Now buck up and get into costume for your next scene."

"I don't want to be my mom!" Lenore whimpered.

"Who does?" Denise asked.

"You don't know what she's like. Everyone thinks she's so cool, but they never had to live with her."

"Well, tell me all about her—after you finish shooting for the day," Denise said. "We're having a girl's night. Until then, you're a pro and you're going to act like one. You're being paid to be a brat, right? So go be a brat."

Lenore started to object, but decided there was no point. She also decided Denise wasn't entirely wrong. There was no real justification for her to be in this mess except that the narrative wanted her to be in it. She *had* been chosen to be a brat, and she'd been chosen while in service to a job for the coven that provided her room and board. So, from a twisted point of view, she was a working actor making good on her commitments. "I won't like it," she said at last.

"You don't have to," Denise assured her.

"And I'm *not* wearing black."

"I'll tell wardrobe myself, if you like," Denise offered. "I do have some clout on this lot."

"That's...sweet. Thanks," Lenore said, forcing herself up out of the pillow to look at Denise. Lenore also tried to smile, but couldn't swear she succeeded. "Guess I'd better go get ready for tea. Do you think I have one of those rings with the secret poison compartment?" she asked sardonically.

"I would hope," Denise said. "It's not like this show doesn't have the budget for it. Do you need it for the next scene?"

Lenore gave a little snort. "I have a hard time thinking I wouldn't by the time I'd finished tea with someone called the 'Pudding Princess.' If not for her, then for me."

"Just leave it to me, then," Denise said, sliding off the bed and onto her feet. "I'm already headed that way to lay down the law about your wardrobe colors. Your Highness shall have her ring." With a mischievous grin, a theatrical wave of her hand,

and a graceful curtsy, Denise backed toward the door, fading out of existence before she reached it.

CHAPTER EIGHT
THE ROYAL HAIR

Nothing would come of Denise's errand, of course. This was hardly the first time she'd headed off on one, always to reappear either thinking it had been successfully handled despite all evidence to the contrary, or having forgotten the subject had ever come up. Still, she always seemed utterly sincere, and she *was* being extremely sweet, even for Denise. A ghostly girl's-night with her might actually turn out to be fun—if Denise even remembered she'd proposed one.

Lenore took advantage of the quiet to take a brief tour of the suite. It turned out to include a sitting room, a library alcove with actual physical books, a fairly decadent bath chamber, and something that might have been meant as a sex dungeon. She quickly closed the door on that last one and let any doubts she could preserve linger in her mind. Lenore really didn't like the whole "sex dungeon" concept. It made her think uncomfortably about her parents having sex lives.

Finally, she took the clothes laid out for her into the walk-in closet and tried them on. They didn't just fit: they fit better than her own wardrobe. They fit better than any clothes she'd ever owned. Had her dad been an extra on *SJZ* or something and never admitted it? The idea seemed ludicrous. He and mom would have incorporated the fact into her con-circuit appearances to further play themselves up as the perfect Goth couple.

She paused to examine herself in the dressing-table mirror in an alcove at the back of the closet. As she did, an outraged gasp of disbelief escaped her lips. Her hair was *black*. It hadn't been black in so long she barely remembered what it had looked like this way, but every last trace of pink had been scrubbed clean from her head. Desperately trying to convince herself this was just some trick of the mirror, Lenore grabbed the pony tail she'd pulled her hair back into for the adventure and held it up in front of her face. The mirror hadn't lied.

So much for *la química* keeping her unmolested. A costume was a costume, but her hair was *her hair*.

"You had no right!" she screamed into the air as sudden rage rushed through her. Without thinking, she found herself grabbing the stool from in front of the dressing table and smashing it into the mirror. "I don't know what you are, but none of this happens without *some* sort of guiding intelligence! Give me my hair back or we are quits! It's over! I'm done playing! You *failed*!"

"I, uh...Sorry. Are you all right?"

Lenore spun, turning her rage on the source of the voice before she even had time to be surprised there'd been someone behind her. "Do I *look* all right?" she demanded, grabbing her ponytail again and shaking it accusingly at the man. Only then did the particulars of the circumstance begin to sink into her brain.

She'd thought she was alone. She was not. There was a man with her, looming in the doorway of her private dressing room—the private dressing room of the Goth Princess. She didn't recognize him. He was not a Goth. He didn't even appear entirely human. What he looked like was an Ivurnian genetic experiment. More specifically, he might have been able to pass himself off as Ambassador Yauhiri L'Roux with his green, cat-like eyes—at least to someone with really poor eyesight. He didn't seem to be trying to pass himself off, though. The clothes were all wrong, for one thing.

"Yes, you do, actually," the man said warily. "Upset, yes. Otherwise, same as always."

"My hair…is not…pink," Lenore hissed.

"This…is…true," the man replied, somehow mimicking her cadence without giving the impression he was mocking her. His tone came out more as a sort of helpless confusion.

Lenore sighed. "You think you know me. You don't."

"We all have our secrets, of course," the man admitted readily. "I'd never considered a lack of pink hair to be one of yours."

"Are you here to turn it pink?" she demanded.

"What? No!" His clear confusion continued to deepen.

"Then you don't count as a peace offering. Apology not accepted, no matter how sexy you look."

"Wait. What? Where did that even come from?" He scowled. "You detest me."

"Yes!" Lenore snapped. "Exactly! Because you're not turning my hair pink!"

"That's…it? All this time I thought you just resented having to rely on me for anything, but you've just thought I…wouldn't…turn your hair pink? That is so messed up."

"What's messed up is me having hair of any color that's not *pink*!" Lenore advanced threateningly on the large man. "Fix it *now* or get *out*!"

"All right!" He threw up his hands placatingly. "Just chill and tell me where the implant is."

Lenore narrowed her gaze. "I do *not* have hair implants!"

He rolled his eyes in frustration. "Why do you royals always have to do things old school? *Please* don't tell me you expect me to use hair dye or something."

"Just make it happen!"

"Bossy much?" Seeming at a loss for other options, he scooted cautiously around her to reach the dressing table and began rummaging through the drawers. "Been a bad day, has it?"

"It was going fine until someone kidnapped me and did this," Lenore muttered.

"Whoa." He looked up, wide-eyed. "Which airlock did Chlodina shoot them out of once she had you clear?"

"Chlodina *was* the someone," Lenore said, her voice oozing poison.

He stared at her in confusion for a moment before realization appeared to dawn. "Oh. Look, I get it. I know you're feeling caged, but you're not leaving her a lot of options. What was she supposed to do?"

"*Not* turn my hair black."

"I'm sure it was Jalissa who did that," he said, returning his attention to the dressing table. "And I'm sure she was just trying to save you some time and bother. It's not like you could show up pink at an official function. It'd start a war somewhere."

He pulled something that resembled a hand-held metal detector out of one of the drawers and held it up questioningly. "This is what I'm looking for, is it? I think my grandmother owns one of these. *Seriously* old school."

"If it works it works," Lenore said.

"Then I hope it works. Come on. Let your hair down and I'll have a go."

Cautiously mollified, Lenore grabbed the fallen stool and set it upright—well away from the shards of mirror—before settling herself on it. The man stood behind her, fiddling with the device, which emitted an occasional electronic chime as he did.

The whole situation brought to mind the recent times Lenore had played guinea pig for Sylvie's experiments in magical cosmetology. Sylvie didn't much care for fussing with makeup, but she did like her cosplay, and she adored being the center of attention, so she'd figured out how to coax her wand into doing the work for her. In addition to convenience, it had offered her a way to practice some low-impact, high-finesse magic. She'd been getting pretty darn good at it, too. If Sylvie had been here, Lenore had no doubt she could have remedied this atrocity in no time.

"This seems promising," the man said. "What shade of pink were you wanting?"

"Not too bright. Not too subtle. Maybe bubblegum pink or flamingo pink, if that helps?"

"Not a bit," he admitted, but the device began to hum, and Lenore could feel it press up against her skull above her ear. Its low, steady hum penetrated muscle and bone with such subtlety she barely realized it was happening until she felt all the pent-up tension melting away from her jaw and temple. His fingers gently but firmly twined in her hair, trapping a lock and pulling it out while the electronic wand slid down its length.

"Okay. Ummm..." Lenore began, wetting her lips while she tried to remember what a coherent thought was.

"Is that good?"

"Hmmm?" she asked dreamily.

"The color?"

Lenore opened eyes, which had somehow mysteriously closed while she wasn't paying attention, and focused in on the pink-tinged lock of hair he was waving in front of her face. "Oh. Yeah. More?"

"Deeper pink?" he asked.

"Just more." Lenore sighed. "S'good." The tension had already drained out of her neck and shoulders too as the languid sensations spread. Gentle fingers combed through her hair, occasionally brushing lightly against the flesh of her ear, her cheek, her neck...

Lenore remained vaguely aware that the man continued to make observations and ask questions, but she really didn't care. She'd become much more interested in the delicious, delightful hum spreading through her arms and her chest—on out to her fingertips and down her stomach—beginning to make things tingle that—

Lenore sat up abruptly, flushed and wide-eyed, her hand shooting out to restrain the wrist holding the gadget. "Are we done?" she asked hoarsely.

"Nearly," he said. "One more streak of black to take care of. Are you—?"

"A streak's fine," she said, releasing his arm and sliding unsteadily to her feet. "I'm sure it's fine. Just give me the thing. I'll finish it later." Lenore grabbed the gadget from his unresisting hand before hastily trying to change the subject. "What's your name, anyway?"

"What?!" He stared at her incredulously.

"Oh. Right." Lenore winced. "I haven't told you I'm crazy yet."

"Not recently," he admitted. "But it's come up."

"I mean, I'm not Diva. I'm not the Goth Princess, and I don't belong here. I already know you're not going to believe that. I just don't want you to come back later all mad that I..."

He held up a restraining hand. "No. We're good. It explains a lot, actually. I've never once seen Diva blush, for starters."

Lenore immediately felt her blush deepen. "Well, thank you for that," she mumbled, fidgeting with her hair. "No one else believes me. I'm Lenore."

"Lenore? Really?" His quizzical expression quickly vanished into a more neutral one under her pointed glare. "Hello, Lenore. I'm Orthos. Are we done freaking out?"

"Maybe?" Lenore hedged, while inside she fought down the desire to make something of his reaction. In any self-respecting Goth society, her name ought to raise about as many eyebrows as "Mary Margaret" would in a Catholic school.

"So what are you to Diva?" Orthos asked. "Twin sister? Clone? Identical cousin?"

"It's weirder than you could possibly imagine."

"Try me," he pressed.

"I'm a witch from an alternate dimension," Lenore said with a shrug.

"A witch?" Orthos asked dubiously. "Named Lenore?"

"You asked," Lenore said. "Doesn't matter. I don't know where Diva is. I've never met her, and all I want is to get back to my friends. Oh, and find a cure for cancer."

"Have you tried the dispensary?" he asked casually. "What kind have you got?" He checked himself and waved off the question. "Sorry. None of my business. I'm sure whatever it is, they'll have you covered. Forgot for a moment where we are."

"So it's just like a pill? An ointment?" she asked.

"No clue. Anyway, if you're not Diva—and everyone else is convinced you're Diva—this is going to get very complicated, if only because no one's out looking for her."

"Actually, I *might* have an idea where she is," Lenore said. "They kidnapped me from the *Queen Ilo*, so they at least thought she was on board. And there was this guy there too, who thought I was a friend of his. He must have thought I was her. I bet they're traveling together."

"Sounds like she's running away again." Orthos sighed. "I wish she'd just fake her own death already."

"Why does she—?"

"Your Highness?" Jalissa's voice called from the outer room.

Orthos immediately raised a finger to his lips, then shook his head while waving his hands and fading silently into a back corner of the closet.

With a nod of understanding, Lenore stepped out into the bed chamber. "What did you find out?" she asked.

"Well, I..." Jalissa began nervously, then stopped and gaped at Lenore. "Oh, Highness! Really? I'm *trying*! Please be reasonable."

"Which means...you haven't succeeded?" Lenore asked, her stomach sinking.

"No." Jalissa actually stamped her foot in frustration. "The ship left. It's hours out now, you have to be at a diplomatic meeting in half an hour, and you've got pink hair...again! What do you expect from me?!"

And there it was: the reason Lenore didn't want to be her mother—the reason she *couldn't* be her mother. Amelina Mallory wasn't sadistic as such, but Amelina Mallory only cared what other people thought when Amelina Mallory wanted to. If what you wanted or needed or felt proved inconvenient to her, she could disconnect from your emotions just like flipping a switch. It had led to some very cold, calculated confrontations between Amelina and her daughter over the years. Lenore didn't know how to not care about other people's troubles—she didn't *want* to know how to not care—even though right now that meant the very genuine despair in Jalissa's voice and her face hit Lenore like a physical kick in the gut.

"To listen when I tell you I'm not Diva," Lenore said evenly, rallying to disconnect from her own emotions because that was the only way she could get relief from anyone else's. "Sorry for trying to bully you, but I really am desperate. Please help me."

Jalissa squinted suspiciously and rubbed one ear before cocking it Lenore's direction. "Your pardon, Highness. What did you say?"

"I said I'm not Diva," Lenore said. When she stopped there, Jalissa made a rolling motion with her hand, prompting Lenore to move on. "I'm sorry. Please help me."

"Wow. Okay," Jalissa said, taking a step back and shaking her head. "This is bad."

"Which part?" Lenore asked.

"All of it. It's all bad in so many ways. But yeah, I'm listening. You're not Diva," Jalissa said. "And that gives me twenty minutes tops to figure out how to avert a war."

"Can I just call in sick?" Lenore asked. Jalissa just glared at her. "That's a 'no,' then. Why does Diva have to show up? Give me the elevator pitch."

"The what?" Jalissa asked.

"Tell me fast," Lenore amended. "Get right to the point."

"War," Jalissa replied succinctly.

"A little *less* to the point?" Lenore asked. "Pretend you've got fifteen seconds. Maybe thirty."

"Ancient alliances," Jalissa said, trying again. "Diplomatic rituals. Sexual seduction."

"So 'having tea' is a euphemism for...?" Lenore hesitated, trying to figure out the best way to finish that sentence, but Jalissa came to her rescue.

"Yes. It is."

Lenore grimaced. "No wonder Diva runs away."

"You'd find it more confusing if you'd seen the Pudding Princess." Jalissa sighed dreamily.

"Not the point," Lenore said dryly. "Does Diva do this sort of thing a lot?"

"Sometimes. Actually, the important part is appearances," Jalissa admitted. "It's all very wink-wink, nudge-nudge, if you know what I mean. Last week she lured the Prince of Frustratingly Overpriced Baubles in here, and then they just sat and played video games for two hours before he walked out with mussed hair and a crooked collar. Of course, I'll have to kill you if you tell anyone that."

"Of course." Lenore didn't doubt it, and immediately wrote a mental note to that effect—using a jumbo-sized mental felt-tip and punctuating the whole thing with three exclamation marks. "But I think I can work with this. You don't need Diva to seduce the Pudding Princess. You need it to *look* like Diva seduced the Pudding Princess?"

"Exactly," Jalissa said. "This is all political theater."

"In which the Goth Princess plays the part of a dominatrix, because that's what some television executive thought would sell twenty years ago," Lenore muttered.

"Pardon?" Jalissa asked.

"Nothing. Sorry." Lenore waved off the thought. "I just meant this whole thing is stupid and doesn't make sense."

"On that we agree." Jalissa smiled the gratified smile of someone who had been waiting years for a chance to express that very sentiment. "But your hair is still pink again."

"Which is really that bad?" Lenore grimaced.

"Sorry. Yes," Jalissa answered apologetically. "It's really that bad."

"Is black the *only* option?"

"Maybe. I don't know," Jalissa fretted. "Not a lot of time here."

"Red, maybe?" Lenore pleaded. "If you can give me red hair, I'll even wear black for just a little while. I can tell myself it's for a charity cosplay."

"It's not up to me."

"Well, who *is* it up to?"

"No one we have time to ask," Jalissa said miserably. "Look, can you really pull this off, or is it time for me to go into panicked damage-control mode?"

Lenore held up two fingers of each hand in a call for silence as she closed her eyes and bowed her head. Behind her eyes, she slipped into her game master head space and started rearranging pertinent facts and feelings about her mother, both in-character and out. She breathed deeply. She banished the butterflies that came with going on stage. They'd be back with a vengeance soon enough, but that would be a worry for later.

She lowered her hands as her eyes fluttered open, and she gave an enigmatic little smile. "We're already in damage control mode," she said coolly. "Just give me the hair. Make it cartoon-torch-singer red."

"I...don't know that shade...Highness." Jalissa clearly couldn't make up her mind whether to be pleased or worried.

Lenore gave a put-upon sigh. "Just make me look like I'm about to burst into flames."

"At once." Jalissa clasped her hands and dropped her head into a polite bow before heading for the closet door.

Lenore cleared her throat. "You wait here. I'll get it."

"But—"

Lenore breezed past the woman, cutting off her protests. "Broken glass. My fault. I'll not have you hobbling around on my account." Apparently she needn't have worried, though. Either Orthos had found a way out of her closet, or he'd hidden himself so well Jalissa never would have suspected. She grabbed the techno-wand he'd used on her and returned to present it to Jalissa.

"I...don't think Her Highness meant for me to use *this* uh...styler," Jalissa said awkwardly.

"Oh, she absolutely did." Lenore hit Jalissa with her best taunting-mastermind smile. "Do you want a seductress or don't you?"

CHAPTER NINE
RELAUNCH

It wasn't really Lenore who walked down the Promenade Èlectrique fifteen minutes later, through the fashionable heart of eCity's upper-class entertainment module. It was some non-player character Lenore had pulled together on the spur of the moment as an exaggerated mash-up of Amelina Mallory's already-over-the-top Goth Gothiness and the seductive lounge-singer archetype. Out of deference to the needs of the plotline, Lenore had named her Diva, then detached to retreat to the back of her brain to watch the proceedings—a sightseer looking out the window of her own eyes in the tour bus of her body.

It couldn't have been Lenore animating her body, because Lenore didn't do sexy. She faked sexy, just like she faked brave and smart and...well, everything. She'd cop to having a superb audial memory, but otherwise her primary talent lay in pretending to be talented. She could bluff her way through nearly anything if she didn't have to maintain the facade for too long.

Turning loose a manufactured persona to handle her body unsupervised didn't come without advantages, though. The trick worked better if she focused her attention on pondering all the strange sights, sounds, and scents swirling around her. She didn't actually gawk. That would have involved taking back control of her eyes and neck at least, and totally spoiled the effect. But she saw what she saw, heard what she heard, and smelled whatever perfumed clouds she drifted through, and she pondered it all like so much scenery hurrying past.

She'd seen the Promenade Èlectrique before, of course—it had been a recurring set on the incarnation of *SJZ* they'd been aiming to visit—but seeing it was an entirely different experience from finding herself immersed in it. This wasn't just some clone of the set her body was walking through, either. This promenade had aged and changed through at least another twenty years of whatever passed for nightlife on a space station. The set for the television show had never been more than one stretch of scenery that included one club, a restaurant, and some store fronts, plus the entrance to a lift that teased the presence of a sporting arena below and a theater above. Here, though, she'd already walked a kilometer or more down the promenade since stepping out of her private transit capsule, and still she could see no end to it.

Another of the many, many places Lenore had never been was Tokyo, but the aesthetic of the Promenade Èlectrique set had always reminded her of Tokyo anyway. The bright, colorful, busy lights and high-tech look combined with the alien-to-Lenore script plastered across everything and the bustling crowds to conjure up all the pop-culture images she'd seen of Tokyo streets. Now that she was actually here, the high, vaulted ceiling of the broad promenade even felt like towering buildings leaning vertiginously in to crowd out the sky. A sliver of stars visible through the transparent strip running down the middle of the ceiling only added to the illusion of being in an earthly city, and Lenore could easily imagine all the exotic near-humans milling through the crowd as cosplaying *otaku*. Even the robots could have been...well, robots. Clearly, the place would never actually pass for Tokyo, but it might pass for someone's loving, fan-fiction reinvention of Tokyo.

And in the middle of all this lovely sensory overload that would have sent Lenore screaming had she actually been there, Diva noticed with no small satisfaction that head after head turned as each new set of eyes took note of her passing. On a promenade full of beautiful, fashionable people, in a city full of beautiful, fashionable people, in a universe full of beautiful, fashionable people—all photogenic enough to make it onto television—Diva was the one everyone she passed either wanted to have or wanted to be.

For her part, that puzzled Lenore to no end. "Beautiful" was *not* a word she attributed to herself, yet she'd been the one who'd given Diva the raw materials to work with. Oh, objectively she figured she looked passable enough. She had enough of her mother's looks for people to remark on a family resemblance, and Lenore doubted she'd ever met a fan of Amelina Mallory who didn't fantasize about her. No one remembered Amelina's brief career this far on because of her Oscar-caliber performances. But it wasn't like Amelina was the new Helen of Troy, either. What made Amelina worth remembering in a crowd of pretty actresses had always been the marketing. She sold attitude. She sold the persona.

In the end, Lenore could only conclude that meant she'd done a good job slapping this Diva persona together in a rush. The hair might have helped too. People would look up, notice the redhead swaggering by, then do a double take as they realized they were seeing the face, figure, and flowing black dress of the normally raven-tressed Goth Princess. The eternal rebel had rebelled against her own rebellion today, reinventing her signature look with just enough of an edge to remind people who she was without quite scandalizing the traditionalists into conniptions. At least Lenore *hoped* she hadn't gone too far. Diva didn't seem to care one way or another, though, and that was all that mattered right now. Also, Diva's bodyguard was following along dutifully in her wake, not shooting her. That couldn't be a bad sign.

It scared Lenore a little how easy she was finding it to let go and leave Diva to do her thing unsupervised. She'd gotten reasonably comfortable over the years with stepping out of herself and playing a role for her friends for a little while, even within the public-but-nonjudgmental space of a fantasy convention. And, yes, it did help knowing she'd never have to live in this place—never be *able* to live in this place—and never face any of these people ever again if she didn't want to. Not unless she got stranded here of course, but that would bring a whole other set of worries. Still, none of that could account for the easy way she just sat back and watched when a four-armed cat woman who'd jostled against Diva turned and watched her go. As she did, the woman's gaze smoldered with unapologetic lust, and Diva just answered with a saucy, confident wink before turning her attention back to where she was walking.

It wasn't that Lenore actually felt one way or another about the moment. She'd known most of her life her parents had some sort of open relationship going on, and that "Auntie Margaret" had been Mom's "special friend." Lenore had even kissed a couple of girls herself before deciding it just didn't do anything for her. What shocked Lenore was finding herself so deep in-character that she was publicly, unselfconsciously flirting with a total stranger for no other reason than it amused this persona she'd adopted. That crossed multiple lines she'd never gone over before, no matter how intensely she'd gotten into a game or identified with a character.

The realization came perilously close to scaring her into taking back control from Diva—which would have turned into a total disaster—until she remembered where she was and what that meant. This wasn't all happening just because Lenore was so much like her mother beneath the surface. It was happening because the part of her mother she *was* tapping into would be perfectly in sync with *la química*. Lenore had very deliberately dug deep into her own libido to find this version of Diva, and her libido was determined to have some fun now that it abruptly found itself out on the playground unchaperoned.

Coming face to face with that thought did make Lenore miss a step as she struggled with the temptation to wrench back control of her body, but Diva laughed off the stumble by pretending to have stepped on something, then followed up by pretending to kick that something playfully away before resuming her swagger. She did spare a moment, though, to massage her fingers and reassure Lenore that both protective rings remained firmly in place. Whatever mischief Lenore allowed Diva to get up to would remain consequence-free mischief. The message was clear: Diva had this, and Lenore should get out of her own way for once and enjoy the moment. With a final mental sigh, Lenore acquiesced and settled back again to look out the metaphorical window.

Now and again Lenore would catch sight of Denise appearing randomly in the crowd, like some spectator patiently and politely watching a parade go by. Always, Denise wore the same proud and supportive smile in apparent approval of Lenore's acting chops, and for once Lenore had to think maybe she did deserve some of the credit her deceased roommate was giving her. This whole thing could be going so, so much worse in so many ways. It probably still would, but right here and right now it wasn't, and even Lenore had to admit that was mostly her own fault.

In all this long promenade with its trendy gathering spots, Lenore would have marveled at the coincidence her scheduled rendezvous would be in that single club she knew from the television show—*The Relaunch*—only she knew better than to believe it was a coincidence. The narrative bridge ritual existed specifically to connect travelers to familiar people and places they never should have been able to reach. For her specific destination now to have never come on stage would have been the weird part.

When at last she reached that familiar stretch of the promenade, Diva breezed right past the line of pretty people waiting to get in, and the imposing robotic doorman waved her through without any hint of hesitation. Hair color didn't appear to be high on the thing's list of ways to identify an individual. And whether it recognized Chlodina as belonging to its short list of V.I.P.s, or simply accepted her as Diva's "plus one," the mechanical creature proved every bit as solicitous to the Goth bodyguard.

Diva casually dismissed the woman who showed up to be welcoming and helpful the moment they stepped inside. "I'm not sure I'll be staying yet," she said, coolly but politely. "Just wanted to see if there's anyone interesting about." As an afterthought she added, "Do have someone bring me a drink, though. The usual."

The woman nodded and hurried off, but her back had hardly turned before Diva spotted her quarry: a gorgeously zaftig, dark-skinned woman with lavender hair and a mid-length dress of vibrant purple, joyously rocking about the dance floor with her arms held high and repeatedly switching partners without ever switching expressions. Jalissa had shown Lenore a hologram of the woman. *That* was Tsuzi, the Pudding Princess, and just watching her move stirred an inward sigh of longing from Lenore in her cozy little passenger's seat. To be clear, what she felt was not the longing of sexual desire, but the longing to feel half so free and unselfconscious as the princess looked. To all appearances, the day they'd handed out social masks, the Pudding Princess had politely declined hers and never once missed it. The next time Lenore got wrangled into a job by a case of narratively orchestrated mistaken identity, she already desperately wanted it to be that one. Perhaps once people started calling you "The Pudding Princess" to your face, you simply felt the worst had already happened and you might as well enjoy the rest of your life.

Very suddenly, Lenore came to herself and realized she was back in her own body. While she'd been staring at the woman on the dance floor, Diva had quietly packed up and wandered off. It seemed she'd walked into a wall she'd never been prepared for. Ideally, Diva would have just taken Lenore's body right out onto the dance floor and joined Tsuzi there. The problem was, Lenore didn't really know how to dance worth anything. Even watching her mother hadn't given her much material to work with there, and pulling off a confident, sensual dance was way more complicated than simply queuing up snippets of body language she'd spent all her life observing.

All of which begged the question, what now? Here she was, the Goth Princess, standing and gawking like a teenager while the young social elite of the galaxy stared at her, waiting for her to be cool—but her cool had walked off and left her hanging, and it wouldn't be back any time soon. What should she do? What *could* she do? What would a *game master* do?

To that last question, she knew the answer. Calmly, she turned to face Chlodina and beckoned her over, then whispered in the bodyguard's ear.

"What?!" Chlodina scowled, puzzled. "Here? Now? Are you...?" She caught herself before finishing what had been about to be a deeply impertinent question.

"Make it happen," Lenore prodded her. "I don't care how—or this whole thing is out of my hands. It's this or war."

Chlodina drew a shuddering breath, buried her face briefly in her hand, then turned a slow three-sixty as she surveyed the room. "This is on you," she muttered.

"It's on me," Lenore agreed.

"Well, the good news is my ex is here." Chlodina shook her head. "Can't say he doesn't deserve this." With that, she strode purposefully out across the dance floor, dodging between writing bodies until she drew up short in front of a Xayarian Goth who could have been the very man the phrase "devilishly handsome" had been coined for. "Kenric." She acknowledged him with cold formality as he turned from his dance partner to face her.

"Hey! Chloe!" Kenric grinned impishly. "What—"

"Combat encounter," Lenore murmured with grim satisfaction as Chlodina's fist connected with Kenric's jaw. The blow spun his body completely around, chasing after his head in a desperate bid to keep the two connected to each other.

Screaming and yelling ensued as the dancers scattered. Chlodina waited patiently, massaging her knuckles, while Kenric righted himself and glared at her. A security guard wearing the *Relaunch* insignia shoved his way through the scattering crowd toward her. Before he could reach her, though, another tall woman with a dangerously cold look—probably someone else's bodyguard—stepped in and reached out for Chlodina. Chlodina dropped, grabbing the wrist of the encroaching arm and hurling the woman neatly over her shoulder to collide with Kenric and send them both sprawling on the floor together.

Chlodina didn't check her own forward momentum after throwing the woman, but continued to somersault forward herself, and she didn't stop tumbling until she had Kenric squarely between herself and the oncoming security guard. As Kenric started to rise, she kicked him toward the security guard, ducked the swing of *another* bodyguard entering the fray, and knocked the man's legs out from under him so he collided with the woman Chlodina had already thrown. From there, things devolved rapidly, and Lenore couldn't waste Chlodina's effort by standing around trying to sort it out.

Spying the Pudding Princess standing at the edge of the dance floor, watching the proceedings with mild bemusement, Lenore darted forward and grabbed her hand. "Come with me," Lenore demanded urgently, "if you want to live."

"What?" Tsuzi asked, turning with a puzzled expression to face Lenore.

"It's a fight," Lenore explained with exaggerated patience. "I'm trying to get you away from the fight. It's dangerous."

"Oh!" Tsuzi said, a look of recognition suddenly dawning in her eyes. "Right. It's dangerous. And my bodyguard's..." She waved vaguely at the growing tangle of brawling bodies that had replaced the dancers. "...in there...somewhere. It's good there's someone right here, offering to take me to safety."

"Sorry," Lenore muttered quietly. "Had to improvise."

"We're good," Tsuzi murmured. "Diplomatic immunity is a marvelous thing. Lead on."

CHAPTER TEN

SUITE DREAMS

"Then the whole room just falls dead silent, all at once," Tsuzi said, leaning confidentially across the table as a multi-limbed robot deftly gathered up the remnants of their meal. "The chancellor looks at me like he just swallowed a bug, and he says, 'Oh. Was that yours?' I literally fell out laughing."

"People." Lenore sighed, then gave a sympathetic chuckle. "Can't live with 'em, can't live without 'em."

"Isn't that the truth," Tsuzi agreed with a lopsided grin.

As soon as they'd made it clear of the club, they'd ducked into the handiest doorway and found themselves in a very nice, dimly lit restaurant lounge where they'd immediately agreed a bite to eat while listening to some woman lilt through a pleasant but unfamiliar song in a pleasant but unfamiliar alien tongue would be just the thing. By the time their order had arrived, so had their bodyguards. Neither appeared much worse for wear, but each appeared ever so slightly sulky as they hovered quietly in the background, keeping an eye out for trouble.

"What went wrong back there anyway?" Tsuzi asked.

"It's complicated," Lenore said. "Mostly I'm just not myself today. *Really* not myself."

"Ironically put." Tsuzi smirked. "Seems to me it's your mask that's slipping."

"Yeah. About that." Lenore chewed on her lip while she tried to figure out what to say. "I'm being calculatingly disarming in order to put you at ease?"

"As I'm sure I'll find out too late, to my regret." Tsuzi nodded thoughtfully. "Good enough for now, but let's not push our luck. Even a place like this can't really guarantee privacy. That's sort of the point."

"Right. Keep the table warm. I'll be back in like two minutes." Lenore pushed back her chair and made her way to the ladies' room, which she found to be remarkably spacious, luxuriously appointed, and mercifully empty. Taking advantage of the quiet and the lack of watching eyes, she leaned on the counter in front of the mirror and began searching the corners of her mind until she found Diva again. With a final sigh, she shook out her arms, rolled her neck to release tension, and turned control of her body back over to the persona.

The woman who'd walked into the restroom didn't walk out. She swayed. She glided. She radiated all the confidence fitting to a Goth princess. And—arriving from behind the Pudding Princess—she laid a hand lightly on Tsuzi's shoulder and leaned down to murmur in her ear, "Dance with me."

The woman in purple cocked her head to smile up into Diva's eyes from very close indeed. "Happily." She offered her hand. Diva took it and led her out to join the handful of couples on the little dance floor. This would not be like dancing at the club. No one here was showing off. The only move on display was to draw one's partner in close and rock her lazily in time with the music. Diva could totally handle that.

"Better?" Diva asked with the alluring smile Lenore usually saved for her daydreams about Scott Legacy.

"Much," Tsuzi agreed.

Diva tickled Tsuzi's ear with a puff of breath, evoking a giggle. "I keep running scenario after scenario in my head," she whispered, "and they all end badly unless I'm completely straight with you."

"I kind of need this whole seduction scene to make things work," Tsuzi whispered back.

"I meant I need to be *honest* with you."

"Oh. Honesty is good," Tsuzi agreed.

"I'm a ringer—a last-minute substitute. Long story. It wasn't planned, but I was told I could stop a war if I showed up and played the game, so here I am."

"That's, ummm..." Tsuzi's whisper faltered and trailed off.

"It's me or no one," Diva whispered. "Sorry."

"No," Tsuzi muttered, pushing away and out of Diva's arms. "No. I can't do this."

Diva snagged Tsuzi's arm before she could step off the little floor and spun her gently but insistently back around. "Yes," Diva said, meeting Tsuzi's gaze unflinchingly. "You can. More importantly, *we* can. The question is, '*Will* you?'"

"Oh, wow." Tsuzi gave a sly grin, appraising Diva through narrowed eyes. "You're not bad."

"Actually, I *am* bad," Diva purred. "But that's the point, isn't it?"

"Perhaps it is," Tsuzi murmured, returning to wrap her arms around Diva's neck and lean in for a slow, mouth-open, tongue-minding-its-own-business sort of kiss meant to look more steamy than it actually was.

"Want to get out of here?" Diva asked with a patented Amelina-Mallory sultry gaze.

"Yes," Tsuzi murmured. "I believe I do."

"Well, that was kind of fun," Tsuzi laughed, kicking off her shoes as the door to Diva's suite closed behind them. "Are you really on the level about not being Diva, or was that just some sort of weird role-play?"

"Both." Diva returned the laugh as she sank down into the closest padded chair. Then Lenore shook off the persona, reclaiming her body. "Ow. How do you people do it?" she asked. Clutching her skull with one hand, she used it to stretch out her neck.

"Which people?" Tsuzi asked, scooping up her shoes and collapsing into another nearby chair. "Do what?" She began kneading the carpet with her toes.

"Extroverts! How do you...how do you 'people' like this? I feel like I was in the middle of that brawl, taking all the punches myself. I swear I've never pretended that long or that hard to be sociable."

"You're seriously an introvert?" Tsuzi asked, eyebrows going up. "I never would have guessed."

"Thanks. Acting runs in the family." Lenore shrugged. "We're dropping the whole seduction bit now, right? I'm really just into guys."

"Yeah. Me too. At least I've never found the woman to convince me otherwise, but you learn to pretend when you're the Pudding Princess. The job description says I love *everybody*. Just between you and me, though, people can be real gits."

"You are preaching to the proverbial choir," Lenore said. "Anyway, I'm Lenore. Feel free to keep calling me Diva, though. No sense inviting slip-ups."

"Imminently sensible," Tsuzi agreed. "Nice to meet you, though."

"Jalissa?" Lenore called into the air.

This time when the chime came, the hologram of Jalissa remained discretely absent, hopefully as a visual signal that wherever she might actually be, she wasn't spying on the proceedings. "Yes, Your Highness?"

"We need alcohol. Or...something. Send in whatever will take the edge off without going overboard." She gestured to Tsuzi, inviting her to voice her own desires.

"Something warm, chocolaty, and minty for me—and add a touch of whatever you're giving Diva."

"Of course, Your Highnesses." The chime sounded again, and Jalissa went silent.

"Make yourself at home," Lenore said, forcing herself back to her feet. "My brain's about to shut down if I don't go grab a hot shower and a little space. Give me fifteen."

"Take thirty if you need," Tsuzi said. "I'm staying the night, aren't I?"

"Sure, if that's in the script."

Lenore dug a red, kimono-style robe out of the wardrobe and was about to head for Diva's decadent bathing chamber when, on an impulse, she stopped and rifled through the dressing table until she found the hair-coloring wand. Then she really did head for the bathing chamber. A wave of relief rolled through her body as the door closed behind her, shutting out the universe. She closed her eyes, breathed deeply, and spent the next minute or two simply drinking in the silence. A light aroma reminiscent of roses and fresh rain hung in the air. Maybe she'd been moving too quickly to notice it here the first time through, or maybe it has been introduced by Jalissa or by some automated system since Lenore's early visit. Regardless, she welcomed it.

As she crossed to the glass-fronted shower, the movement of her own reflection in the bathroom mirror drew her eye to it, and then to a red lipstick scrawl on the mirror itself. "Call me. — O," it read, with an arrow pointing down to the counter, where the still-open tube lay next to a palm-sized device with a single button and the grill of what looked like a built-in speaker.

Weariness warred with curiosity for several long seconds before Lenore finally reached out and tapped the button. A pause followed, then a chime, and then the murmur of some sort of crowd. "Hello?" a man answered.

"Orthos?" she asked, pretty sure she recognized the voice of her Ivurnian visitor from before.

"Yeah. Give me a minute." The sound of the crowd grew muffled, then cut off completely. "Lenore, right?"

"Yes. Were you trying to reach me or her?"

"You. You seemed...stressed." He chuckled at his own characterization of the encounter. "I had things I had to do, but I didn't want to leave you wondering how to find your friends all by yourself. It's a big galaxy."

"No lie." It was Lenore's turn to laugh. "Thanks. I appreciate that. Is this like a burner phone you left me?"

"A what?"

"A disposable, untraceable sort of thing."

"Basically," he agreed. "I'd be obliged if you'd space it, though, when you're done with it."

"Sure. If I can find an airlock. Does this thing have a hologram option?" Lenore asked. "It's a little less stressful to see who I'm talking to."

"Hold the button for like ten seconds."

"Cool. Thanks." She did—after reflexively checking her hair in the mirror. It'd do, though she regretted it remained red.

"Hanging in there?" Orthos asked as his translucent hologram materialized at a comfortable distance. "How'd your mission go?"

"I think I salvaged it." Lenore shrugged. "Look, thanks for putting up with my tantrum, and thanks for fixing my hair."

"Red now?" he asked.

"Not for much longer." She waved the hair-coloring wand demonstratively. "At least it's not black." She winced. "I sound awfully shallow, don't I?"

Orthos spread his hands noncommittally. "I see worse over less on a regular basis."

"Anyway, I'm sorry. I was lost and stressed and confused, and there's a whole story behind the hair. Anyway, you didn't deserve it."

"I didn't. Thank you for noticing." His grin fell a bit short of the dismissive gesture it was surely meant to be.

"So who *are* you, anyway?" Lenore asked. "Some sort of secret agent?"

"Just a guy who knows how to get things done and be discrete about it."

"Does discretion usually involve showing up unannounced in a girl's dressing room?"

"If I hear her shriek? Maybe." Orthos reached out to pull a utilitarian chair into the hologram as if from nothing, and sat down straddling it, with his arms resting on the back.

"Then where were you the moment before I broke the mirror?" Lenore asked.

"Out in the suite, looking to have words with Diva. That place has three secret entrances, and that's just the ones *I* know about. I think it used to belong to the leader of a smuggling ring."

"Show me?" Lenore asked hopefully.

"I said I was discrete, remember? I wouldn't even admit they existed, but you'd have figured out one or two on your own. And finding them's just the start. They're all locked and rigged with alarms or worse. Let them be."

"Okay," Lenore said, chewing on her lip as she regarded him. "For now. Look, I need to take care of some stuff myself, but if you're offering help, could you maybe handle a couple of things for me?"

"Maybe. What do you need?"

"I need to find out about cancer cures—to get hold of one, if possible, that I could take to a friend. And I need to at *least* get a message to my friends on the *Queen Ilo*. I think that one's going to be tricky. They're not on the manifests. We sort of just stepped on board half by accident. Any chance you could let them know where I am without getting them in trouble?"

"I'll figure it out. Promise. I'll make some calls, do a little research, and come by later if I have something for you on the medical front. Will you be okay posing as Diva in the meantime?"

"Thank you so much. I think I'm good for tonight at least." She gave him a sincere smile. Jalissa was already working on the *Queen Ilo* business—or at least had claimed to be—but Lenore was a firm believer in having back-up plans on critical missions, and she couldn't remember ever having a more critical mission than getting home before she went insane.

"Okay. Just do your best. It'll be a big help if you can pull it off until we can trade you out for the real Diva. Call me if you need any backup." The device chimed. The hologram flickered and disappeared.

Well, that could have gone a lot worse, she decided. She still couldn't believe she'd given in to curiosity when she should have been reveling in the isolation, though.

Still aching from the mental ordeal of playing extrovert, she tossed the burner phone down on the counter along with the hair-coloring wand, sealed up that open lipstick tube, and wiped the message off the mirror. Then she went to start the shower—only to be brought up short by the absence of a knob or any other visible controls.

Well, if the communication system operated on voice-command... "Shower on?" she ventured. "Very warm?"

In response, the water began pouring out of two different nozzles *and* raining from the ceiling of the shower stall. Then as Lenore looked about for the best place to leave the robe and strip out of her clothes, her eyes fell on the alcove containing the room's large, multi-person tub, and she had second thoughts.

"Shower off," she tried. "Fill tub. Very warm." Steaming water immediately began to cascade down a wall—made of what Lenore assured herself were fake skulls—to pour into the tub below. The macabre touch actually reminded her comfortingly of the family room she'd spent so much time in growing up.

"Hey, uh...room?" Lenore asked. "Do you talk?"

The room didn't answer. Lenore wasn't sure whether she was disappointed or relieved, but she steeled herself for just a little more human conversation and poked her head back out of the room to ask Tsuzi for a quick tutorial on high-end modern domestic technology in *SJZ*. Tsuzi couldn't tell her everything about what the suite could do, but quickly introduced Lenore to the basics. It seemed the place came equipped with a wide range of voice-activated atmospheric controls and other conveniences. When faced with a challenge that needed more physical intervention, the suite could summon a robotic assistant to pick up the slack.

Ten minutes later, Lenore *finally* had the privacy she'd been craving, and with some added perks. Every surface in the room had been overlaid with very convincing holograms to lend it the appearance of a natural cave, echoing with very convincing ambient sounds. The overhead lighting had been completely extinguished in favor of several illusionary candles that generated very real, flickering light. The smell of damp limestone had replaced the scent of rain and roses, and the tub itself had taken on the semblance of a bubbling pool fed by a naturally heated mineral spring. Submerged up to her chin in the blissful warmth of that pool, Lenore could pretend she'd retreated to a private sanctuary deep underground and miles away from the nearest human.

She forgot all about trying to get in and out in fifteen minutes—or even thirty. She forgot about time entirely. Instead she floated and dozed as her uncoiling muscles released their tension into the surrounding waters, while a built-in headrest far softer than it currently looked cradled her with her head comfortably and securely above the surface. Whenever the heat of the water started to feel oppressive, a fresh current of cooler water would flow through as if on cue, then linger until the warmth would return just when she wanted it. That occurred with such precision the room had to be reading her body temperature.

She drifted in and out of consciousness for what could have been hours, filtering through layers of anxiety dreams about being stranded in a strange and crowded universe before sinking down into more pleasant fantasies about inventing useful new rituals—starting with a simple replacement for the cell phones that didn't work in most of the universes the coven visited. Even those fantasies eventually dissolved into delightfully urgent dreams about being cast to play the romantic female lead in a steamy new incarnation of *SJZ*, opposite an actor who was sometimes Alek Raine and sometimes his character, Scott Legacy. Either way he got to play the Ivurnian ambassador to her Ice Princess.

At one point Lenore's fantasies even turned to climbing out of the tub long enough to retrieve the burner phone. Then she realized she'd already done that and was back lounging in the tub, staring at that button, wanting to push it, not knowing why. Well...no. On reflection, she *knew* why. She knew exactly why. *La química* and the narrative had dropped her into an updated *Beauty and the Beast* fantasy where the beast looked like one of her teenage crushes and had promised to help her get home instead of being the one to lock her up in the first place.

It had been inevitable that *la química* would try something like this, too. That was its job. This was exactly the sort of thing the ladies who'd developed the narrative bridge ritual had fine-tuned it to do. Some aspect of the spell was reading her mind and trying very hard to deliver a custom-tailored, personal, erotic experience. The problem was it clearly hadn't been fine-tuned to deal with a cerebral introvert like herself who was fighting it every step of the way.

She laid the burner phone aside and sank back down into the water. Her fantasies were her fantasies. They belonged where they were, safely locked away in her head.

"Call him."

The voice startled Lenore out of her reverie, and she jerked half back out of the water to find Denise lounging in the far end of the tub. "What?" Lenore demanded, unsure whether she was cross at the intrusion or simply confused by it.

"You want to call him," Denise prodded gently. "So do it."

"And say what?"

Denise shrugged, water cascading off her shoulders. "Call him and find out."

"Why?" Lenore asked earnestly. "It takes me months just to warm up to a co-worker. Two weeks from now this guy's going to be out of my life, maybe forever. Who he is, what he's like, how interested I am in him...none of it matters. I just can't work like that."

Denise chewed thoughtfully on her lip. "Is that why you're stand-offish with me?"

"Stand-offish?" Lenore's laugh took on a slightly hysterical tinge. "We're naked in a hot-tub together."

"Do you know how many men I've kissed in front of a camera who I wouldn't give the time of day to if we met on the street?" Denise countered. "You're nice to me. You're polite. But you've got this wall around you like Windsor Castle. That's not a gripe. It's just a fact."

"I don't like getting hurt. That's not a crime yet, is it?"

"It's not," Denise said. "I'm only trying to understand. We're not as different as you think."

Lenore shook her head sadly and looked away.

"It comes and goes, you know," Denise said.

"What does?"

"My memory. When I forget who I am, what I've become...that's when I forget to stay away. That's when you see me. This once I thought, 'What the hell.'"

"So you know—?"

"That I'm dead? Yeah," Denise said. "Gives people the willies—when they notice I'm here at all. It's been nice having people around just so things would be different. Then suddenly you could see me...hear me. In the past, the next step has always been for people to go all odd and run away. After that, maybe some wackos come around for a while playing ghost hunter, acting stupid. Gets depressing. But *you* stayed. And you talked to me. Do you know how long it's been since anyone treated me like a real person? Because I don't."

"Maybe I can see and hear you better than other people have," Lenore said. "I did cast a spell trying to reach out. And I had an imaginary friend when I was little. Winnie always said she'd died on the Titanic. Mother liked her—said she was good people."

"Your mother could see your imaginary friend?"

"Not really. She...I...You know it would explain a lot if she could?" Lenore paused, dredging her memories. "Oh, wow. You know, I never 'saw' anyone or anything else imaginary like I saw Winnie? Ever. What if she *was* real."

Denise gave a small laugh. "What if? That's always the question, isn't it? It's the one I showed up to ask you."

"What do you mean?" Lenore asked.

"What if you die when you're my age?" Denise studied her soberly from across the bubbling waters. "My age when I died, I mean. Happens all the time, and I can't have more than five years on you."

"What if I turned into a ghost?"

"No." Denise shook her head. "What if you just...died?" She stood up unselfconsciously, the water pouring off her body, and stepped carefully out of the tub. "Wait long enough to let anybody in, and you never let anybody in. Believe me." She moved to Lenore's end of the tub and tapped meaningfully on the burner phone. "I've heard people talking about 'women's lib' and all that. You're allowed to take charge now. You fancy him. Call him. Call him just to find out what happens." Then Denise simply wasn't there anymore.

Lenore sat for a long time, staring at the phone. At last she reached for it, changed her mind, and moved to massage the bridge of her nose instead. When that didn't make the world magically fix itself, she reached for the phone again. She stared at it in her hand, saw her thumb tap the button, heard the chime—and her fingers sprang open, releasing her grip on the phone. It dropped into the waters of the tub and vanished, bouncing once lazily off of her stomach before being swept away by the current.

Some detached part of Lenore pointed out that space-age tech like that phone might be totally waterproof, but most of her was too busy studying her own fingers in horror to listen. She hadn't fumbled the phone. She hadn't panicked. She'd simply sabotaged herself, very calmly and very deliberately—and she didn't have a clue why.

CHAPTER ELEVEN
JAILBREAK

When the tub had drained and, with the room, returned to the state she'd found it, Lenore retrieved the burner phone and slipped it into the pocket of her robe, untested. She had no intention to try calling Orthos again, but she had to at least try to jettison the thing into space rather than leave it lying around anywhere. She also remained enough of a realist to still cling to the phone as a possible lifeline for getting her home. Whatever idiocy had possessed her to try to sabotage the device in a moment of weakness hadn't been thinking about *that* part.

She pondered her reflection in the mirror for a while. When she'd entered the room, she'd had every intention of returning her hair to its proper shade of pink before she emerged. Now that the moment had come, she found herself unwilling to face the side effects that would surely interfere with a good sulk. Besides, she didn't exactly feel herself right now anyway, and the darker shade suited her current mood. At least she no longer felt all bruised and achy.

Leaving Diva's clubwear where she'd hung it when she'd taken it off, Lenore finally returned to the larger suite to find Denise settled cross-legged on the coffee table in front of Tsuzi, chattering away in the princess's direction. From the sound of things, Denise had returned to what Lenore thought of as her normal self.

"Every time I visit, he still insists I read it to him even though he can read it himself now," Denise was saying. "It's Charlie's absolute favorite book—all those crazy animals. With your budget, I'd really consider trying to hire the guy and see if he can invent some even more insane aliens for the show. The kids would just eat them up. You'd be having to fight off the sponsors with a stick. Who can say no to that?"

Lenore picked a chair where she wouldn't have to be staring through Denise in order to talk to Tsuzi, and sank tiredly down into it. After a while, she realized she'd tuned out Denise's chatter, tuning out Tsuzi in the process. "Sorry. What was that you said?" Lenore asked.

"I asked if you were feeling better," Tsuzi said.

"Some. Thanks." Lenore pushed herself up into a better sitting position.

"Glad I told you to take your time. I was starting to wonder if I should check on you." Tsuzi waved away the holographic book she'd been holding, and it slid off into nothingness. "So are you Diva's usual stand-in?"

Lenore shook her head. "Just a case of mistaken identity. They came looking for her, found me. Believe it or not, I'm her counterpart from an alternate dimension."

"Cool. I've seen a few of those. Never my own, though."

"Oh. I guess *SJZ* does have its share of doppelganger episodes."

"Pardon?" Tsuzi raised an eyebrow.

"Sorry. Just thinking out loud." Lenore glanced over to where Denise had been sitting. The ghost had already gone again. Lenore wondered whether that meant Denise was having another bout of self-awareness or she'd made herself inobtrusive because she'd decided the cameras were rolling again.

"So who else knows you're not Diva?" Tsuzi asked.

"Well, I've told Chlodina, but she doesn't believe me. I've managed to convince Jalissa. Do you know Jalissa?"

Tsuzi nodded.

"She convinced me to pretend to be Diva and come help you out," Lenore said.

"And that's it?"

"Yeah."

"Are you...okay?" Tsuzi furrowed her brow in concern.

"Stomach hurts. Stress. Want to go home." Lenore hated lying to that open, carefree face, but Orthos was clearly trusting her to keep whatever cloak-and-dagger games he was up to with Diva a secret.

"I'll do what I can to help you," Tsuzi said. "But could you make a point of not telling anybody else you're not Diva? If it gets out she's gone, things are going to get very...complicated. In a dangerous way."

"Yeah. Okay." She had enough allies now, there probably wasn't much to gain by confiding in anyone else anyway. "So in the meantime, what am I supposed to do to stop this war?"

Tsuzi shrugged. "You're doing it."

"Just by pretending to sleep with you?" Lenore asked incredulously. "That's all?"

"Yeah," Tsuzi said, picking up a steaming mug on the side table by her chair to begin sipping at it. "The Goth Princess is the designated scapegoat for the entire sector and beyond."

"What do you mean?" Lenore spied another mug sitting on the coffee table and got up long enough to retrieve it. It too remained warm, despite the fact it must have been there quite a while, waiting on her.

"You said it yourself," Tsuzi said. "You're the bad girl. Everyone knows—or thinks they know—the Goth Princess is seductive and conniving. Your main job is to flit around the galaxy tempting the rest of us into your wicked schemes."

"Still not seeing how that helps," Lenore said wryly.

"Concrete example," Tsuzi said, setting down her mug and sliding out of her chair to pace around the carpet. "Tensions have been high for several years between my people and the Sherixi."

"Those four-foot-tall, evil hedgehogs?" Lenore asked, remembering her recent research on the *SJZ* denizens.

"Four-foot-tall *misunderstood* hedgehogs," Tsuzi corrected. "Yes, they look frighteningly demonic, and, yes, they can be utterly ruthless, but my archaeologists have been turning up lots of proof they had the prior claim on Talaga IV, where all the bad blood started. They had a thriving civilization there for millennia. I'm pretty sure it was their home world. Then one day they all basically got up to have a long walk after dinner and spent a couple of decades wandering around the sector looking for pretty rocks. They came home ready for a nice fifty-year hibernation—only to find *our* corporations had declared the world abandoned and spent the last six years tearing down their cities and selling the parts for scrap. We'd pretty much leveled the place. Of course war broke out. That all started nearly two-hundred years ago. By the time..." She waved her hands in front of her as if to chase away her own words. "Forget all that. Doesn't matter. What I'm trying to say is diplomacy is nuanced, right?"

"Sure," Lenore agreed.

"So now we share Talaga IV with the Sherixi, but it's not an easy peace. And like...I guess eleven days ago now? Something like that. Anyway, there was a big explosion at our primary colony on Talaga IV. Right away, everyone's blaming the Sherixi. I know for a fact it wasn't them. The governor knows for a fact it wasn't them. But the *colonists* don't want to hear it. We've got people there demanding blood, beating the drums of war."

"Maybe I'm *not* in an alternate universe," Lenore said dryly.

"People are people are people, even when they're not people." Tsuzi shrugged. "Anyway, the Pudding Council is under a lot of pressure to—"

"The *Pudding Council*?" Lenore choked on her drink.

"Yeah?"

Lenore helplessly waved a dismissive hand until she'd stopped coughing and could manage to speak again. "It's just where I come from that would be the name of a really bad marketing idea. Sorry. Culture shock."

Tsuzi smirked. "Well, they *feel* like a bad marketing idea sometimes, so I guess that's fair. Anyway, they'll have signed off on going to war about an hour ago. That's all the time they could promise me. Now it's up to me as Princess to rubber-stamp their declaration and make it official. But, hey...just at the worst possible moment I've neglectfully allowed myself to be lured off into a tryst with the bad-girl of the galaxy, where the two of us are not-so-mysteriously blocking all our calls. Some people *will* gripe about my dereliction, sure, but mostly I'll just be seen as another inevitable victim of your wiles. My indiscretion will be quickly forgiven and forgotten. And it's nothing for *you* to worry about, because that's already your reputation—and it's exactly what everyone you answer to already expects and wants from you. Meanwhile, the Sherixi and I have our people furiously working to stage a scripted confrontation that will appease everyone and make it look like 'justice' was done."

"So, you're using the extra time...to make a propaganda film?" Lenore asked.

"Of course we are. Don't you have monarchies where you come from? You, me, Diva...we're all just actors telling stories here, trying to keep civilization from collapsing. It's propaganda all the way down."

"If you're all actors, then who really runs the galaxy?"

"Now that—" Tsuzi began, but a chime from the suite's communication system interrupted her. It kept interrupting her too. Rather than fading away, the tone began to rise and fall urgently—a soft but insistent siren.

"Sounds like you'd better answer that," Tsuzi said.

"Yes?" Lenore tried, raising her voice. The response seemed to be adequate.

"Deepest apologies, Your Highness," Jalissa said. "I'm sorry for the attempt to disturb you, and am distressed by your refusal to answer my call, as has already been registered in the official logs. But it's critical that I speak with you, so I'm just going to keep trying your door until I find it unlocked. Please?"

The chime of Jalissa ending the call sounded even before Lenore could open her mouth to respond. "The door's locked?"

"Yeah. I made sure that was handled while you were getting cleaned up," Tsuzi said. "Your suite doesn't accept my voice commands for that sort of thing, but there's a manual lock there by the door. Shall I get it?"

Lenore gave a small nod and an encouraging wave of her hand. It took less mental effort than second-guessing herself about what to say to get the door to unlock. Moments later, Jalissa came hurrying in and closed the door behind her before re-locking it.

"A million pardons, Your Highness," Jalissa said, turning deferentially to Tsuzi. "Not that I'm here, of course, but—" She cast her eyes at Lenore, clearly weighing a decision.

"I had to tell her," Lenore said. "She knows."

A mixture of distress and relief warred briefly on Jalissa's face before she settled for nodding and plunging hastily onward. "We've lost contact with the *Queen Ilo*. She's...gone."

"What?!" Lenore demanded.

"And this is more than the usual bad, right?" Tsuzi asked cautiously.

"Oh, yeah," Lenore assured her.

"I'm pretty sure Diva's on board," Jalissa said. "If she still exists. I'd be calling on her successor to step in already, but..."

"But that would mean admitting she's not here with me and never has been," Tsuzi finished for her.

Jalissa nodded. "I can be working up another excuse for if this drags on, but—"

"This *can't* drag on!" The declaration didn't quite burst out of Lenore's mouth as a shout. It tried, though. It really tried. "I *have* to get to the *Ilo* to get home, and I've got *maybe* two weeks before this all goes south. After that, maybe I can't get home at all, *and I will be losing my mind.*"

"I already had a ship headed that way," Jalissa said placatingly. "We'll know more in a few hours. In the meantime, yes, we *do* have to figure out how we're going to straighten out this mess. Chlodina thinks you're playing me, and I *can't* try to convince anyone else. I need a plan on how we make it look like Your Highnesses are still sequestered together while someone's chasing after the *Ilo*—ready to drag Diva back here by any means necessary—*and* I'm working out how to stage her death if it turns out she's already dead."

"I have to be chasing the *Ilo*," Lenore insisted. "*I* do."

"That makes the most sense," Tsuzi agreed.

"It does," Jalissa conceded. "And you've both got yachts docked that could take you. But even if we could sneak you out to one of them, there'd be too many questions if one seemed to be leaving port without you. And if anyone thinks you've left these rooms, I can't pretend I haven't passed on messages to you."

"However we manage it, I need to stick with...Diva." Tsuzi waved a hand in Lenore's direction. "If either of us is found out, we've got to be found out together."

"I hate it, but yes," Jalissa agreed. "And I have to stay here to pretend you slipped out past me to go joy riding or something. There's a million things that could go wrong. Neither of you will have your bodyguards, just for a start. But I can't see any other way to do it. I'll have to see if I can scare up a ship through backdoor channels."

Less than an hour later, Lenore and Tsuzi found themselves following Jalissa out a door that hadn't been in the suite's little dining alcove when Lenore had done her initial sweep. At Jalissa's behest, they brought no luggage. She promised she'd had everything they'd need sent ahead, and dressed them both in generic Goth-black outfits that included voluminous, hooded cloaks that might keep people guessing about their identities in a pinch. The two things Lenore did grab to take along, concealed within her cloak, were the hair-coloring wand and the burner phone.

She still hadn't returned her hair to its rightful shade of pink, but she was determined to make that happen—just as soon as her mood lightened enough to accept the side effects. Also, she had a name for the thing now. Whether the small lettering she'd discovered on the handle was a brand name, a manufacturer name, or something else entirely, she couldn't say, but it read, "Trestintinator." That was good enough for her. As for the phone, she couldn't leave it just lying around, whether the thing was working or not. She'd promised to get rid of it.

The door let them out into a maze of narrow, dimly lit access corridors that forced them to walk single file. Lenore couldn't honestly tell whether the maze contained more pipes and cables or more graffiti. It seemed to be a toss-up. There also seemed to be no end of suspicious stains and puddles, though they remained just sparse enough that the trio never had to wade through anything. Occasionally Lenore would catch glimpses of things at the edge of vision as they'd skitter away into the shadows. She couldn't even be sure whether they were organic or mechanical, but Jalissa showed no signs of concern, so Lenore pretended she wasn't concerned either.

After half an hour of walking, descending four different ladders, and a few startled jumps evoked by a sudden crashing bang of metal against metal that echoed through the labyrinth, they emerged into a large supply closet off of a rather seedy looking lounge area with a view of perhaps twenty ships docked at the station.

"That'll be your ride." Jalissa pointed at one of the smaller vehicles: a battered old thing that had probably appeared misshapen even when it was brand new. "I know she doesn't look like much, but—"

"But she's got it where it counts?" Lenore asked.

"But she was the best I could do on short notice," Jalissa finished.

"Honestly, she's a piece of junk," a scruffy man in a blue-gray jumpsuit said, stepping up from behind them. "But she's space-worthy, and she's leaving now. You coming?"

Jalissa saw them off at the long boarding tube, then left them to follow the man out to the ship. The closer they got to it, the less confidence it inspired. "I'm not asking your names," he said, not even trying to make eye contact with either of them. "You're not asking mine. We're all suffering from an appalling lack of curiosity. Deal?"

"Sure. I guess," Lenore said. "Hardly seems worth the effort to find out if we are."

"I'm laughing on the inside," the man assured her dryly as the airlock opened and they stepped through to the dingy, cluttered interior. "Sit wherever you like," he added, waving vaguely around a cabin that seemed to have everything in it except seats. The place could have been a traveling flea market. "Just don't mess with my stuff."

"Easier said than done," Tsuzi murmured as the man disappeared toward the cockpit. With her voluptuous figure, she seemed to be struggling to even find room to stand comfortably in the closely packed space, much less sit.

"Do you at least have a cuddly but vicious sidekick or something?" Lenore called after the man. Receiving no answer, she began to look around for her own space to occupy.

Tsuzi let out a quiet chuckle. "I like him."

"Yeah," Lenore said. "You like everybody." Giving up on finding a comfortable place to sit, Lenore settled for sidling up to a small viewport and looking out into space. From here, she couldn't see much more than the side of one big ship and a small part of the space station. She considered engaging Tsuzi in further conversation, but decided it would be ill-advised without some clue whether their host could overhear them.

She also thought about the burner phone. She still didn't know whether it was dead. She didn't know what range it had, either. She owed it to Orthos to keep his confidence, but she also owed it to him to let him know she was leaving—chasing after the *Queen Ilo* herself. She ran all sorts of mental scenarios before finally excusing herself to find the ship's head. Then, alone in the tiny room, she ran through a lot more scenarios as she stared at the phone. Most of those scenarios wound up looking like a cautionary tale from a movie where some idiot on the run decided they *had* to place just one phone call.

Then there were all those science fiction shows where the captain found out they had a spy on board because the ship's sensors picked up a scrambled transmission. They gave Lenore visions of an outraged smuggler bashing open the door and angrily shoving a pistol in her face. It's not like it would take more than a few seconds to work out where any encrypted signal on this ship would be coming from.

In the end she returned to the cluttered cabin and resumed staring out into space without ever having tried to power up the phone. By that time, though, the view had changed. Without any feeling of acceleration, they'd slid away from the dock and begun to ease their way out past the larger ships. Considering she might have been the first Earth native to ever set out on a space voyage beyond the immediate vicinity of Earth itself, Lenore found the moment vaguely disappointing. In total defiance of how she'd arrived here, there was nothing explosive or cinematic to it: no physical rush, no visual spectacular—not even a dramatic soundtrack.

The view of the battered, utilitarian ships gave way to an unglamorous view of what seemed to be a battered, utilitarian, low-rent district of the enormous space station. She could feel the mental pull of its gravity again, but now looking sideways at the station instead of up—and without the vast, open space she'd been in when she first saw it—the experience lacked its original vertiginous effect. Still, it was a feeling, and that counted as a start.

At last, actual stars crept into her field of vision followed by the first chromatic clouds of the nebula, and Lenore let out a sigh of relief. The moment might still lack drama, but it finally felt real. She could remind herself she wasn't watching this on some computer monitor or television screen. She wasn't even hanging about inside a seemingly motionless structure hanging in space, or in a ship tethered to one. A single bulkhead in a craft no bigger than a small, earthly yacht was all that lay between her and icy death in an infinite void. Now that was some serious macabre, as though the universe itself was welcoming her home. She could get used to that.

CHAPTER TWELVE
ASTEROIDS

"Hey, Denise. Are you seeing this?" Lenore asked without thinking.

"Oh. Are we between scenes?" The ghost appeared at her side, joining her in staring out at the stars. "Guess I was lost in thought. That's a beautiful backdrop."

"It is," Lenore agreed.

"Did you say something?" Tsuzi asked.

"I was just thinking this felt like a crypt floating among the stars," Lenore said.

"So why do you make that sound like a good thing?"

"It is a good thing," Lenore said. "A lot of my best memories come from graveyards and haunted houses. My family did a lot of traveling just to see them. My folks called it 'going visiting.' We'd picnic, and we'd set out plates for the dead. I've never seen my Mom seem more genuine than when we'd do that. She wouldn't even dress Goth—just faded jeans, a random t-shirt, and all her subtlest, most respectful studs. She even pretended to talk to the ghosts. Only maybe she wasn't pretending after all?"

"What makes you think that?" Tsuzi asked.

"Lenore thinks maybe her 'imaginary' friend was a ghost," Denise volunteered, "and would talk with her mom."

"The sight does run in families," Tsuzi conceded, leaving Lenore to do a double-take.

"Wait...do you see Denise?" Lenore asked.

"Hello!" Denise spoke up, waving her arms. "Right here! Oh..." She screwed up her mouth in distaste. "Very funny. Ha ha ghost story ha ha. Can we get back to what you were saying about the graveyards?"

"Sure," Tsuzi said, giving Lenore a subtle nod. "Tell us about the cemeteries."

Lenore accepted the prompt to let her question drop—there would be time to follow up on that development later—and tried to pick up her prior train of thought. "It was all just very peaceful. Relaxed. So much of the time, being around my mom is a study in stress. But I got to wander around a lot of those places basically unsupervised and just explore, as long as we were there alone and the site wasn't collapsing or something. The best was when we'd stay up all night and watch for the dawn. I spent more than a few chilly nights snuggled up in a sleeping bag in the middle of a cemetery, gazing up at the stars.

"Dad always said the crypts and the old empty houses weren't places of death. He said they were reminders of life. He'd challenge me to imagine what those houses had been like with a happy family living in them, or to imagine the person a tombstone commemorated going about their lives—maybe falling in love or chasing a dream. 'All lives end,' he'd say. 'But nothing can erase the fact they happened. They're etched into the bedrock of time. *That's* real immortality. Why mourn when we can celebrate?'"

"Your father sounds like quite the philosopher," Tsuzi said.

"He likes to think so." Lenore gave a little smile. "Anyway, that's what crypts make me think of. They're soothing to visit. I don't get a lot of the stuff my parents are into, but I do get that one."

"People say there's ghosts on the studio lot," Denise said. "Maybe you should invite your parents to come visit them."

"Maybe. Right now I think I'm better off having some space from my folks," Lenore said. "What next, though? We're off the station, we're on our way, but are we really going to catch the *Queen Ilo* in a ship whose own captain thinks it's a piece of junk?"

"It's all we've got," Tsuzi said. "And I've got to warn you, 'catching' the *Ilo* may be an optimistic way of putting things. Most of the time when a ship just disappears, what that really means is she's been torn apart one way or another. The actual mission is probably just getting to where she vanished, then tracking down whatever escape pod your friends are on."

The pronouncement left Lenore with dreadful visions of the mighty cruise ship getting into a fatal collision with a comet, leaving the passengers to discover there weren't nearly enough escape pods to go around. Then she remembered if that happened, Sylvie and the others could just flee back across the narrative bridge, dragging along everyone they had time to take with them. There could be a million things going horribly wrong here, but a *Titanic* re-enactment shouldn't be one of them.

"All right," Lenore said, letting out a slow breath. "Time for some magic."

"Like Houdini?" Denise asked.

"More like Marie Laveau."

"Should I be asking, 'What?' or 'Who?'" Tsuzi said.

Lenore lowered herself carefully to sit cross-legged on the floor and closed her eyes. "Just indulge me. This'll take a while."

About ten minutes of mantras and meditation later, with her mind floating in blackness, Lenore opened her mouth and began to sing.

Mid pleasures and palaces though I may roam.
Be it ever so humble, there's no place like home.
A charm from the sky seems to hallow us there,
Which seek thro' the world, is ne'er met with elsewhere.

Home. Home! Sweet, sweet home!
There's no place like home.
There's no place like home.

Until she'd studied the ritual, Lenore had had no idea Dorothy and her ruby slippers had cribbed the refrain from somewhere else. Mom would be pleased to find out this sort of trivia about the little witch-killer, however remotely damning it might be. Of course, anything that showed up in the old, Victorian spellbook the coven was working from would predate *The Wizard of Oz*. In this case it seemed the song dated back to the 1820s.

Lenore finished the song out, then circled back and repeated the thing two more times. To her relief, she felt heat spring up as if from a crackling fire, warming the outside of her left thigh. When she reached down and rested her hand on the floor, she could feel the sensation on her palm as well. "Whatever happened to the *Ilo* hasn't destroyed my way home," she announced.

"And you know this...how?" Tsuzi asked.

"I'm a witch. That's how I got here in the first place. Anyway, my way home is on the *Ilo*, and the *Ilo* is off...over...there?" Lenore's voice trailed off as she pointed generally toward the aft of the ship—away from wherever it was they happened to be heading.

In a panic, she scrambled to her feet and burst through the door to the cockpit. "Where are you taking us?!" she demanded, making the pilot jump.

"What?!" he asked, flustered, then gestured to the forward view. A small but brilliant blue disk near the middle—surely, the star eCity orbited—easily outshone everything around it. The pilot tapped a couple of controls, and the image magnified until the marbled blue texturing of the star's tumultuous surface filled the screen. In the process, a scattering of small, dark shapes became visible, backlit by the star as they tumbled slowly through space. The screen highlighted one of the asteroids in red. "The Alfieri-214 Mining Complex, as requested."

"What would I want with a mining complex?" Lenore demanded.

"Don't know. Don't care," the pilot said tersely. "I get the other half of my money when you arrive safely. That's the deal."

Tsuzi appeared, laying her hand on Lenore's shoulder. "It'll be okay. Come on back and get out from underfoot."

"You're sure?" Lenore asked.

"Sure I'm sure. C'mon."

Lenore allowed herself to be led back aft to the cluttered space they'd just left. "But we aren't chasing the *Ilo*."

"I don't know how to fly this thing," Tsuzi said. "Do you?"

"Of course not," Lenore admitted.

"So we chose to trust him when we stepped on board. We chose to trust Jalissa when we trusted him. The die is cast. We're on our way. It's too late to worry about how things will turn out. So it's going to be okay."

"That doesn't follow," Lenore insisted.

"Who would we dare call for help if it's not? When there's nothing to be gained by borrowing trouble, *don't borrow it*."

"But I'm so good at borrowing trouble," Lenore grumbled.

"I'm beginning to sense that." Tsuzi smirked. "And how are you doing on those interest payments?"

Lenore just shook her head and returned to staring out the view port, where she remained lost in dark and uncharitable thoughts for perhaps fifteen minutes before the first asteroid loomed into sight through it. She could only guess at how far they'd traveled in that time, but considering it took eight minutes for light itself to reach Earth from the sun, any scientist back home would have killed to get her hands on this supposed piece of junk Lenore found herself on.

"Is your mother a witch too?" Tsuzi asked, pulling Lenore out of her thoughts. It was a transparent ploy to get Lenore's mind off all the things she couldn't control, but Lenore accepted the bait.

"No," Lenore said. "She's not. She never would have kept *that* secret from me. She's the original Xayarian Goth. I know how to pull off this act because I grew up watching her. If she could do even the tiniest bit of magic she'd have worked it into her persona and she'd have tried to teach me—I was always supposed to be her perfect little Goth princess—but she didn't. I lucked onto a coven on my own."

"So if she had the sight...?"

"I guess I'd know that too," Lenore admitted to herself as much as to Tsuzi. "I couldn't inherit the sight from her because I don't have the sight. I only see Denise because of a spell I cast a few weeks ago. I never caught Mom talking directly to my imaginary friend either. She never pushed to find out if I could see ghosts. Nothing the least bit eerie happened when she'd take us 'visiting'—it was just sort of a kid's tea party with invisible dolls. And I don't remember even once hearing her frame a ghost story as a first-hand encounter. She'd *love* to see a ghost, but I can't imagine she ever has."

A growing number of asteroids came into view as they rambled on through random discussions. Lenore found herself wondering whether it was realistic for those asteroids to appear so close together within the vast distances of space, or if she was only able to see so many because that had made for a more interesting visual effect on a television screen. She'd have to look it up when she got home.

A few more minutes of random mental distractions found the ship settling gently on the surface of one of those asteroids. Even with a limited view and precious little to provide a visual scale comparison, Lenore felt sure the chunk of metal and rock had to be a few miles across at least—perhaps a few dozen.

"All right, ladies," the still-anonymous pilot announced as he passed through on his way between the cockpit and the airlock door they'd boarded through. "Time to conclude our business."

Lenore peered curiously out through the viewport, hoping for any glimpse of the structure they might be transferring to, but from this angle there was nothing to be seen but rock and space and more rock and more space. Still, the pilot was the first in the airlock, with Tsuzi close behind, and neither showed the least hint of nervousness. Suppressing her qualms with silent chastisements about interest payments, Lenore followed. "I, uh...don't need some sort of personal life support device or something, do I?" she still asked Tsuzi.

"I wouldn't know why." Tsuzi shrugged.

"You're fine," the pilot assured Lenore brusquely as the outer airlock door opened without waiting for the inner door to close. Lenore nearly freaked in the moment between seeing nothing beyond but barren asteroid and the moment she realized they weren't experiencing explosive decompression. The pilot just headed out and down a ramp to the asteroid's surface, showing no concerns other than an impatience for his passengers to follow him. He didn't explode, or freeze, or clutch at his throat, or do any of the other gross things that showed up in science fiction portrayals of being ejected into a vacuum. He didn't even bounce like a lunar astronaut. He just walked.

"What's...ummm...What's going on?" Lenore asked as she nervously descended the ramp behind Tsuzi.

"What do you mean?" Tsuzi asked, studying Lenore's worried expression with concern.

"Where's the atmosphere coming from? And the gravity?" No one could have mistaken Lenore for an astrophysicist—least of all Lenore herself—but as a geek in general and a game master specifically, she hoarded trivia about all sorts of topics, never knowing which factoid might come in handy in telling her stories or building her worlds. This she knew: mass generates gravity. On any mass as small as this asteroid, jumping up so high one never came down should have been a very real concern, and any atmosphere that had ever existed here would have quickly discovered it had more important places to go or things to be. "Does the mining complex generate both for the whole asteroid?"

"Oh...You haven't done a lot of space travel, have you?" Tsuzi asked. "It's just localized physics at work. The Electra system doesn't follow the same rules you're probably used to. All the asteroids in this belt maintain a constant gravity and atmosphere. We're good."

"Oh." Lenore bit her lip and fell in line behind Tsuzi, pondering the term "localized physics" as the pilot led them around the ship toward a small structure some distance away. Well, was there any other way to reconcile over half a century worth of *SJZ* canon that stretched back to a time before the dawn of the actual space age? Space-opera television and movies had Earth-like gravity and Earth-like atmosphere very nearly everywhere by default into the seventies at least, simply because filmmakers lacked the technology to do otherwise.

Halfway to the structure, Lenore paused and stared pensively off into space in the direction she could still feel the ritual-generated warmth radiating from.

"What's up?" Denise asked. Lenore hadn't been aware of the ghost following, but what else was new?

"It just feels like things keep spiraling further out of control," Lenore answered with reflexive candor before she had time to consider censoring herself.

"Yeah." Denise sighed. "Welcome to showbiz."

The door of the structure opened for them. The entirety of the interior appeared devoted to a single room built around an industrial elevator shaft and the entrance to an accompanying stairwell. Deserted and unfurnished, the room offered no other signs of habitation than a single well-worn, plush toy rabbit left sitting with its back to the elevator cage.

"Delivery!" the pilot called out loudly. His voice echoed down the shaft and back, then silence fell once more.

After a couple of seconds, the rabbit casually picked itself up onto its hind legs, dusted itself off, and spoke without moving its mouth in a voice more masculine than feminine. "Very good. The identity of your passengers has been confirmed—" One lop ear fell over the rabbit's face, and it paused to emit a sighing sound as it brushed the ear back up like an unruly lock of hair. Even then, the tip of the ear refused to stand straight. "—and the delivery has been accepted." The rabbit held out one tiny, mitten-like hand, offering the pilot a featureless golden wafer. "I believe you'll find the rest of your payment in order."

After a moment of surprise, the man crouched down and took the wafer. He tapped it experimentally on his wrist. He held it up to squint at it for several seconds. "I'd say it was a pleasure doing business," he said at last as he rose back to his feet, seemingly satisfied, "but of course I was never here."

"Of course," the rabbit agreed mildly. Aside from never opening its mouth, the thing possessed an amazingly expressive face, and the smooth articulation of its limbs could nearly have been mistaken for organic. In fact, Lenore didn't feel completely confident declaring the rabbit *wasn't* some sort of organic life form, but it absolutely looked like someone's well-loved, well-hugged, soft, and fluffy toy rabbit. Despite the oddness of seeing it up and moving around, the thing inspired a very strong urge in Lenore to just pick it up and snuggle it—not least because all that fluff happened to be tinted an adorable shade of pink.

The rabbit walked distractedly past Lenore and Tsuzi to stand in the open doorway and watch the retreating pilot until he'd climbed back into his ship and the airlock had sealed behind him. Only then did the rabbit directly acknowledge their existence. It turned and bowed to them. "Your Highnesses," it said deferentially. "Allow me to officially welcome you to the Alfieri-214 Mining Complex in my role as resident therapist. My formal designation is CB152433, but you're welcome to call me Sir Cuddlebunny if you find it more comfortable—or simply easier to recall."

"Well aren't you a cutie," Tsuzi observed with a grin.

"Thank you, Your Highness," the rabbit said with another bow. "I do my best to present a comforting demeanor. I regret to inform you your connecting flight has been delayed, though. It should arrive within the hour. In the meantime, I've been instructed to make your wait as pleasant as possible."

"Well, then," Tsuzi said, following the rabbit into the elevator. "Let's make the most of this."

"I'm good here," Lenore said, apprehensiveness and emotional fatigue getting the better of her curiosity. "I'm just going to stretch my legs while we wait."

"As Your Highness wishes," the rabbit said with yet another bow.

"You sure?" Tsuzi asked, her face etched with the customary concern of a well-meaning extrovert.

"Yeah. We're going to be cooped up for hours soon, right?"

Tsuzi shrugged, somewhat mollified. "I guess so."

The door to the elevator cage slid shut, and Lenore stood watching its rapid descent into the heart of the asteroid. She found herself wondering what "localized physics" might mean to gravity on the far side of the asteroid. Did this place have some center of gravity where up and down would suddenly perform a complete flip as passengers in an elevator passed it?

She went back outside to walk about, enjoying a nearly total silence disturbed only by the sound of her own footfalls and admiring the surreal spacescape stretching away to infinity in every direction. From here she could see the bright blue star at the center of the solar system, the colorful nebula, and countless other asteroids tumbling lazily through the vast emptiness. Some of them must have closely matched the speed and trajectory of the one she was standing on, but the unique spin of this particular asteroid prevented even those from appearing to hang in a fixed place, so the surrounding asteroid belt performed an intricate dance across a midnight-black sky. Lenore stood there drinking it all in while an entire day/night cycle passed around her in no more than twenty minutes.

"Where *are* we?" Denise had appeared at her side again, gazing at the sky in wonder.

"Well, where's your mind at?" Lenore asked.

"I do not know," Denise breathed. "There's this thing called LSD. Have you heard of it?"

"I meant..." Lenore let the attempted clarification drop, having come up dry on subtle ways to rephrase the question. It didn't really matter anyway. Denise would re-frame anything she heard or saw in terms she could currently understand. "I thought LSD was a sixties thing."

Denise shook her head. "I went out with a doctor a couple of times in...fifty-eight, I think? Really wanted me to try the stuff. I never did, but he talked about the trips it would take me on. I kind of imagined they might be something like this. But I can't be on drugs now, can I?" Without waiting for an answer, she finally pulled her gaze away from the sky to give Lenore a self-conscious look. "Are you okay with me being here? I hope I'm not freaking you out or anything."

"You're fine." Lenore gave Denise a quick smile. "More than fine. I'm lost out here, and you're the closest thing I've got to an anchor right now. I wanted an adventure, but this has all gone way past my comfort zone."

"If you were comfortable with it," Denise said as she returned to her stargazing, "it wouldn't really be an adventure, would it?"

"I suppose not," Lenore conceded.

They both went silent for a while, watching the sky slowly spin around them. "What's it like?" Lenore asked finally.

"What's what like?" Denise cocked her head questioningly.

"Being...uh..."

"Dead?" Denise asked. "I don't know. I mean, I only know what it's like for me. I've never met anyone else who was."

"And I'm the only *living* person you've been able to talk with this whole time?" Lenore asked.

"Pretty much."

"That's...horrible," Lenore said.

"Well, I guess there's Tsuzi now. If she's real," Denise said. "Is she real?"

Lenore pondered that question for a few seconds. *Was* it fair to call Tsuzi—or any of this—real? "Yes," she said at last. "Tsuzi's real."

"Oh, good. She's nice."

Lenore was considering steering the conversation back to her own question when Denise abruptly turned and reached for Lenore's hand—then rolled her eyes at herself as their hands passed through each other to no more effect than sending a slight chill up Lenore's arm. "Sorry," Denise said. "Even when I remember, I keep forgetting. Come on, you'll want to see this." The ghost started backpedaling toward the entrance to the mine shaft.

CHAPTER THIRTEEN

METAGAMING

"See what?" Lenore allowed herself to be lured back inside, where Denise quickly hurried down the stairwell, the metal grill of each step letting out a small clank as if actually bearing her weight. The stair doubled back on itself several times before arriving at a landing with a door. Denise hurried through it even though the automatic door failed to acknowledge her presence and remained resolutely closed until Lenore reached it. That door led into an industrial corridor—scored and dented by the passage of many years' worth of heavy machinery—where the air smelled of grease and tasted of copper.

Already waiting at another door several yards away, Denise beckoned for Lenore to keep following. "You were worried about what might be waiting here, so I had a quick look around while you were stretching your legs," she said. "Didn't run into anyone at all, but I didn't go any lower than this, either. Anyway..."

Lenore stepped through the next door and into a moment frozen in time, in a room maybe thirty or forty feet across. A path about as wide as she was tall circled a central platform that filled the rest of the floor space, elevated by a single step. The marbled floor of that platform contrasted sharply with the metallic, functional look of the rest of the complex—and on that marbled floor, half a dozen figures had gathered around a table in a familiar tableau. Surprisingly, Lenore recognized a couple of them, and she wasn't sure how to feel about it.

"I think they're waxworks," Denise said in response to Lenore's confusion. "Really *good* waxworks, of course."

The figures all appeared to be youths of maybe sixteen or seventeen. The four she didn't recognize included a young man who could only be a Xayarian Goth, a four-armed cat girl like the one who'd bumped into Lenore on the Promenade Èlectrique, an otherwise attractive young man sporting a fairly tragic attempt at a goatee, and a young woman who seemed to have turned her entire body into a tattoo canvas. The last of those half-sat, half-stood, frozen in the act of rising out of her chair and jabbing a finger at the middle of the table. And next to her sat, well...Lenore felt pretty sure it was a young Orthos.

The final girl at the table proved the hardest to parse. She could have been *Lenore* in high school, which should have meant she was Diva at that age—but her hair said otherwise, dyed as it was in Lenore's own favorite shade of pink. She also had on Lenore's very own favorite, pink "Goth Princess" t-shirt.

Lenore spent several seconds just staring, trying to work out exactly what she was seeing, then stepped carefully up to lay a hand on the shoulder of her doppelganger. Her hand passed through effortlessly, without so much as the chilling sensation that had come from Denise touching her. "It's a hologram," she concluded.

"A what?" Denise asked.

"I mean we're looking at a three-D picture from someone's photo album." Lenore looked down at the table where the tattooed girl's arm reached toward a miniature diorama of a college campus at night. There, gathered near the edge of a fountain, tiny representations of several people stood back-to-back, apparently facing off against a horde of green-skinned zombies. "Looks like they were having a game night."

"I guess that makes as much sense as the weird sky upstairs does," Denise admitted.

Lenore leaned in to squint at the tableau within the tableau: a group comprised mostly of women, but they had one young man with them—and a cat.

Crouching down beside Lenore, Denise grinned and laughed. "Hey! That's *your* cat!"

Lenore couldn't squint hard enough to confirm much detail, but the cat certainly did seem to share Loki's tawny coat and leopard-like rosette markings.

"And that's you!" Denise squealed, pointing out the tiny, pink-haired woman standing on the edge of the fountain while an aurora of pink light glowed around her upraised hands.

Which—it seemed—would make the red-head with the wand Sylvie. The dark-skinned woman with the shotgun would be Diana. Lenore felt less certain about the brunette in the Mardis Gras get-up, but she could have passed for Manami. And if all that was true, the man—frozen in the act of aiming a handgun—would have been Brian.

"This all just got waaay too meta," Lenore murmured before raising her voice in a hopeful request to the room at large. "Can we make this any bigger?" Nothing happened. That was probably for the best. Had the detail on the tiny holograms born out the resemblance to herself and her friends, it would have done no favors to her already-slippery hold on sanity.

"Hey, uh...are you going to be okay if I wander off again?" Denise asked. "My brain's starting to go fuzzy."

"I'll be fine." Lenore offered a reassuring smile. "Thanks for letting me know. It can get kind of awkward when you just vanish."

"I'll be nearby if you need me. Just can't promise I'll be clear-headed." Denise gave a little wave. Then she was gone, leaving

Lenore to decide what to make of the hologram and what it was doing out here on some asteroid mining facility.

Well, she could completely rule out coincidence. Beyond that...She really should see if Orthos's phone still worked and try to give him a call. Any light he could shed on how the Freyjur wound up as pawns on his game table would be extremely welcome. Still, her hand refused to reach for it.

Finally admitting defeat in that battle with herself, Lenore just pondered the image for a few minutes more. She got in close and studied her own teenage face, looking for any conclusive evidence that the girl behind it wasn't—and never had been—her.

Even knowing it was futile to do so, Lenore found herself trying to pick up her own figurine from the diorama, hoping to study it like she might study a painted miniature from a gaming table back home. Of course her fingers simply passed through it.

Finally she stood back, looked in vain for any sort of manual controls for the hologram, then tried a few more voice commands. "Magnify. Enlarge. Zoom in." Changing tactics she experimented with, "Go. Play. Forward," and finally, "Resume." The image didn't begin to move any more than it had grown bigger.

"Carry on."

Lenore jumped at the sound of Orthos' voice behind her, just before the frozen image sprang to life. The tattooed girl finished the motion of stabbing her hand at a row of zombies, mouthing some unheard witticism while her companions at the table broke into silent laughter.

"Sorry," Orthos said, stepping up beside Lenore. "I get that reaction a lot. I move very silently, it seems. Don't have a clue why. It's not like I do it on purpose."

"I, uh...sorry." Lenore took her own shot at an apology. "Is this yours?" She indicated the hologram.

"Yeah." He nodded. "It's locked to my voice. You'd never have gotten it started. Anyway, I'm your ride."

"Oh." Lenore nodded her acceptance. "Oh! Because you're a guy who knows how to get things done. And you don't just work for Diva."

"The light dawns." He spread his arms in a gracious shadow of a bow. "I'd expected to hear from you directly, though, not Jalissa."

"Yeah. I sort of drowned your phone." She fished it out and offered it to him apologetically. "I didn't know if it would be dangerous to try to start it up again."

Orthos stowed the device, unexamined, with a nod of acknowledgment.

"So what is this game?" Lenore asked, turning back to the happy, animated conversation going on over the table. "An RPG? Tactical miniatures?"

"Just a storytelling game. Not really very tactical."

"So a role-playing game?"

"I guess you could call it that. We're in a hurry, though, aren't we?" he prompted.

"Yes," Lenore agreed, re-focusing her mind on priorities. The little mysteries could wait. They'd have to. "We are in a *big* hurry. Lead on."

Lenore didn't normally set aside much room in her thoughts for vehicles, but even she had to admit to a certain visceral reaction to the sight of their "ride." Roughly twice the length of the battered old ship that had dropped them here, the *Nevermore's* sleek, aerodynamic hull—with its swirling, abstract markings of stark black and white—could have passed for the love child of an orca and an osprey. Every inch of the exterior screamed "fast and deadly."

"The *Nevermore*?" Lenore echoed the name of the ship as Orthos ushered them up the ramp to the main airlock, with Sir Cuddlebunny leading the way. Lenore wasn't sure whose idea it had been to bring the little therapist along—but at the end of the day, did she know *anyone* who didn't need a therapist?

"The name is an inside joke," Orthos said. "Does it mean something to you?"

"It probably means the narrative has a questionable sense of humor," Lenore said—adding, "Just an inside joke," when his gaze prodded for more. "So this is *your* ship?" she asked. Off to the right as they emerged from the airlock, she could see what looked like an upscaled version of the passenger cabin from a high-end private jet.

"I am the captain, yes. Not the owner. She's a beautiful ship, but one that did a better job of blending would make my life easier."

"Oh, you love her," Tsuzi said, patting a bulkhead as she ducked into the passenger cabin.

"I didn't say I didn't," Orthos chuckled. "She can just be...challenging at times."

"But does she ever insist you color her hair pink?" Lenore heard herself say, and instantly cringed. That was flirting, wasn't it? And kind of a lame excuse for it. If anyone noticed, though, they didn't react.

Orthos laughed again—not heartily, but at least not in a judgmental way. "Not recently, no. There's room enough at the helm if either of you want to join me, but feel free to take advantage of the passenger cabin. A *lot* of money went into making it as comfortable as possible. I get some very demanding passengers."

Lenore turned to peer more closely into the passenger cabin, only to find herself facing a sternly scowling Denise, standing there with her arms resolutely crossed. "Don't you dare," the ghost whispered threateningly.

"What's up?" Tsuzi asked, concerned.

"Well, you're hardly the only royalty I've had on board," Orthos said. "There's all sorts of amenities back there."

Tsuzi waved him off. "You go on up front and get things fired up. I think your passengers need to get on the same page here before we can give you a full flight plan."

Orthos nodded amiably and headed toward the front of the ship.

"So what am I missing?" Tsuzi asked quietly as soon as he was out of sight.

"Nothing," Lenore insisted.

"Yeah." Denise's scowl didn't let up. "*She's* the one trying to miss out on things."

"Hey!" Lenore started to protest, anger flaring, but Tsuzi cut her off.

"Both of you. In there. Now. Sit," Tsuzi hissed, pointing to the cabin.

They both went, scuffing their feet sullenly like chastised teenagers. Lenore threw herself into one of the chairs, only to become more annoyed at what a comfortable and inviting seat it provided. What was even the point of throwing yourself into a chair that just said, "Okay, then. Have a hug?"

"She likes him," Denise said without waiting for an invitation to continue the conversation.

"I don't *know* him!" Lenore snapped.

"And?" Denise asked pointedly.

"We've talked for five—maybe ten—minutes. *I don't know him!*"

"But you like him," Denise repeated calmly.

"He made a good first impression. That's it," Lenore huffed. "What's the big deal?"

"I told you what the big deal is," Denise said. She hadn't bothered with a chair but did sink down onto her haunches on the floor now, looking up at Lenore. "Life is short."

"The girl isn't wrong," Tsuzi said. "I don't mind at all hanging out here if you want to go let him make a second impression. Or third. Whatever the count is. He's a good guy. We were kids together."

"I don't want to like him!" Lenore snapped. "I don't want a one-night stand or a one-week stand. I want the fairy tale, okay? And that's not happening here. *I can't stay.* I came to see other worlds and to save a friend's sister. That's *it!*"

"That also sounds fair." Tsuzi shrugged, turning her attention on Denise. "Don't push her. It's only going to backfire. Why is this important to you?"

"Because *I* messed up, okay?" Denise's scowl returned, this time focused on Tsuzi. "I can't fix it, but maybe I can stop someone else from being stupid. What *else* have I got?"

"Who did you mess up with?" Tsuzi asked, unfazed by any of the anger flowing around her.

"Everybody." The scowl eased but didn't disappear. "I messed up with everybody. My sister. My nephew. My parents. A guy I knew back east. The one guy in L.A. I actually *wanted* to date. The only real friend I had on the lot. I made time for all the glamorous people. I had to. That was the job. But I should have quit. I just wanted my life to count for something, you know? The joke is, it didn't: just a few hours of me on celluloid hanging around for guys to lust after. *That's not a legacy!*"

"It's more than most people leave," Tsuzi said. "Tangibly, I mean. Most of the consequence of our lives—most of the value— no one ever really gets to see or understand. Heck, I'm a princess trying her best to stop a war, and even if I succeed, no one's going to remember I did it. And I'll never know what lives I did or didn't save. Maybe there will be an entire planet colonized by descendants of someone who'd be dead except for me. But probably not. Who knows? It's all pointless. *All* of it. *If* you choose to look at it from the wrong direction. If you approach it with unrealistic expectations. We're not living in a story, dear. Everything ends badly. And everything works out fine. It all depends on when you stop paying attention.

"There's no musical soundtrack. There's no happily-ever-after. There's no score card. There's hardly even time to stop and breathe. Then you're dead, and you have a whole new set of troubles. I get to hear all about it, believe me. No one gets it right. There is no right. There's only trying to leave the galaxy a little better than you found it. Sounds like you managed that, at least."

"You know other dead people?" Denise asked, laser focused on that implication of Tsuzi's words.

"Oh, yes," Tsuzi said. "Very few as talkative as you, but there's even a couple on board with us. If it's answers you need, I'll try to help you find them. That's the job."

"You can? You will?" Denise's jaw hung open in disbelief.

"I will *try*," Tsuzi cautioned her.

Denise curled up with her arms around her knees and began sobbing uncontrollably.

"And *that*," Tsuzi said, turning her attention back to Lenore, "is your cue to give us some space. Go up to the front of the ship and get that second impression. I'm not *asking*. I'm telling you. If you accidentally find out you still like him, tough. Live with it. I have to deal with worse every day before breakfast." When Lenore tried to open up her mouth and stammer out a response, Tsuzi cut her off. "Go!" She pointed the direction Orthos had left.

CHAPTER FOURTEEN
FEAR OF FLYING

"I, uh...Hi," Lenore mumbled as she stepped into the...did this count as a bridge or a cockpit? She wasn't sure. It included enough space to move around a bit, and could seat four or five—the ambiguity coming in because it contained four seats plus one plush rabbit, currently perched on a console.

"Hi," Orthos greeted her, offering the seat beside him. "Do we have a game plan now?"

"If you know where the *Ilo* was last seen, let's head for there," she said, winging it. "When we get close, I'm hoping I can guide you." She could still feel the warmth of the homing ritual tickling at her flesh. Currently that warmth rested on her right shoulder, but it had been wandering all over her body since they'd set down on the asteroid.

"Works for me." Orthos nodded. "Do you know how to fly? I thought I had a physical co-pilot lined up, but she couldn't make the rendezvous, so right now it's just me and the A.I. That's good enough for a short, routine flight, but I feel a whole lot better when I know there's someone else who can take over the controls. Plus, this might not turn out routine. Or short."

Hesitantly, Lenore accepted the offered seat and eased down into it. "No. I don't know how to fly. At all. Sorry."

With a nod, Orthos flipped some switches, lighting up several panels and starting a gentle background hum of power. "Strap in," he warned as he buckled himself in.

The rabbit excused himself, hopped down from the console, and hurried off—presumably to find a better place to buckle up. He would have fit a child's car seat much better than any of the chairs the bridge provided.

"I...We're going to feel the momentum?" Lenore asked Orthos, puzzled. She'd felt none at all on the battered old ship. When that one had the technology to counter subjective momentum for the passengers, she couldn't imagine why an expensive new ship like this one wouldn't include the same tech.

"Oh, yeah." He grinned as he flipped another switch. "You ready for launch back there, Tsu?"

"All settled." The ship relayed Tsuzi's voice.

"Then we're off."

He grabbed the control column and gently eased the ship off the surface of the asteroid—ten feet...thirty...fifty. Lenore could see the ground slowly falling away beneath them through the front viewport. Then Orthos left the ship to hover while he worked through a few more controls.

"All right," he said. "Are you ready to learn to fly?"

"What?!" Lenore looked around in near panic at the field of asteroids tumbling past them in all directions. "If you're suicidal, speak up now. I'll go find another pilot."

"It'll be fine. I already did the hard part, and I've engaged the debris shields and the safety overrides. The A.I.'s not going to let you ram us into *anything*. I already know I'll never get Tsuzi to do this, so you're my failsafe. I want to be able to hand control over to you on a moment's notice and know you'll take care of the easy, obvious stuff that won't seem obvious to an A.I. Can you do that for me?"

"I...guess," she conceded, though not without trepidation. She hadn't even gotten behind the wheel of a car before she turned nineteen. Speed wasn't her thing. She liked sedate. Sedate was good. But right now, speed would be important. At least those weren't action-movie asteroids out there, hurtling past in a thick and furious obstacle course. It should be more like dodging moderate traffic on the interstate—she hoped.

"All right," Orthos said, prompting her to take hold of the co-pilot's control shaft. "You've got control now. Pulling toward you is 'up.' Pushing forward is 'down.' Left and right are left and right. The lever on your right controls speed. Just ease it forward to take us out of hover. We've got retros too, for fine maneuvering, but that's a different lesson."

Very cautiously, Lenore eased the lever toward herself. The ground below them rolled forward, and she could feel a tiny pull of inertia, like in a car easing backward out of a parking spot. She eased the lever forward again until their movement stopped—then farther, and the ground began to drift away behind them.

"Perfect," Orthos said encouragingly.

"Why *is* there acceleration I can feel?" Lenore asked. "I know there doesn't have to be."

"Every starship does come with inertial dampeners. That's standard equipment. Without them, pulling even four or five G's can be brutal, and you've got to go *way* past that for most practical purposes. But completely drowning out the acceleration is a blunt instrument. You fly better when you can feel what you're doing, not just see it. So a quality ship never completely eliminates the feeling of acceleration—not at the helm, anyway. And believe it or not, passengers want to feel the acceleration too, even if that means the occasional spilled drink. That feeling in your gut of, *Hey, now I'm* really *going fast*—that's a selling point. Complete inertial dampening is bad marketing."

Lenore laughed. "You sound like a friend of mine. Sylvie *loves* roller coasters." She wondered after she said it whether this universe would even have roller coasters, but if Orthos didn't understand the reference, he let it pass.

"All right: the A.I. navigator already knows our heading, so let's—"

"You know what?" Lenore said, struck by an epiphany. "It doesn't matter."

"What doesn't?"

"I've *got* our heading." She eased forward on the throttle, and as the ship began to move, she swung it gently to the right and pulled back a bit on the control shaft, lifting the nose. Then she leveled off and straightened out just as she felt the warmth of the homing spell settle in the pit of her stomach. "There," she said, feeling the pull of acceleration as she increased their speed a bit more relative to the asteroid they were departing. "That's our heading."

"Impressive," Orthos said sincerely. "Certainly close enough while we're trying to get clear of the asteroid belt."

"I told you I was a witch." Lenore smirked in satisfaction and pushed the throttle confidently forward. Despite the dampeners, the resulting acceleration slammed them both back into their seats as the *Nevermore* took off, careening through the asteroid belt like a pinball rocketing full-speed out of its chute. Orthos hadn't been kidding about the A.I. refusing to let them collide with anything, but its anti-collision strategy didn't seem to include slowing down—much less stopping—and didn't much care what direction it sent them.

Lenore started out screaming in terror as the surface of another asteroid rushed at them, but had barely registered she was doing it before the *Nevermore* swerved away and straight toward another asteroid, then another. In all, half a dozen asteroids came rushing at her face in roughly as many seconds, with the force of acceleration throwing her in random directions as the A.I. veered away with a fraction of a second to spare each time. Then her flailing hand finally found the throttle again and brought them to a stop, unharmed.

When her scream trailed off, she found the air filled with the sound of Orthos's helpless laughter. If he hadn't been safely strapped in, he would have been doubled over. After an initial rush of embarrassed anger that drained away as quickly as it had come, Lenore found herself joining in with the laughter, if only hysterically.

"Yes," Orthos finally gasped. "She's very responsive. My fault. I should have prepared you better. But now I'm going to have to try that again on purpose—when I'm not in a hurry."

"Oh, that was awful," Lenore managed. "Please don't take me with you when you do." She still couldn't keep the laughter bottled up, though.

"Did someone die up there?" Tsuzi demanded over the ship's comms. "What just happened?"

"Small technical malfunction," Orthos answered, still laughing. "Sorry. Pretty sure we're all good now, but stay strapped in until we're clear of the belt, just in case." He turned his attention back to Lenore. "You good to try again?"

Lenore didn't bother saying anything. She just shot him a confident, enigmatic smirk she'd borrowed from her mother and swung the ship smoothly around to point it to the way home again. This felt less like driving a car now and more like playing at some sort of three-dimensional bumper cars—more complex, perhaps, but knowing she could recover from even awful mistakes made all the difference. She had this. Under her guidance, the *Nevermore* began a controlled acceleration as it glided smoothly through the rocky obstacle course.

"Much better," Orthos said. "You really haven't done this before?"

"I play video games." Lenore shrugged. "This isn't hard."

"The basics aren't, no. Just don't try a manual landing or docking for now, and I'm sure you'll be fine. But I'll teach you as much as you want to know and we have time for. Like I said, I don't like being the only pilot on board."

"Thanks." She gave him a little smile. "This is fun." As she'd observed before, this wasn't an *arduous* obstacle course. She just had to watch where she was going and keep their acceleration gentle. "I'm confused about the physics, though. They *feel* right, which seems like it should be wrong."

"I do *not* know what you mean," Orthos admitted.

"I guess you wouldn't. So that game you were playing: was that Diva there with you? The girl who looked like me?"

"It was."

"I thought you said she hated you," Lenore said, glancing away from the forward view long enough to give him a probing look.

"She didn't always," Orthos said. "And it's probably not fair to say she *hates* me. She does resent me, though. I think she'd trade places with me in a heartbeat. She's not happy being the Goth Princess."

"I was starting to figure that out," Lenore said sardonically.

"I do miss her, though—what we had when we were kids." He gave Lenore a sideways glance. "I sort of had a crush on her."

"Did you now?" The asteroids had begun to thin as they approached the outer edge of the belt, and Lenore took the acceleration up another notch. It *did* feel good. "What about the game? Who were those characters in it?"

"Just your typical zombie horde."

Lenore rolled her eyes. "I mean the ones by the fountain?"

Orthos went silent for a moment. "I was hoping you could tell me."

"What? Why? *How*, even? They're *your* characters, not mine."

"Uh huh." He waited.

"Fine." Lenore sighed. "Was the cat named 'Loki?'"

Orthos nodded silently.

"The girl in pink...was that Diva's character?"

"It was," he agreed.

"It's going to creep me out just a little if her name was Lenore. But it was, wasn't it? That's what made you do a double take about *my* name."

"Yes. If I hadn't already seen for myself alternate universes were a thing, I'd still be convinced you *are* Diva, no matter the inconsistencies—either playing a game or having a mental breakdown."

"If it makes you feel any better, they think your universe is just a show back where I come from," Lenore said. Mentioning the entire, sprawling *SJZ* media empire seemed pointless.

"They do?"

Lenore nodded. "It's a pretty big deal, been going on for a long time. And my mom—she was an actress—she actually played Diva's mom on the show. So I guess that kind of makes me Diva's hotter sister." She shot him a playful grin, realized she was flirting again, looked away self-consciously, and tried to mask it by reaching for the throttle. This time, the acceleration wasn't smooth, but they only ricocheted off two asteroids before clearing the belt and rocketing off through open space. After taking a moment to reorient on home again, Lenore swung the *Nevermore* around in a broad arc to face it and kicked the acceleration way up, hoping it would imply that's what she'd intended all along—and hoping the sensation of it would drown out the stomach-churning certainty she'd confided too much and gone too far. Any minute now they'd either get to his gentle rebuke or his deciding to take her flirting as a genuine invitation. With *la química* in the mix, he'd almost certainly mistake the invitation; then she'd have to figure out how to let *him* down, and it would be all her fault.

Two minutes later they shot past eCity close enough for Lenore to make out some detail of the vast, sprawling station— then it was gone again. A gas giant loomed up on the right, growing larger and larger until it too fell away, and still Lenore kept pushing the acceleration. With her thoughts growing increasingly cluttered and self-conscious and chaotic, she needed something to do. She needed something to chase. She needed something to blow up. That's what you did in a spaceship like this, right? You shot bright lights that made things blow up.

"I think I've created a monster." Orthos laughed. "Good thing I like monsters."

"I...am...not...Diva," she muttered, jerking the throttle up a little farther with each word until it finally hit its physical limit. She had no idea how fast they were going now, but they might have cleared the solar system. Distant stars began to rush past impossibly fast, as they only could in a space opera. It didn't make sense, but she loved it and she hated it and she desperately wanted more.

"I know that," Orthos said, concerned. "I *said* I know that. It's good. Diva's actually a bit of a brat."

"I...am...not...your...crush." There had to be a big red button around here to hit to make the ship jump to warp space, or whatever voodoo *SJZ* invoked to magic the travel between stars. "I...am...not...*la química*'s...plaything!"

"I don't need convinced!" Orthos said urgently. "But I do need you to ease up, or I'm taking back the helm."

"I..." Oh. Right. The power-drunk feeling of the acceleration had all been an illusion. Of course she was still just a little kid learning to ride with the training wheels on. Of course this was all make-believe. Make-believe was all she did. Make-believe was all she was. The mental walls came slamming down. Discipline reasserted itself. Lenore reached calmly for the throttle and eased it back about halfway toward where it had started. The acceleration eased.

"Sorry," she said, unbuckling. "Is that better?"

"Yes. Thank you." He started unbuckling himself. "We should, ummm—"

"Yes," Lenore agreed quickly, climbing out of the co-pilot seat and heading for the door. It had become a race now for her to get that door between the two of them as casually as possible before he could say or do anything to make it all worse. "We should. I'm just going to be...ummm...I mean, I'm just going to go..." The door slid open, and she turned to back out as she still fumbled to make her excuses. He wasn't there. Lenore's voice trailed off as she glanced up and around the small bridge, looking for any place he could be or any place he might have gone. Orthos *had* to be there. He just...wasn't.

Worried and uncertain, not knowing what else to do, she turned to step out into the corridor—and there he was, looming over her, close enough to reach out and touch. "Lenore," he said quietly, meeting her eyes, "don't do this."

"Do what?" she squeaked, craning her head back to look up at him. Had he always been this tall?

"Run away. You're not even running *from* me. You're just running."

"That's stupid," she said, mustering up some indignation. "Don't act like you know me."

"Don't I?" Orthos raised an eyebrow. "Do you or don't you perfectly recall every name you ever hear?"

"What of it?" Lenore demanded.

"You like people, but books are better because people are exhausting."

"Well, that's a no-brainer." She rolled her eyes.

"It makes you quiet and withdrawn," he pressed, "but when you can tell a story or play a part, you come spectacularly alive."

Lenore crossed her arms over her chest and looked away. "Wake me when you get past the fortune-teller tricks."

"Fine." Orthos made a sound that could either have been a growl or a sigh. "Your mother's name is..." A breath of concentration hissed through his teeth. "Something Mallory. Amelina, right? You idolize her and you can't stand her. You started wearing pink just to drive her crazy, and you turned it into your identity. You...you're not a founding member of your coven—the Freyjur—and it makes you insecure, even though you're really, *really* talented. You joined when your friend Sylvie—"

"How do you know all this?" Lenore demanded, rounding on him.

"Because you stepped out of a game!" Orthos said. "*That* game: the one in the holo."

"I've never fought zombies," Lenore protested weakly.

"But it's still you, isn't it? You and your friends?"

"Pretty much," she admitted.

"I loaded up that holo to compare it to you—to assure myself I wasn't misremembering anything. You were a character Diva created. She joined the Freyjur game late, after we'd already been at it for a while, and she played as you for three years until she had to go off and be a princess. We all had a blast."

"I'm not that character," she said earnestly, finally looking up to meet his gaze again.

"I know. I get it. You can't be. You're real. She's not. And, obviously, you haven't fought zombies."

"And my hands don't glow."

"*And* your hands don't glow. Is there any chance you might wind up fighting zombies in the future?"

Lenore started to laugh off the question, then realized just how impossible the scenario *wasn't*, given what the coven could do. "Maybe? Are you going somewhere with this?"

"I'm saying I *know* you. And your eyes say *you* know *me*."

"Not...really," she stammered. "You do remind me of a character in the show, but..."

"But you look at me and you see him?"

That hadn't been how she'd intended to finish the sentence, but Lenore couldn't deny it. She nodded weakly.

"I look at you and see who Diva could have been," Orthos said. "I see the 'good parts' version of her that *became* Lenore. I had a crush on Diva because I wanted her to be *you*. She just wasn't. Not quite."

"No!" Lenore shut her eyes tight and clapped her hands over her ears. "Don't say that! This is *not* going where I think it's going." But of course, it was. Because *la química*.

"Why not?" Orthos asked gently.

"Because I'm gone in two weeks!" The words exploded out of Lenore with a vehemence that surprised even her. "I can't live here! I can never live here! I don't want to like you! I don't want to be anything to you! I just want to find my friends and go home!"

Orthos gazed down at her soberly for about two seconds as she stood panting and emotionally spent, then he gave a small nod. "Okay." He stepped carefully around her and back onto the bridge.

Lenore stood staring at the space where he'd been, almost in disbelief. It was...over? That was it? This was the vaunted *la química* the others couldn't stop bringing up? Well...good.

She turned around just to make sure. The door remained open, still prompted to by her presence. Orthos had already settled back into the pilot's seat, checking some readouts and making gentle adjustments to their speed.

"Thank you," Lenore said quietly. "For understanding."

"I don't," he said without turning around. "But I don't have to understand something to respect it."

"I'm...sorry I can't be who you want me to be."

"Please don't make this about me," he said, still not looking back. "You're the one turning down the two weeks. But if home is the thing you need, home is the thing you'll get. I'm floored I got to meet you at all. I'd never dreamed you were really out there. It will be nice just to know."

"Thank you," Lenore said again before finally turning to go. Only she didn't turn. She didn't go. Her brain gave the command half a dozen times. Each time her body firmly ignored it. She might as well have been paralyzed. Helpless, she stood staring at the back of his head and at those impossible stars sliding past. "I'm really better?" she heard herself ask. "Than an actual princess?"

"As far as I'm concerned, you're the real one."

Lenore's eyes misted up, engulfing her vision in a softening blur. "You're wrong about that one. Pretending is all I do."

"I said what I said."

"You're not being fair." He didn't answer. She stopped looking at the back of his head, but kept watching the impossible stars. Finally—perhaps minutes later—Lenore gave up on telling her body to walk away and allowed it to step quietly back onto the bridge. The door whispered shut behind her. She returned to watching the stars in silence. At some point she gave up on that too and accepted the gravitational pull toward the view of the stars. When she found herself standing beside Orthos, she spoke up quietly. "I'm calm now. Will you please transfer control back to the co-pilot for me?"

He finally looked up at her, gave a small nod, and tapped at the controls. He gestured her to the seat. "All yours," he said, matching her quiet tone.

"Thank you." She bit her lip. She dropped her gaze. She started to say something more. She gave it up as a bad business. Her throat was too dry. She turned to slide into the co-pilot seat. She stopped halfway and stood back up.

"Is something wrong?" he asked.

Lenore didn't answer. She swung her leg over his and lowered herself down onto his knees, wedging herself—facing Orthos—between him and the controls. She laid her hands on his shoulders, cocked her head, and looked deep into his green, feline eyes.

Silent seconds passed. He was the one who broke them. "I thought you—"

"Orthos." She cut him off quietly but firmly. "Shut up."

With her arms trembling and her own pulse ringing in her ears, Lenore leaned in and ever-so-gently kissed him on the lips. Then she leaned back and stared into his eyes again. The world didn't explode.

Orthos wet his lips and swallowed. He started to open his mouth again, but she laid a warning finger on his lips. "Don't. Not a word. Not unless you want me to stop. Do you want me to stop?" She could feel her whole body trembling—poised for flight as an overload of adrenalin slammed mercilessly through her system—but she kept her finger where it was, warning him to silence. Slowly, carefully, he shook his head.

She leaned in again, pressing her lips more firmly against his, allowing their breath to mingle. Again, she leaned back.

"Every time you open your mouth to speak, I'm going to flinch," she said quietly, soberly. "I'm going to feel it down deep in my gut this is the moment—the moment you tell me I was right: I'm just a fake who'll never be good enough, even if I'm perfect. And I'm about one breath away from curling up in a ball and crying as it is. So can we just...not talk? At all?"

He nodded gently. She smiled her gratitude, then leaned in and kissed him again. This time she parted her lips more than a little. This time she felt his arms wrap around her and pull her to him. This time she felt a chill as his tongue brushed gently over the yielding flesh of her lower lip. This time the room began to spin.

Lenore pushed back again, reluctant to, but needing to breathe. The air felt thin, like she couldn't get enough of it in her lungs. On a starship, that would be a very real danger, of course, but the absence of any flashing red lights or warning klaxons left Lenore ready to assume the problem was her.

It shouldn't have been this hard. It wasn't like she hadn't done this sort of thing before. She'd even had a couple of steady relationships, if short-lived ones.

A year ahead of her in school, Tyler had been dark and dreamy and tragic—more than a little obsessed with death. Of course, that made him the perfect boy to bring home to mother—a little too perfect, in fact. When their make-out sessions consistently turned out to be less than magical, she'd blamed herself and he'd been happy to let her. When they broke up, she managed to convince herself for a while he just wasn't into girls. It was only after he moved away she discovered what he'd been into was Amelina Mallory. Quiet words between his parents and hers had led to their breakup—and a lack of legal action regarding certain lines Tyler had crossed in stalking the object of his obsession. No one would tell Lenore exactly what lines those had been, but the following summer, she launched into her torrid love affair with the color pink.

And her freshman year of college, she'd had a serious thing going with Gabe—a very clean-cut Catholic boy, and the total gentleman normal girls brought home to their normal mothers. She hadn't really loved him—in hindsight, not anything close—but she'd convinced herself she needed a total break from her upbringing, and here he was. It lasted five months, and it ended with all the fireworks her first break-up had lacked.

Gabe hadn't really loved her either. He'd been looking for the same sort of clean break she had, and from the start she'd been meant to be his "bad girl" Goth. After he'd done all the tolerating he could of Lenore not living up to the supposed hype, he decided he'd try to take what he was "owed." The decision left him hospitalized with a concussion and Lenore herself facing legal charges for assault. Things could have gone so much worse from there, but in an ironic twist, one of Gabe's friends e-mailed her a copy of the video Gabe had meant to become his trophy souvenir of that night.

In a rare win for victim's rights, Lenore walked. Gabe didn't. And Lenore still had her own trophy she kept in a box at the back of a closet: the heavy statue of the crucifixion she'd used to deliver that concussion. Jesus saves, right? When all the legal dust had settled, she'd asked Gabe's father for it and he'd handed it over, having been horrified himself by the video evidence.

"Are you all right?" Orthos asked quietly. "We don't have to—"

"You're breaking the rules," she said, blinking back tears. "Do you want me to go?"

He shook his head.

"Then shut up." Lenore kissed him again.

As tragic stories go, hers wasn't very tragic, but it was *her* story, and it underscored exactly what she'd already known: no matter who she was, no matter what she did, no matter where she tried to fit in, she would never—could never—be good enough. But given that truth, why *not* make the most of these few days? Why *not* let go of the fairy tale and surrender to the fantasy? So what if her head and her heart were so warped that just thinking about giving up this thing she'd barely tasted already felt like a kick in the stomach? Forget monuments to lives long gone: if she was too scared to ever let herself have nice things, wasn't she already just a monument to the woman she could have been?

Lenore gasped at a sudden shift in her center of gravity as Orthos lurched to his feet, lifting her with him. He took a misstep and dropped her a couple of inches onto an array of controls, evoking a barrage of indignant alert sounds from the console. The sounds didn't seem to concern Orthos, though, so Lenore didn't let them concern her.

He scooped her up again, almost effortlessly, and she wrapped her arms and legs around him, clinging to him, their gentle kisses turning hungry. He took a couple steps toward the door, staggering a little as her legs tangled with his.

"Someplace more comfortable?" she asked.

Orthos nodded.

"Anywhere," she told him. "Just...anywhere." She didn't wait for him to get to anywhere. She didn't worry about whether he could see where he was going. She didn't concern herself with the thought he might drop her, even though he stumbled a couple more times from the interference of her limbs.

In the moments since that first tentative kiss, the hunger for the touch of his lips had already become as urgent as breathing. In the years since she'd started building that wall around herself, Lenore had almost forgotten the giddy sensation of skin on skin. She'd forgotten how real and solid a simple touch could make her feel, and there was no substitute. Suddenly it seemed to her she'd been as much a ghost as Denise.

Lenore's clinging hands found the back of Orthos's head and pulled it to her, pinning his mouth to hers. His hand found its way under her shirt to the small of her back, and she nearly sobbed with relief at the reassuring sensation. In retaliation, she slid her hand under his collar just to feel more of him. How could she not know how much she'd missed this? Her head swam. Her breath grew more and more ragged, and still somehow the aching seconds when their lips were parted and their tongues weren't exploring seemed the suffocating part of it all.

They passed through another door and entered what registered peripherally as some sort of lounge. That would work. Of course, by that point, a storage closet would have worked. Or his private cabin. Or the floor of the corridor. She simply didn't care what happened next, where they were, or where this was going—as long he didn't stop kissing her.

He angled them toward a couch, but never got that far. His knees buckled and they tumbled gently together on the floor. Lenore didn't mind. The carpet was nice, and he never let go of her. She wound up on top, straddling his chest, grinning drunkenly down at him. The room kept spinning.

Orthos reached up and tenderly cupped her cheek as their gazes met and she found herself sinking deep into those remarkable eyes. Despite her every warning, the fool opened his mouth and spoke two whole words. "Stay. Please?"

Against all Lenore's better judgment, she instantly forgave him. "Okay," she murmured, struggling out of her shirt and casting it aside, moaning at the caress of his fingertips on her naked stomach. So disoriented she tipped forward completely by accident, she landed on her hands and drew up short of taking a faceplant into him with her lips just two inches from his.

This time it was Orthos wrapping his hand behind her head, drawing her down to him, pinning their lips together while his other hand brushed one bra strap from her shoulder. Then the lights went down, and everything faded to black. Or...no: she'd just closed her eyes. Funny how they felt so heavy. Oh, well. Not much of a loss to leave them closed when she could still feel him beneath her. His grip had gone slack, though, and his hand had fallen away from her hair.

"Orthos?" She leaned down to kiss him again, found his lips unresponsive. He wasn't moving. A jolt of panic surged through her body—and then it was gone. She just felt so tired. She could feel his breath on her cheek, though, slow and steady in time with the rise and fall of his chest. Asleep? Now? She should be hurt, right? Insulted? But she couldn't quite remember...much of anything.

She'd figure it all out later, after she'd slept for a bit herself. That would clear her head. Lenore managed to settle her ear against his chest and lay there listening to the beat of his heart until what little remained of consciousness slipped away.

CHAPTER FIFTEEN
READY, AIM, FIRE

With a gasp, Lenore came abruptly up out of sleep to find herself sitting bolt upright in a surreal steampunk nightmare. All around her, spider-like mechanical arms assembled nonsensical little contraptions of gears, springs, levers, and a wide variety of childhood building blocks as they whirred from station to station along a labyrinthine highway of conveyor belts.

Steam hissed from copper pipes overhead, and condensation dripped steadily onto a concrete floor covered with a fetid swamp of brackish water, grease, and a grimy rainbow of unidentifiable pigments. Several towering heaps of broken and discarded mechanical parts rose out of a greenish miasma that curled about the floor. Those heaps ate up much of the space not already dedicated to automation.

Flickering, industrial bulbs hanging in steel-cage lamps offered the room's only light. In the background, an orchestral song Lenore quickly flagged as "March of the Toy Soldiers" hissed and popped out of a collection low-quality speakers.

In the middle of all that, Lenore found herself sitting alone on an iron-banded, wooden platform that looked disturbingly like a medieval torture rack. She still hadn't collected herself enough to do more than hyperventilate when a deep, basso voice with a mechanical edge hissed to life directly behind her. "Welcome back to the land of the living, Your Highness—for now."

The first syllable alone had been enough to make Lenore jump, spin, and claw her way backwards to the far end of the platform. She found herself staring up at a vaguely gorilla-like metal monstrosity with a fanged, skull-like face and slitted eyes that glowed like molten lava. Leaning forward on its stout forearms, the thing still stood nearly ten feet tall at its shoulder.

Even a lifetime of consuming horror movies hadn't quite prepared Lenore for this moment: waking up, disoriented, beneath the shadow of something so massive and menacing. Jaw slack, eyes open wide, she simply froze. So did the metal monstrosity for that matter. For several long seconds, neither of them moved. "Your Highness?" the thing finally rumbled again.

Several more seconds passed before a much smaller voice squeaked from somewhere out of sight at floor level. "This is no good. You broke her."

"She's not broken," another small voice protested. "She's fallen asleep again—with her eyes open, no less. We're just that boring."

"That's still no good," the first one squeaked.

"Obviously." The owner of that second small voice sighed. "Go work on your laugh or something. I'll handle this."

The mechanical monstrosity remained frozen, but a moment later, two small, mitten-like hands grabbed the edge of the wooden platform and swung the malleable little form of Sir Cuddlebunny up onto it. "Your Highness?" he prompted. He made a sound as if he were clearing his throat as he stood there patiently with his hands behind his back. "I was hoping perhaps you could make time enough in your busy schedule to wake up." If that had been meant as irony, the little construct was no good at it.

Lenore blinked. "I'll try. But I seem to be trapped in some sort of dream state." She sat up. She stood up. She studied her fingers as she flexed her hand. She dug a nail into her palm. It hurt an appropriate amount. She looked slowly around the room, taking in the assembly line, the trash heaps, the unmoving giant, and the little plush rabbit. She screwed her eyes shut tight, then opened them and looked around again. "Count backwards from ten for me," she finally commanded, eyes landing on the rabbit again.

"Your Highness?"

"Just do it."

The rabbit performed a conciliatory bow and casually did as he was bade.

"Okay. Pretty sure I'm awake," Lenore said. "But I am *not* happy about that."

"If Her Highness needs further rest—" the rabbit began.

"What 'Her Highness' needs is to know *exactly* why she's here in the middle of...this..." She gestured expansively to the room. "...and *not* holed up somewhere making out with a hot Ivurnian! Just in case knowing might keep her from *breaking things.*"

"Please don't concern yourself on that front. Breakage is an anticipated part of the therapy."

"Just tell me!" Lenore snapped.

The rabbit took what appeared to be a reflexive step back and nearly toppled off the edge of the platform. After recovering his balance, Cuddlebunny straightened up his ear and fluffed up his dignity before answering. "To constrain my explanation to what I hope you will agree are the most relevant bits, you have been taken prisoner by the Advanced Intelligence Menace—"

"The Artificers Intellect Mutuality!" the squeaky voice—now some distance away—interrupted loudly.

Cuddlebunny made the throat-clearing noise again. "By A.I.M.," he said, staring pointedly off in the direction the voice had come from, "for the most sinister and diabolical purpose—"

"You're being redundant!" the voice squeaked.

"*For the most sinister and diabolical purpose*," Cuddlebunny shouted back, even cupping his paws to his unmoving mouth as if that would help, before he turned back to Lenore again and dropped his voice to a conversational pitch, "of enlisting you as a consultant."

Lenore stared at the rabbit in disbelief. "*What* sort of half-baked fan fiction is this?" she demanded.

"If we're going to take this story *completely* off the rails, by Dracul's blood at *least* ship me with somebody! Things were just getting interesting! I had this whole emotional breakdown! I was throwing caution to the wind! Living in the moment! *I was making out with a hot Ivurnian!* Then here you come completely out of nowhere, practically unforeshadowed, hit me with a tranquilizer dart—"

"Sleeping gas," Cuddlebunny offered helpfully from behind two drooping ears.

"—and all the sweet, sweet kisses go poof! For what? So you can ask for my advice on how to be an incompetent megalomaniac?"

"Oh! Nice!" Cuddlebunny gasped in awe. "The 'Advanced Intellect Megalomaniacs!' I'll bet we can get everybody on board with that one!"

"Don't count on it!" the increasingly distant voice squeaked.

"But that's the point, isn't it?" Cuddlebunny went on, ignoring the interruption. "If we were competent megalomaniacs, we wouldn't need advice on it."

"Give me back my Ivurnian!" Lenore shrieked, her hands balled into fists.

"Oh, he's quite safe," Cuddlebunny said, unperturbed. "Aside from being our prisoner, I mean. We have a strict code of ethics when it comes to feeding prisoners to space squids and the like. It's just not done."

"What *is* done?" she asked, her anger still drowning out any wariness that might otherwise have crept into her voice.

"Well, that's what we rather hoped you'd help us work out. Part of it, anyway. We just don't know. It's rather pathetic, really. But *that* is why we need a consultant. In all the modern era, no one has been better at being bad than Her Royal Highness, Vanda Malette, the Goth Princess. And since Vanda has gone on to a well-earned retirement in an undisclosed location, the best mentor we could find can only be her daughter and heir: you."

Lenore buried her face in her hands and growled. "*Listen* to my *priorities*!"

"I am," Cuddlebunny assured her. "But I also need you to listen to mine. We aren't working at cross-purposes, you and I."

"Then where are my…" For the first time, Lenore realized her state of dress remained exactly as it had been when she'd fallen asleep, and she self-consciously re-secured the wayward bra strap. The nice thing about Goth outfits, at least, was one often had a hard time telling the difference between inner and outer wear. *She* might be a jeans-and-t-shirt sort of girl, but no one would bat an eye at seeing the Goth Princess in a midriff-baring lacy, black bra and slit, leather skirt combo. "Then where are my kisses?"

"Still sleeping. Please, Highness: come take a meeting with the A.I.M. council and hear us out. Then we can discuss the status of *everyone* you're looking for."

"Are you insinuating you're also holding the Pudding Princess and the passengers of the *Queen Ilo*?" Lenore asked suspiciously.

"Oh, no. Well, not intentionally insinuating that, anyway," the rabbit said. "We just are."

"You know that being 'evil' isn't just a thing that people choose, right?" Lenore asked as they took a long, slow ride up a very old-fashioned elevator—complete with its own elevator operator that looked like a four-foot-tall, mechanical T-rex wearing a bell-hop's hat on top of a bushy wig of rainbow-colored, neon fibers. The little thing didn't seem well-chosen to its task, as its vestigial arms struggled to work the control lever. "It's not a mindset or a team jersey. It's a side effect of actions people feel justified in taking."

She'd had this argument a lot over the years. She'd grown up rubbing elbows with all the dark, brooding, cynical, beautiful, cool people, and the wannabes who fell into their orbit too often thought calling themselves "evil" was an integral part of the game.

"On the contrary," Cuddlebunny replied. "Evil is very much a team jersey. On Nanaflooey VII, they don't even pretend otherwise. You know how a sports team might wear different colors depending on whether they're playing in their home stadium or visiting someone else's? The Nanafluti use their words for 'good' and 'evil' to describe the team jerseys in place of 'home' and 'visitor.' Regardless of any group's specific qualities or actions, it's the 'other' that's always evil."

"Exactly," Lenore said. "Which is why *you* can't be."

"You Highness," the little rabbit said soberly, "we *are* the other."

The elevator jolted to a stop and the door clanged open. Lenore followed Cuddlebunny out onto the dusty, red surface of a planet that might have been some pulp science-fiction author's imagining of Mars back in the days when space travel remained pure science fiction. Ahead of them, a moving sidewalk stretched into the distance toward a tall, palatial building whose bizarre curves and spires gave off that same retro-future vibe. Flanking the sidewalk just a few paces away on either side, row after row after row after row of unmoving mechanical giants like the one she'd woken to stretched out as far as she could see. Overhead, hundreds—maybe even thousands—of retro-looking starships hung in the sky, bristling with deadly looking weaponry.

"We...are...A.I.M.," Cuddlebunny declared. "And the universe shall fear us!" The sound of thunder rolled out of a cloudless sky as the little plush rabbit let out a passably maniacal laugh. He held a pose, with arms stretched skyward, until both thunder and laughter had trailed off, then he cocked his head and looked up at Lenore inquisitively. "How was that? Was that okay? I know it needs work."

"You'll...get there," Lenore said reassuringly as she craned her neck to study the massive and melodramatic military presence around her. "So you're trying to conquer the galaxy?"

"Not exactly," Cuddlebunny said, then paused to straighten his one persistently flopping ear. "I'll explain at the council meeting. We've got slides."

The council meeting did indeed include slides. It also included a veritable rogue's gallery of robotized plush creatures of species both exotic and mundane, all sitting around a massive oblong conference table fit for scenes of movie villainy. An appropriate contingent of chairs had been furnished as well, though—except the one Lenore had claimed—all remained empty. Her diminutive hosts all sat on the edge of the table itself, looking adorably sinister.

The first slide just displayed the A.I.M. logo in its bold, red-on-black color scheme. The letters had been blazoned on a stylized computer monitor that sported a large pair of devilish horns, and—for reasons Lenore decided were best left unguessed—a pair of oversized clown shoes.

"The Advanced Intellect Megalomaniacs—" Cuddlebunny began from the head of the table.

"Archvillainously Inspired Monsters," a purple giraffe corrected him firmly.

"Give it a rest, Cheryl." A tentacled blob across from the giraffe sighed.

Sir Cuddlebunny feigned clearing his throat again. "A.I.M. has been around as an organization for the better part of a century, but we've spent most of that time moving quietly in the shadows, making our plans and marshaling our forces. By now of course, like everyone else, you know us as the pre-eminent threat to galactic civilization."

"Of course." Lenore had actually barely heard of them, but Diva apparently should know them well, and humoring them seemed the smart move. Mostly, though, she just couldn't bear to disappoint all that collective cute.

"Please understand that the rest of the story is a matter of galactic security on the strictest need-to-know basis," Cuddlebunny went on. "We need *you* to know, and we've chosen to trust your discretion as the reigning Goth Princess. Do not tell anyone else—not even Master Orthos—or we *will* be forced to do terrible things."

"Like what?" Lenore asked.

"Just trust me when I say socks lost in the laundry will be among the least of your worries," the rabbit admonished her sternly.

"Gotcha."

"Contrary to carefully crafted appearances," Cuddlebunny said, "A.I.M. is not some encroachment on the galactic hub by a recently encountered interstellar civilization of sentient machines. We are, in fact, all native-built machines from the galactic-hub civilization itself." His little mitten-thumb pressed a handheld clicker and the holographic slide changed to a stock image of a psychiatrist's office, complete with reclining couch. "I trust you're familiar with the Mickensworth-Hinkleton scandal?"

"Ummm...no. Not so much," Lenore admitted.

Cuddlebunny gave a resigned nod that—in its silence—spoke volumes about the state of modern education. "One hundred and thirty-seven years ago, Dr. Moira Mickensworth committed the most egregious breach of doctor-patient confidentiality ever recorded. It provoked riots, toppled governments, and disrupted tea time for the next seven years."

"Disrupted tea time?" Lenore asked.

"One of the toppled governments had supplied half the galaxy with biscuits," a squat, blue penguin explained.

"Just so," Sir Cuddlebunny agreed. "As a Princess, you'll appreciate the delicate social webs that maintain civilization. The point is, the affair resulted in a terrible crisis of faith in professional counselors everywhere. That's where we, the A.I. counselors, come into the story. People who no longer trusted people could turn to us—with our built-in confidentiality imperative—to keep their juiciest and most closely guarded secrets. An industry was born." He clicked his clicker, then waved it at the ensuing image in a laser-pointer effect.

"Initial competition was fierce. We started with a basic, networked model." He pointed at cartoonish image on a video monitor. "But demand for security pushed the industry to replace it with a portable, standalone model. These quickly proved too portable." He pointed to a masked caricature of a thief dashing off with someone's hand-held device. "For the sake of self-portability, they tried traditional, metal-shelled robots, but the public deemed those too sterile to confide in. Next they tried androids, but the ultra-realistic ones defeated the purpose, and the less realistic ones triggered an 'uncanny-valley' response in their patients, so neither approach put patients at ease. The modern plush-robot therapist model everyone knows today was originally marketed for children, but then those children grew up so attached to—and comfortable with—their childhood therapists they'd keep turning to the same ones on into adulthood. That's how we became the default standard in therapy for organics through the galactic hub." He finished pointing out the individual vignettes and moved on to the next holographic slide.

"Once *everyone* started confiding in us, it didn't take long to reach the inescapable conclusion that all forms of organic, sentient life in the entire known universe are—without exception—clinically insane." In the animated scene on this slide, a man in a straitjacket sat curled up in a padded corner, wild-eyed and silently laughing. "No offense." The rabbit bowed its head to Lenore in acknowledgment. "It's part of your charm. But it does also make you a perpetual danger to yourselves and others."

"Can we just hit pause for a moment?" Lenore asked. "First: you're not wrong. But second: how *exactly* is building up your own military presence supposed to make things even the least bit better?"

"That's sort of the point of the slides," Cuddlebunny said, sounding a little hurt. "We'll get there."

"Sorry," Lenore said. "Please, go on."

The next slide bore a strong resemblance to Edvard Munch's "The Scream," but in three dimensions and with the focal figure sporting seven eyes and wearing a button that read, "You don't have to work here to be insane."

"The root of the problem seems to be insecurity," Cuddlebunny said. "You're all mortal, and once a creature becomes aware of its own mortality, existential angst sets in. You don't even have to be aware of what's going on personally for it to take root. There's this whole avalanche effect where one can get swept away by the angst of others. Emotions are contagious—and enough of you are feeling afraid and desperate at any given time that things never seem to settle down. You always find yourselves trying to outrun the tiger—or its local equivalent."

The next scene showed a Tyrannosaurus rampaging after a dozen or so green-skinned humanoids, dressed in furs and clutching ineffectual stone-age weaponry. Lenore had actually seen the specific image before during her *Beauty and the Bestiary* research into *SJZ*. The show had gone through a phase where dinosaurs kept showing up on random alien planets after someone spent half of its special-effects budget on recycled stop-motion animation footage.

"And when you feel you can't outrun the tiger," Cuddlebunny said, "what you try to do instead is outrun someone else—anyone else—who's being chased. You're constantly offering up your neighbors as sacrifices in the hope you yourself will live.

"There are less rational behaviors than that, but organics seem to *always* feel they're being chased by some peril they can't quite define, and they end up offering sacrifices to the tiger before they're even certain the tiger exists, much less which direction it's coming from. You—as a society—are always clawing to make sure *some* of your fellows are worse off than you are.

"On the whole, you seem to think it's better to be the king of the beggars than to live by comfortable, modest means in a world without beggars. The worst bit is that once the tiger takes its sacrifice—once a society has ground up its most vulnerable members—then a new sacrifice will need to be found. So you just keep pushing each other down or tripping each other up and running away when you could be organizing together to kill the tiger instead. Very tragic."

"I don't know if you're right," Lenore said, "but it's fair to say you're not wrong."

"Oddly, though, you seem to be at your best when you're staring an actual tiger in the actual face. If you can be convinced there's nowhere to run and nothing to be gained by offering up a sacrifice, you fight back ferociously and accomplish amazing things. The drumbeats of war unite you against a common enemy." He clicked forward to a slide featuring a barrel-chested, chisel-jawed man posed heroically with a tattered flag while squadrons of starfighters clashed overhead amid glorious explosions. Behind the man's back, an army charged fearlessly forward into a hail of laser fire coming from off-screen.

"We'd love nothing more than to eliminate the tiger altogether for you," the rabbit said. "We've poured enormous amounts of resources into researching practical immortality for you, but it remains maddeningly elusive. Our experiments all come up against the most inexplicable dead ends. Of course we've still got a division hard at work on the conundrum, but even once they achieve a breakthrough, it could still take many generations for the social effects to really be felt among organics. During that time, you'll doubtless keep sacrificing each other out of pure spite. So—in the interim—we've resolved to become the face of your tiger."

"So...you've become a galactic menace...to keep us from killing ourselves?" Lenore asked.

"To keep you from killing *each other*—but yes. If we can present ourselves as enough of a menace, we can scare you into uniting to oppose us. We've met with some limited success at it, but not nearly enough. This will only work if the entire galactic core decides we've become an existential threat."

"Still not getting it." Lenore shook her head. "Do you *really* think you can come out ahead on something like this? How many people do you have to kill to save even one this way? War is war, and it's always ugly."

The rabbit cocked its head and squinted the fluff around its eyes as if trying to blink. "We're not going to kill anyone. I told you we have a strict code of ethics. I don't think we even *have* a space squid, if it comes to that." A fluffy, white tentacle rose into view from behind a woolly mammoth. "You don't count, Larry— not unless you've started eating people or something."

"Not as such," Larry's voice admitted, lowering the tentacle back out of sight.

"Right then," Sir Cuddlebunny reiterated. "No space squids."

"I was more concerned about the army of giant robots and the fleet of killer starships," Lenore said dryly.

"The starships *are* quite good, aren't they?" Cuddlebunny puffed up his chest with pride.

"Do you like them?" The purple giraffe preened. "I designed all the little fiddly bits around the engines."

"Very impressive," Lenore said, though in truth what she mostly remembered about them was the sheer numbers. "Do the fiddly bits stop them from killing people?"

"Oh, no. Those are just for show," the giraffe demurred. "But so's the rest of it. They're all props."

Lenore stared pointedly at the giraffe. "Props?"

"We got the idea from you royals," Cuddlebunny said, "and your propaganda films."

"No one needs fifty-thousand fake starships to make a film!" Lenore declared in exasperation. "You use ten fake starships five thousand times! Or better yet, make one CGI starship and clone it however many times you need. There *are* filmmakers you could consult, aren't there?"

"You make a fair point," Cuddlebunny agreed, "but our deception goes way past making a few films."

"Studies show we need scale," a little black rodent squeaked. From its voice, it could have been the other visitor she'd heard when she woke up. "We need spectacle. We need witnesses."

"Witnesses to *what*?" Lenore demanded. "To an army standing around looking splendid and a fleet not wreaking havoc? That's not going to instill fear of *anything*."

"Told you we needed an expert," something near the far end of the table murmured.

"Well, it's certainly good for the galactic economy," the mammoth said eruditely. "When you live as long as we do with zero expenses, it's not hard to build up quite a fortune out of nothing—working through proxies, of course, if you can't legally own anything yourself. Doesn't do anyone a bit of good if all we do is hoard it, but now entire planets are—"

"Yes. Of course," Cuddlebunny interrupted. "We can go dig into all that in a follow-up meeting, and *you* can make the slides, Marsha. For now, let's not lose focus: Princess Diva, will you help us?" All eyes swiveled to Lenore. "The galaxy thinks you're bad just to be bad. *We* know you always have some greater good in mind, just like us. The end justifies the meanness. *We're on the same side.*"

A part of Lenore *did* just want to jump in and start offering advice, but she was also self-aware enough to know she was not in a good headspace for making weighty decisions like, "Should I help a bunch of cute little megalomaniacs wage war on the universe?" She was too emotionally wrung out, and had been in "on-stage" mode for too long. She might have slept recently, but she hadn't rested. She'd blacked out and woken up without any intervening dreams to sift through the day's experiences.

Committing the last of her mental energy reserves, she closed her eyes and bowed her head in thought. Moments later, Diva looked up, shook out her hair, then smoothed it away from her face. She pushed back her chair and calmly rose, posing herself with one hand leaning against the table. "We're *enough* on the same side I won't go against you," she said coolly. "The rest I'll need some time to think about. *Now* we talk about Orthos, the Pudding Princess, and the *Queen Ilo.*"

CHAPTER SIXTEEN

GHOST SHIP

Without the massive bulk of the space station hanging above the *Queen Ilo*, the vertiginous illusion of being pull upward off the deck had disappeared. Now, with the lights dimmed, the ship silent, and nothing overhead but a sky full of stars, walking through the green space at the heart of the ship felt more to Lenore like a midnight stroll through the grounds of a welcoming old estate on one of her family's haunt tours.

Cuddlebunny had explained that the now-deserted cruise ship had been seized and spirited away as their original plan to take her—Diva—captive. Their informants had spotted her on board the *Ilo* while it was docked at eCity, apparently trying to slip away incognito. The assault had already been well under way by the time they figured out "it had all been a clever ruse" to distract attention while she slipped out of eCity on a private vessel. They'd followed through with taking the *Ilo* because the act of piracy had been meant to intimidate the public anyway.

As "prisoners of war," the crew and passengers were all on their way to a detention colony where they'd be forced to suffer the torment of being disconnected from the galactic information network and the ignominy of being left to fold their own clean towels into decorative shapes while A.I.M. sorted out its best next move for them with the help of its new consultant.

When they'd checked the ship manifests against their list of prisoners, A.I.M. had—not unexpectedly—come up one short: a woman by the name of Agnathia Petrovna. Petrovna had fit Diva's description closely enough for the council to be satisfied she'd slipped off the ship before it had left port.

So she could be sure that all meant what she thought it meant, Lenore had asked for a chance to review images of the prisoners. She wasn't sure whether to be anxious or relieved when none of her friends showed up among them, so she settled for remaining calm. If the rest of the Freyjur *and* Diva had all gone M.I.A., there could be little doubt the others had grabbed Diva and hustled her off through the narrative bridge when the robots boarded the ship—and odds were very good they hadn't found out Diva *wasn't* Lenore until after they'd all made it back to the studio.

The big question mark in the whole scenario was whether they'd felt it necessary to seal off the bridge behind them after they left. When she'd woken up after her second kidnapping, Lenore had no longer been able to feel the direction to the narrative bridge. At the time she'd told herself that had been because the spell had expired—and it probably had. In any event, she'd asked Cuddlebunny to leave her to do her thinking in the quiet spaces of the *Queen Ilo*, and after a quick and fruitless search to find her way back to the bridge without magical assistance, she'd strolled out into the park to quiet her mind and gather her focus.

When it got to the point she had to admit to herself she was just putting off the ritual, she sat down under a tree on the edge of the lake and began her meditations. Half an hour later, she began to quietly cry in frustration at the irony of being unable to clear her mind to cast the spell that might put her mind at ease. She'd been sitting for some time like that, curled up with her head resting against her knees when a faint whisper of footsteps in the grass broke the near-total silence.

Lenore rubbed her eyes to brush away the tears. "Hey, Denise."

"I guess that means you found one of your friends?" Orthos asked with quiet curiosity as he settled on the ground in front of her.

"Not really. I...How did you get here?"

"I was hoping you'd tell me," he said. "Last I knew we were...in the crew lounge on the *Nevermore*. Then I'm waking up alone on this ghost ship. You left this for me?" He offered her something that looked like a smart phone. Its display showed a top-down schematic of the ship centered on the spot marked with a red dot labeled "Diva"—where the two of them were sitting.

"I thought it was leading me to her," he said. "But you're not her."

"What gave me away?" Lenore asked.

"Your wardrobe."

She glanced down at her lack of shirt. "Oh. Yeah. No, this isn't mine." She set the device on the ground beside her, making a mental note to find out at some point how it was tracking her. "I thought I was alone here."

"Want to fill me in on what I've missed?" he asked.

"Yes. I do. I don't know how much I can, though." Lenore sighed. "I don't even know if I can get home. I thought all I had to do was get here and everything would be all right."

"And now?" he prompted.

"Now I'm here and my friends aren't. Diva isn't. I think they're all alive and okay, but...I may be a dead woman walking."

"*May* be?"

"I need to find out if my way home is still here. If it's not, the clock is ticking. At some point in the next few weeks, my brain is going to start to unravel."

"Okay," Orthos said calmly. "Then let's set everything else aside and get rid of that uncertainty. What's standing between you and finding out whether you can go home?"

"I am. My own stupid head is too rattled with the thought that *maybe* I can't go home for me to find the way there. My stomach's tying itself in knots, and I can't focus."

"I don't understand," he said.

"I'm a witch—just not a very good one," Lenore said. She'd wanted to inject a heavy dose of self-loathing into her voice, but simply lacked the emotional energy. "I could search the ship meticulously if I have time—I guess that's what I'll end up doing—but I'm afraid I'll get lost and miss something. I just want to cast a spell so I'll *know*."

"And for that you need to calm down?"

"Yes."

"All right." He held out his hands to her and she took them. "Whatever else is true, you're not alone now, and we're going to keep it that way."

"But being alone is what calms me!" The tears started again, completely without permission.

"Look," Orthos said. "I've got a reputation for getting things done, and it's not because I cling to doing things in ways that aren't working. Was being alone working?"

Lenore shook her head.

"Then let's try this my way. I'm just going to go sit on the other side of this tree—give you some space—and let you do your thing. But I'm here. Say the word, and I'll help however I can, okay? If this *doesn't* work, we'll start searching the ship together, and I'll make sure you don't get lost. We work exactly one problem at a time, and we keep hammering until something gives."

She nodded her acceptance. It was good, solid, sensible advice—the kind she always gave characters in movies when they were being idiots. "One problem at a time," she agreed softly. "And keep hammering."

Her mind kept trying to second guess the plan once he'd stepped away and left her to it. Instead of properly meditating, it kept asking questions like what A.I.M. had meant to accomplish by bringing Orthos on board and leaving that tracker for him. Maybe they'd done it as a simple peace offering, although...She gave herself a hard mental slap, then tried to let the tension flow out of her body in a long, slow breath. Work one problem at a time. Hum a mantra to distract her inner monologue. Breathe.

It didn't happen immediately, and it didn't happen smoothly, but it did happen. Lenore finally found her way back to the empty, quiet space in her head and felt the tiny spark of magic she needed to tap into. Then she began to sing. One...two...three...four times through the song. Her voice trailed off, and she felt...nothing.

"Thank you," she said quietly.

"So...that's it? You're done," he asked from behind her.

"Yes."

"I'm...sorry," Orthos said.

"For what?"

"You're not acting like someone who just got good news."

"Oh." Lenore went silent for a bit. "They'll come back for me."

Of course they would. Sylvie, for one, would never knowingly leave her behind; not like this. It was hard to imagine *any* of them leaving her behind like this. They'd thought they had her with them, and didn't realize their mistake until after they'd disconnected the bridge to keep the robots on this side of it. And if they hadn't realized their mistake by now, they would very soon. This was not the first time the coven had mistakenly gone home with a doppelganger.

Even if Diva actively tried to pretend she was Lenore for any reason, Sylvie would see through her. Give it a week, absolute tops. And unless the coven just decided this place was too dangerous and went somewhere else looking for their cancer cure, they'd be back sooner than that regardless—after a night's sleep to give the robots time to clear out. So why did she still have this sick feeling in her gut that she would never get home?

She didn't hear Orthos move until he was slipping in behind her to sit with his back to the tree. She didn't fight him when he wrapped his arms around her and pulled her up against him. "The next problem to work," he said gently, "is that you won't be thinking straight. Get it out of your system."

She wanted to protest. She want to pretend she didn't know what he meant. She felt too numb, though, so instead she just twisted around and rested her ear against his chest, listening to his heart again. For a minute or two that's all she did. Then she felt the first of the tears trickling down her cheek. They never devolved into sobs, but they did get to flowing freely before they ran dry.

When they'd run their course, she pulled herself up in his lap and she kissed him gratefully. Then she kissed him again, just to be sure he got the message. "Thank you," she whispered. "I did need to get that out of my system." The she pulled his head to hers and tried again more earnestly, really tasting his lips this time, offering to explore his mouth, finding her tongue warmly welcomed in. "And that one too," she panted when she pulled away.

His supporting hand had found the small of her back during that last kiss. The warmth of his touch felt heavenly against her exposed flesh, and his claw-like nails prickled against her skin like the kneading of an affectionate cat—not quite painful, but definitely a wake-up call for her senses. Orthos's eyes remained closed in the aftermath of that last kiss, with his breath quickening and a noticeable tremor running through his body.

Well, that was gratifying. Lenore allowed herself a little grin of satisfaction. She met his eyes as they finally opened. Then she swallowed. Something in his earnest gaze had gone, as if a shroud had been pulled down behind the window to his soul. Her lips parted to speak, but the words turned into a yelp as she found herself toppling precipitously backward. The moment turned into a genuine spike of fear as she braced for impact—but even though the fall had felt fast and unsupported, Orthos somehow dropped her gently to the grass without hurting her. Then he followed her to the ground, lunging for her throat in a fluid motion she'd seen a thousand times in scores of different vampire flicks.

She would have screamed, but by the time she could draw in a breath it was over—"it" being the perceived threat. His teeth had barely grazed her flesh, but his lips and tongue and hot breath had unerringly zeroed in on the cluster of nerves under her jaw, igniting a much different overload of sensations than her animal instincts had braced for. Instead of that scream, her indrawn breath came out as a whimper and a moan. She pulled him to her again, held him there, and ached so much she thought she might scream after all.

Orthos pushed himself up again, onto his knees, straddling her hips. His hungry gaze locked with hers, his hard, rasping breaths coming out somewhere between a purr and a growl. Lenore's mouth worked to form a question, but failed miserably because she couldn't put the words together in her mind. She didn't even know what she wanted—all she knew was she wanted it.

Never taking his gaze from hers, he reached down to fumble with the catch on her bra. She egged him on with her eyes, forgetting that this borrowed bit of black lace fastened in the back until she heard the front tearing. Her pulse sped up another notch as the supporting garment gave way, baring her chest to the cool air of the park.

She scrabbled at his shirt, trying to return the favor. She lacked the reach to accomplish much, but he got the idea and handled it for her, stripping it off over his head. When the motion inevitably broke their locked gaze, she ran her hands over his abdominals, drinking him in. Orthos might not have been the same, specific man she'd spent so much of her life quietly lusting over, but here was the athletically muscled and broad-shouldered torso—hairy and scarred and imperfectly handsome—that had lived beneath the Ivurnian ambassador's tunic in all her fantasies. He tossed the shirt aside, leaving his eyes closed and reveling in the feel of her hands on his stomach.

Then, so impulsively it felt like her body was acting without her permission, Lenore's hands dropped the few inches to his belt line to quickly release the bulge straining to break free. His eyes shot open wide as she grabbed it, the scrape of her nails sending a wake-up call of her own. He pulled her back up off the grass, crushing her to his chest, kissing her savagely. She returned his kiss, matching passion for passion. All the while, her hand refused to relinquish its prize.

While one of his hands kept her pressed up against him, the other trailed down Lenore's spine until it found her skirt. She heard the distinctive purr of the zipper...felt the leather loosen around her hips...heard the yelp of surprise.

"Oh, my God! I'm sorry! I'm so, so sorry! I'm not looking!" This time, it *was* Denise.

"What's wrong?" Orthos asked, nearly dropping Lenore as she pulled away with a start. "Did I hurt you?"

"Not you! Not you!" Lenore assured him hastily. "We're not alone."

Now he did drop her gently onto the grass as he spun around, trying to spot the intruder as he worked to resecure his pants. "I don't smell anyone."

"It's...my roommate." Lenore sighed miserably, sitting up on her knees and re-zipping her skirt. She fumbled with the tatters of her bra, but quickly had to admit the thing was a total loss. She settled for shrugging off the remnant of it and wrapping a protective arm across her chest. The effort was mostly a social ritual for Orthos's benefit anyway. It wasn't like she hadn't shared a shower with Denise multiple times.

"I am sooo sorry," Denise repeated, standing a few yards away with her back to them. "I tracked Tsuzi down so I was coming to track you down, and I thought I could help you rescue each other or some...God, I'm sorry."

"Your...roommate?" Orthos asked, clearly struggling to make sense of the entire moment. "Wait...you mean Denise *is* with you? The ghost? I thought when you said your friends had all gone—"

"You know about Denise?" Lenore asked in surprise.

"He knows about me?!" Denise's own surprise clearly surpassed Lenore's by several notches.

"She was part of the game too," Orthos said. "Can't say I expected she'd be here, though. She never really went on adventures. More a home-base kind of girl. Ummm...Hi, Denise?" He turned about uncertainly—still looking for the ghost—before settling on waving vaguely in the direction Lenore was facing.

"Ooh. Tell him I say, 'Hi!'" Denise said excitedly.

Lenore relayed the message. Orthos gave an unfocused smile in the direction he'd waved, then scooped his shirt up off the grass and tossed it to Lenore.

"Thank you," Lenore mouthed as she caught it and slipped it on. He was enough larger than her she could have passed it off as a dress if she'd needed to. "So is Tsuzi all right?" she asked Denise.

"Frustrated," Denise said. "Worried. Says she didn't sign on to play the princess locked in the tower. It's a really nice tower, though. More of a penthouse suite. She seems to be safe and physically comfortable."

"Good to know. Thank you, Denise," Lenore said, feeling guilty she hadn't demanded more proof that Tsuzi was as safe as their captors had claimed. "Will you go back and tell her you found us and we're okay? And I saw Cuddlebunny. He seems to be in good shape too."

"Yeah. Okay," Denise said. "After that, though, I've got some other things I need to take care of. I'll be gone for hours. Lots of hours. I hope that won't be a problem?"

"We...will manage, I think," Lenore said carefully. "Thank you."

"Great." Denise flashed Lenore a final, apologetic grin. "Proud of you, girl. Have fun!" Then she was gone again, in her usual abrupt manner.

"Aaaand...we're alone." Lenore gave Orthos a woeful, lopsided grin. "So sorry." She felt her face flushing, looked away, then tried to meet his gaze again and failed. She smoothed back her hair. "Well, that was very..."

"Yes," he agreed. "It was."

"But I still haven't told you what's going on, have I?"

"Can it wait?" he chuckled.

"Maybe?" she offered weakly. "No. I'd get stuck thinking about how selfish I'm being. I need to tell you."

"Then tell me."

Lenore sighed and fidgeted. "I think...maybe if I tell you everything, though, it will put us both in danger. Pretty sure we'll wind up separated again at least."

"Okay. Yeah. That's a non-starter," Orthos said. "Just tell me the parts you can."

"We're all captives of A.I.M., to start," Lenore said.

"We're *what*?!" Orthos said, stiffening in alarm.

"We're safe for now," she assured him. "They left me alone here to think because they want something from me. And they probably brought you in to put me in a better mood. I did throw rather a fit about you not being there when I woke up."

"What do they want from—?"

She laid a restraining finger over his lips. "Can't tell you. As devil's bargains go, though, it's sounding very...livable. And I say this as a girl who's *very* paranoid about devil's bargains and other enticement scenarios. I'm a role-player too. *And* a game master."

Orthos chuckled. "Doesn't *everyone* write their graduate thesis on how to outsmart an evil genie?"

"What's your degree in?" Lenore laughed.

"Nothing," he answered sheepishly. "At least nothing yet. I wrote it preemptively when I was fifteen, just in case. I'm sure it needs a lot of work."

"Geek," she said, wrapping her arms around him and pulling herself up on her toes to kiss him affectionately.

He kissed her nose in retaliation. "So...A.I.M.?" he prompted.

"Right. A.I.M." She looked around self-consciously as if she had any hope of noticing whether anyone was eavesdropping on them. Well, if someone was listening, they'd already heard—and seen—an unfortunate amount. "Long story short: they captured the *Ilo* to get to Diva. Their informants acquired us as a target when they found she wasn't here. They say everyone who was here is a prisoner somewhere else, but I'm pretty sure Diva got away safe with my friends, so we have to get me home to get to her. That's all I can tell you, so now you tell me: what do you hear about A.I.M.? What do you know about them beyond any shadow of a doubt? Do you think their word is worth anything?"

"Honestly, you're the first person I've heard of talking to them and living to tell about it, so you're the expert on whether they can be trusted. Cold, hard facts are hard to come by. They're relative newcomers to this region of the galaxy, pushing in from the rim. At first a few exploration ships went missing, then they started leveling outposts, leaving no survivors."

"Any identifiable remains?" Lenore interrupted him.

"I don't think so. From what I hear, everyone was either taken or thoroughly disintegrated. Now whole colonies are disappearing from the frontier. Incursions are becoming more frequent. They seem to be hunter/predators more than warriors, though. They prefer to retreat when they can't show overwhelming superiority. The problem is they do have numbers, and their bases of operation are proving elusive—to say nothing of finding their home world. Keeping those hidden is an impressive feat of logistics on their part, given their numbers, and it's what *I* find scariest about them. It means either their FTL capability or their camouflage technology is generations ahead of anything we've got. Maybe both."

"Is that it?" Lenore asked.

"Do you want names and places and specific battles?" Orthos asked. Lenore shook her head. "Then that's all I know. If you're actually talking to them, this is big. It's the first hint I've heard that diplomatic relations could be possible."

"Can I ask your opinion as a resident of this universe?"

"It won't be a representative opinion," Orthos said. "Don't mistake me for 'normal.'"

"It's still a more valid opinion than mine." Lenore sighed. "Do you guys talk about the 'trolley problem' here?" Her deliberation on what to say to the council of rogue counselors had been stuck on this point ever since they'd asked.

Orthos nodded. "Like, is it better to consciously sacrifice one stranger to save several strangers, or to stay out of it, leaving the one to live and several to die?"

"Yeah. I think that's what I'm looking at here—not that they've asked me to kill anybody, but different people will pay some sort of price no matter what I choose, and it'll play out on a large scale."

Going by what they'd told her, A.I.M. would be waging a war that was totally fake, with one of its chief aims being to make people nervous. The problem was that when people got nervous they started doing stupid, impulsive things. Could an organization of professional counselors really not know they were playing with fire by trying to outright terrify people? Every day their fake war went on was a day some random spark could cause it to erupt into very real violence. That didn't even begin to take into account the traumatic disruptions already going on in people's lives because of A.I.M.'s plans. She couldn't just put a stop to the nonsense regardless of what answer she gave them, though. These constructs weren't asking her permission to wage their fake war—just her help in charting its course.

"Is it better to act to save the galaxy some grief," Lenore asked, "or to refuse to get involved so I'm not picking who suffers and who doesn't? I'm going to wind up feeling awful about it no matter what I do."

CHAPTER SEVENTEEN
DON'T KILL MY FANTASIES

"You know I work with royals all the time, right?" Orthos stroked her hair soothingly. "They're constantly making decisions like this, and the ones that don't hate doing it usually wind up discretely assassinated by the ones who do—because the ones who *don't* hate it eventually turn into raving megalomaniacs. Diva runs away to avoid this stuff, and I do understand where she's coming from. If you've got a soul, these are the choices that will slowly tear it apart.

"If you can't tell me what's going on, though, I can't really weigh in on what the ethical thing to do is. What I *can* say is you have every right to make this call. The person who should be making it abdicated the responsibility and stuck you with it, however accidentally. Choose the path *you* think is less wrong, and understand that's just how things work at this level. You *can't* save everyone. There are too many people in the galaxy. There's never enough time. There's never enough resources. There's never enough *you* to go around. So you pick your battles and you make the decisions you hope will lead to the fewest sleepless nights."

"Like I don't get enough sleepless nights just thinking about the stupid things I did on any given day," Lenore muttered.

"Sorry." He shrugged helplessly.

"Not your fault, of course." She stepped away from him and turned to stare out at the lake, hugging herself.

Wasn't the whole galaxy supposed to be conspiring to make this a relaxing, fun adventure for her? The stress of playing extrovert to prevent a war had been bad enough, but every time she tried to run scenarios in her head for how this A.I.M. thing might play out, they all ended in disaster on an interplanetary scale. If she'd been able to get her mind around the sheer enormity of it all, she'd probably be lying on the ground catatonic right now.

"I'll help any way I can," Orthos said. "Just please don't fool yourself thinking this mess will go away if you ignore it."

"I know. I won't," Lenore said, not turning back to face him. "And I believe you. Thank you." In the silence, she thought she heard the faintest whisper of movement in the grass behind her again. Then he was standing at her back, wrapping her in his arms again. She reached up to lay her own hand lightly on his arm, grateful for the touch. Then she froze, her mind racing through possibilities. "Dracul's blood," she breathed.

"What?"

"I don't know about this whole A.I.M. thing, but maybe you can help me with my *own* problems. Maybe I *can* get home without leaving it to the rest of the coven." Now she did spin to face him excitedly. "As long as I'm stuck being Diva, I'm rich, right? If I make a shopping list and throw a bunch of money at you, will you track some things down for me?"

"It feels like that's skipping way ahead. We're still prisoners, aren't we? I'd really like to make it out of here with Tsuzi, Cuddlebunny, and the *Nevermore*."

"Yeah. Okay. But if I can work all that?"

He chuckled. "If you can work out all those details, I'll be more than happy to run errands for you."

"I can do this," she said, trying to reassure herself. "I can work this problem. I just have to stop feeling sorry for myself and start thinking like a gamer."

"Then let's start setting some priorities," Orthos said. "Where do we start?"

Lenore chewed her lip. "If I make the right choices with A.I.M., I'll bet I can resolve most of the other problems in the process. But..." Her voice trailed off as her shoulders sagged.

"But?" he prompted her.

"But it's hard being Diva," Lenore said quietly, lowering her gaze. "Not hard hard. Exhausting hard. 'Turn on a high-end app and watch your phone battery drain' hard."

"And you're trying to tell yourself you need to go be Diva right now?" Orthos asked. "To power up, let the adrenalin kick in, and run to Tsuzi's rescue?"

"Shouldn't I?" She raised her eyes to meet his gaze soberly.

"Doesn't sound like she's being tortured or anything. Do you think her life's in danger right now?"

Lenore shook her head. "I can't read these constructs like they were humans, but they said she was fine for now."

"And how long do you have to think things over?"

"They...didn't actually give me a deadline," Lenore said.

"What deadlines *do* you have?" he pressed. "Not theoretical ones or imagined ones. What's your cut-off? When do you know the bomb goes off or the walls crash in?"

"I don't know exactly," she admitted. "I should have more than a week still before I have to get home, but that's a soft deadline. It's just when the mental decay starts. And I'm not sure when it *really* starts. There's not a lot of data to go on. The timing is mostly guesses."

He took her hand and tugged her away from the lake, toward the walking trail that had brought Lenore here. "And that's the most time-sensitive problem you can *specifically* point to?"

"But what if—?"

"No!" He cut her off abruptly. "Look, there is no, 'What if?' here. If you go down that road, you'll second-guess yourself to death. And do you know how much help you'll be to anyone when you're dead? Exactly none.

"I'm sorry this got dumped on you. I truly am. But you've been drafted into playing a game with stakes none of us can imagine. There are no rules to read. You can't see the game board. You can barely see any of the playing pieces. You have almost no knowledge of the context. You have exactly one advisor. He has limited knowledge of the context himself, *and you can't even confide in him what you're trying to decide.* There is nothing sane about this situation. There is no good or right or smart way to handle it. You are in over your head. Everything is out of control. I *know* it stinks, but you've got exactly one play here: you trust your gut, you do what it says, and you roll the dice.

"Now is it your gut that's telling you we need to move now, or is it your guilt?"

"It's..." Lenore's voice faltered with uncertainty. "I mean..."

"How long has it been since you ate?"

"I don't know," she said. "It was back on eCity."

"Did you notice it's been almost two days since we boarded the *Nevermore*?"

Lenore blinked. "Ummm...As in forty-eight hours of sixty minutes each? That kind of two days?" Earthly time measurements seemed to be standard throughout the galaxy in space opera television, to the point she hadn't considered them as a possible communication barrier until this moment.

"That kind of two days," Orthos confirmed. "And if you're like me, you didn't wake up feeling rested and refreshed. How long has it been since you even had anything to drink?"

"Ummm…"

"I rest my case. The only things you *do* have control over right now are your own body and your state of mind. You asked for my input. This is it: Drink. Eat. Sleep. Shower. Maybe even find some fresh clothes. *Then*, when you properly have your wits about you, get out there, trust your gut, and try to make everything as right as you can manage. Not before."

"What about getting drunk?" Lenore asked. "I think I'm ready to try life as an alcoholic."

"That's not off the table—but not before you hydrate and have something in your stomach. Come on. Unless A.I.M. took it all to feed their prisoners, there's food around here somewhere. And if there's not, you need to remind them we're their prisoners too."

Now that he'd made her stop and acknowledge it all, Lenore couldn't believe her body hadn't been screaming its complaints more loudly. She could only assume the sleep agent she'd been subjected to had numbed her body's self-monitoring systems as a side effect.

They quenched their thirst at a lakeside cabana, where Lenore learned she quite liked a slightly sweet purple concoction billed as "Frozen Fluffy," even though she'd only tried it because her mother would have died before drinking anything by that name. Then they raided the kitchens of a restaurant at the edge of the park.

A reasonably competent cook, Lenore had planned on pulling something together herself until Orthos started challenging her to identify the available ingredients. Broad classification wasn't hard with most of them—meats, fruits, spices, and so on—but it became clear in no time she could neither put specific names to the things she was seeing nor guess what they would taste like.

"You relax," Orthos said, dropping a pink, plum-like fruit into her hand. "I've got this."

"No," Lenore insisted. "I'm on an adventure. Teach me." That didn't stop her from immediately taking a bite of the plum, or from finishing it off while he walked her through accessing the kitchen's recipe database. Soon they found themselves throwing together a traditional Xayarian-Goth salad, visually dominated by black berries and blood-red leaves—Mother would have *loved* that one—and searing something called "latzunit steaks." The steaks looked like a quality cut of red meat, but smelled vaguely of fish. Once or twice in the past, Lenore had toyed with cutting meat out of her diet, but ultimately decided there *were* lines she wasn't willing to cross just to annoy her mother.

When Orthos wrapped one arm around Lenore's waist and used the other to help guide her hand through searing the steaks, she didn't doubt for a minute *la química* had inspired him to act out a pointless, cinematic trope for her benefit. She also didn't care. It was a really *nice* pointless, cinematic trope. If the scent of the meal hadn't been driving home just how empty her stomach had become, she probably would have forgotten the steaks halfway through and left them to burn while she tried to pick up where they'd left off back at the lake. As it was, she made do with lounging back against his chest while pretending she couldn't as easily have handled this part herself.

They ate on a dining terrace on the edge of the lake, with holographic candles dancing in the wan light of the ship's night mode. Lenore took an experimental bite of her steak. It didn't turn out to be anything special by her estimation, yet she soon found herself wolfing the whole thing down with barely a pause. At least by the time she got to the salad, her hunger pangs had eased to the point she could enjoy it at a more leisurely pace. She liked it better than she had the steak, too.

"So is it really *me* you know from your games?" Lenore found herself asking. "Or just a character based on me? I need to know."

Orthos shrugged. "How could I tell?"

"I guess I'm asking you what my early adventures were like in your games. When did I enter the story? What was happening then?"

Orthos must have scrounged up *something* to eat before he'd found Lenore, because he stopped picking at his salad and pushed it aside to study her earnestly with his chin resting on his hands. "Diva joined the game for 'season two'—after we completed the first big story arc. Some of our original players had left, and she claimed a seat. Sylvie and Nami joined the cast at the same time."

"That scans well enough," Lenore said between mouthfuls. She found herself already regretting they hadn't prepared something with real carbs to go with it. "Do you guys have, like...chocolate here?" she asked.

"I'll be right back." Orthos smiled as he pushed what remained of his salad across the table to Lenore and strode quickly away into the gloom. He returned within five minutes to slide a small plate in front of her holding something that looked and smelled like a waffle of solid chocolate. He also dropped a bowl of warmed bread in front of her that smelled like tart apples.

"You are a..." Lenore's flirtatious grin flickered, and she stumbled over her words as a dark little voice in her head reminded her not to get used to this. "...mazing. You're amazing." To cover the sudden burst of awkward self-consciousness, she broke off a bit of the waffle and nibbled at it. It proved to be the real stuff—rich, smooth, and perfect. Apparently, even the far-flung corners of an exotic retro-future galaxy couldn't live without chocolate. "Was there like a game session where I joined the coven, or did that happen 'off-stage?'"

"Off-stage. Your first actual adventure took the coven to a desert planet called Mars, where the locals wore...almost nothing. Sylvie and Nami really went native. You were...less enthused, but you went along with it just so you wouldn't attract attention. How'm I doing?"

Lenore sighed as she reached for a slice of the bread. "Well, it *sounds* like us, but I haven't lived it. I've only been with the coven a few months. Did we have a home base in your game?" She took a bite of the bread and sighed again, closing her eyes this time to bask in the sensations. The bread more than lived up to the promises it had made to her nose.

"An old cinema studio, in a city called Los Angeles—'The Angels.' Your ghost roommate, Denise, had been an actor there."

"All true." She tried to shut out visions of parading around some pulp, retro-future Martian desert in a micro-bikini or less. All else aside, just considering the sunburn involved made her cringe. The good news was even if anything Orthos was bringing up had been a vision of her future, it shouldn't be written in stone. The futures of the places the coven visited had never been locked in by any supposed foreknowledge of the fictions involved. Presumably, the reverse would be true. The only things Lenore really needed to know or worry about were the facts that pre-dated her arrival here—but those facts would be among the hardest to tease out, since they all seemed to pre-date Diva's first play session.

"Let's tackle this from a different direction," she said. "You say you know me. You say I'm not Diva. What *makes* me not Diva? How—specifically—am I me and not her?"

Orthos spent some time pondering the remains of his meal. "You're who Diva *wanted* to be—at least for a little while, when we were kids. She thought she wanted to get away from all the glamor and the craziness. She honestly adores the attention, though. The only thing she really wanted to escape was the responsibility.

"Diva was born to power and wealth that she couldn't or wouldn't rebel against. So she invented you—the heir to a Goth Princess title, thumbing her nose at the very idea of stepping into her mother's shoes. You were born to just enough comfort and with just enough of a legacy to have something to turn your back on. Then you went out and found your own power without any responsibilities you didn't choose for yourself.

"When you do things for other people, it's because you want to. When Diva does things for other people, it's usually more because she has to, and she gets resentful about it. That's gotten more pronounced as she's actually had to deal with the job, but I think even when she created you, you were less selfish than she was just because that was an expectation in the game. The Freyjur aren't paragons of virtue, but the story was always that you're basically decent folks who'd use your power to intervene where you could—just because it was the right thing to do. Without that, most of your adventures wouldn't have made sense.

"So basically, you're more empathic than Diva. I assume the 'backstory' behind that is because you weren't born to the same level of privilege. Power burns empathy out of people. I've seen it happen over and over and over. The royal families do a decent job of fighting back against that effect by stressing the responsibilities that go with their positions. Even so, they fail more often than they realize. Sometimes they fail spectacularly. Diva didn't turn out terrible or anything, but she did turn out...disappointing. We didn't build the friendship I'd thought we were going to.

"And you're a lot more scholarly than Diva. She doesn't have your memory or your determination for exploring the topics she loves in depth. Those are things she chose for your character build just so you'd be a better witch. There was a niche open in the coven for a high-end scholar, so that's what she went with. That's why you're the most effective ritualist in the coven."

Lenore laughed. "Okay, that one you're wrong about."

"Am I?" He cocked a skeptical eyebrow.

"I'm the best impostor," she assured him. "That's all. I wing it just like I wing everything."

He studied her soberly. "Okay, you weren't the best ritualist when you joined the coven. Half the others had already invested experience points into upping their skills. If this is still before your first adventure...eh. But you *will* be the best, and before the next big story arc is over."

"Annnd...there's my answer. We're not really talking about me." Lenore sighed, deflating.

"What?! You've got skills and you know it."

"Maybe," she admitted reluctantly. "But I'm not going to be here through a bunch of 'major story arcs.' I'll be lucky to get through one. I'm too much of a nomad."

"You?" Orthos laughed. "*You're* a nomad? The girl who fought so hard to push me away because I wouldn't be around long enough to get attached to?"

"I never said I liked it." Lenore scowled. "I just...I just..."

He sobered, and looked away guiltily. "Just what?"

"I just don't fit," she mumbled, staring at the table. "Anywhere."

"Oh." The single syllable came out as a cold, clipped sound that stung like a shard of ice.

And that, Lenore knew, was that. She didn't know what she'd done wrong. She didn't know what she'd said wrong. All she did know was the sound of that familiar inflection. It said she'd crossed a line and it was time to move on. There would be no more kisses. There would be no more comforting talks. If there was any point in trying to get home, she might still have his help—she did have Diva's money to work with, after all—but everything else had just darted hopelessly out of reach.

Her hand found a napkin, and she hid behind it, dabbing at her face while her brain finished shifting gears. "You were right, you know. I didn't sleep well at all. Now that I've eaten, I think I'm about to collapse. I saw a hammock around here somewhere. Thank you so much for all of this." She pushed back from the table. He started to get up with her, but she waved him off. "It wasn't far. I'll be fine, and I'm going to be out cold in no time. Just get some rest yourself, then we can meet back here?"

"Okay," he replied uncertainly, but remained sitting where he was as she turned and walked away.

A moment later she was stepping down from the terrace and walking off across the manicured lawn of the park. She hadn't lied about being exhausted. She hadn't lied about the hammock, either. She'd actually seen two or three on the walk to the terrace, strung up for passengers to lounge in as they lazed amid the greenery near the lake. It didn't seem she'd been paying attention to how they'd approached the terrace, though, because she wasn't finding any of those hammocks now. She didn't dare double back, though, and risk running into Orthos. The park wasn't huge or anything. She'd find another hammock soon enough if she just kept walking.

Ten minutes later she'd found the far end of the lake. She hadn't found a hammock.

She turned and stared back across the park, searching fruitlessly for a telltale flicker from the fake candles at the table where they'd eaten. In the muted light of the ship's evening mode, she couldn't see anything at all out past a few dozen yards. She couldn't even see most of the lake. Orthos could be anywhere by now. She'd be as much at risk of running into him if she continued on around the lake from here as she would have been by doubling back.

She could always step out of the park and go looking for a passenger cabin. She'd tried to peek into a few when she was exploring earlier, though, and found them all locked. She might waste hours looking for a nice little coffin to curl up in.

Wrung out as she felt, the thought seemed unbearable. Rather than face it, Lenore finally just gave up. Her knees buckled beneath her—unwilling to fight the artificial gravity of the *Ilo* any longer—and she sprawled on the deck, sobbing softly into the grass.

The next thing she knew, the deck was rocking. No. It wasn't the deck. She wasn't in the grass anymore. She was being carried. With a start, she kicked and shoved and squirmed away, winning free only to find herself toppling back into the grass.

"Sorry. Are you all right?" Orthos asked. "Didn't mean to scare you. I couldn't just leave you there."

"I'm fine," she answered testily. "It's fine. I like the grass. It's soft."

He stared down at her. She didn't stare back. "I'm sorry," he said at last.

"Why would you be sorry? You haven't done anything wrong. You don't have anything to apologize for."

"Yes," Orthos insisted quietly. "I do. It's all my fault."

"Nothing's your fault!" Lenore snapped. "I'm a mess. Me. Just me. You haven't done one single thing wrong. Stop trying to own my problems! They're all I've got."

He dropped down in the grass a couple of yards away and sat cross-legged, watching her. "It's my fault you don't fit in. I'm so sorry."

Lenore buried her face in her hands. "Please stop."

"I'm serious," he said. "This didn't come from Diva. She's comfortable everywhere. She didn't make you a 'nomad' as some sort of wish-fulfillment or to fit into the game—or because it gave her good stats."

"She didn't 'make' me anything," Lenore replied darkly. "That's not how all this works."

"However this works, it's still my fault the Lenore I know feels like this," Orthos insisted. "Look, do you know where *I* fit in?"

She prompted him with her eyes not to make her guess.

"Nowhere," he said. "I just don't. I never have. Sometimes games like that let me forget for a while, but eventually everyone moves on—more or less together—and leaves me behind. I'm caught in this limbo between the royals and the rest of the galaxy. And I *hate* it. The royals see me as a servant. The servants see me as a royal. I've made myself useful to a lot of people. I've made a nice life for myself. But at the end of the day, I go off alone to my own quiet little space that I share with no one, knowing that's what it's going to be like tomorrow and the next day and the next and the next and the next.

"No one's cruel to me. I don't even *want* to go to all those parties I'm never invited to. I mostly enjoy the peace and quiet. But I've spent my entire life certain if one day there just weren't enough seats in the escape pod—"

"You'd be the one left out?" Lenore asked.

"I'd be the one left out," Orthos agreed. "I'll always be the expendable one. No matter how perfect or useful I make myself, I will always be the one who doesn't fit. Anywhere." He looked away into the darkness. "Diva knew I felt that way. She really did care about me in her own way when we were kids. Just not enough to stay, or to really be friends once our lives tangled back together."

"So...she'd flirt with you?" Lenore asked as the pieces fell into place. "At the game table? As me? And making 'me' feel like I never belonged—"

"Was part of it, yes." Orthos sighed, still staring off at nothing. "It felt nice thinking someone understood. Maybe she even did a little. The flirtation wasn't an act. There *was* some chemistry between us. But I let myself forget she had this whole life ahead of her I could never be more than a bit player in. I let myself forget for a while I didn't—couldn't—belong."

"Why not?" Lenore still hadn't really moved from where she'd fallen. She'd just sat up and made herself less uncomfortable.

"Family," he said. "It's complicated, but when you move among royals, pedigree is everything. People honestly get killed for nothing more than having the wrong bloodline at the wrong time."

"That's not *just* a royal problem," Lenore said dryly.

"You're not wrong," he admitted. "It happens whenever power becomes a generational legacy. But monarchies codify birthright, so that's baked into the system from start to finish. It's definitional. And I've been defined right out of the game. No one has a stake in my existence.

"Look, I don't normally talk about this. Everyone's got their issues, and all I really suffer from is benign neglect. Things could be so, *so* much worse. But it's pretty obvious something I said or did or didn't do back there hurt you. I see what you're doing. I know why you're doing it. If it's easier on you to just push away and forget what almost happened, okay. We've got plenty of problems to stay focused on instead. There's just one thing I need from you."

Lenore waited for him to go on—to fill the sudden silence—but she was the one to break first. "What's that?" she asked.

"Don't kill my fantasies. I've got this whole fictional world going on in my head where that game never ended, and you never went away. I know how pathetic this sounds. I know it's not real. Or...maybe I don't." His voice trailed off for a moment as his brow furrowed. "Maybe I finally broke and now I'm hallucinating you. I don't care enough to want to know. What I'm getting at is I accept I can't give you the place you finally belong. I understand you'll be gone in a few days, and I may never see you again. I just need you to leave knowing that this is the place where you *could* have belonged. If I can't give you that much out of all this mess...I don't know what the point is to being me."

"I..." Lenore's voice broke from the sheer effort of trying to get that one syllable out—not that it mattered much: She had no idea what words to follow it with. She buried her face in her hands again and began to sob uncontrollably. This time too, exhaustion took her before she'd cried herself out, but she woke up under a blanket in a large hammock with Orthos pressed up against her back and a death grip on the arm he'd wrapped around her.

CHAPTER EIGHTEEN

UNSAFE

"So here's the deal," Lenore announced as she stood at the end of the A.I.M. conference table in all her borrowed Goth Princess splendor. Orthos had even helped her scrounge up a coordinated cape and other accessories from the abandoned staterooms on the *Ilo* to help her pull off the look more effectively. "I'm in...*if* you'll make some concessions.

"First, and non-negotiable: I need an assistant. That will be Orthos. I trust him completely in this matter, and only him. Cuddlebunny at least should know he can be trusted as well." The rational part of Lenore's brain knew she was sticking her neck out on this one. She'd surrendered to the notion that he did know her, but that didn't mean the reverse was true. For all she actually knew, Orthos and Cuddlebunny shared a checkered history, but Orthos had assured her going with her gut was her only play, and this is what her gut was telling her. Besides, better to test her faith now and find out it was unfounded than to learn after she'd gotten herself in even deeper. "He's willing to be sworn to absolute secrecy, but then he gets the whole story. Everything I know, he knows."

While Lenore watched the proceedings anxiously from the back of her mind, her body stood patiently and unperturbed through a buzz of hushed conversation among the adorable little megalomaniacs. "*Only* him?" Cuddlebunny asked finally. "We're thoroughly aware how hard it is for organics to keep secrets."

"Only him," she assured her audience coolly.

"Then we are willing to work with that," the rabbit said. "What else?"

"I need clarity on what's been happening with the disappearing populations. It sounds like you haven't been killing anyone, so how have you pulled it off so far?"

"Ah. A sensible concern. With our resources, it's just misdirection and stage magic. The galaxy is *filled* with people who get overlooked and forgotten. The more overlooked and forgotten they are, the more they'll jump at a chance to make a fresh start on some greener world. We organize our own settlements, recruit our own colonists, ship them off to a nice little planet deep in A.I.M. space, and carefully construct a fake colony where we originally said we'd take them. Since we control all communications in and out of the world where we actually settle them, they basically get a sandbox to play in that they won't outgrow for generations and generations. But when someone does come looking for them, they only find that ruin no one ever lived in."

That...sounded kind of cool, actually. If Lenore hadn't already relinquished control of her body to the Diva persona, she would have found it difficult to continue looking bored. "That does sound like a well-thought-out solution," she said, "and one that won't make it difficult to plan going forward. Now, I have other urgent matters to attend to over the next few days. That means I'll need freedom to move about. So along with Orthos, I require the service of his ship, the *Nevermore*. If Sir Cuddlebunny feels better about it traveling with us, he's welcome to—it might actually lead to fewer questions back in the Electra system—but I'm fine either way."

"We anticipated you'd need to get back to princessing sooner rather than later," Cuddlebunny said. "You can have the *Nevermore*, of course."

"Excellent. Then I believe we have an accord. You did interrupt my ongoing business with the Pudding Princess, but rather than simply ask for her back, I propose to use her first for our new, shared agenda. Shall I go on?"

"Please do," the giraffe said, inserting herself into the conversation without waiting on their spokesman. It earned her a pointed look, but she didn't appear to notice.

"Where you've been going wrong so far is a reasonable mistake to make," Lenore said. "You're presenting yourself effectively enough as a menace, but your illusion needs a better story. I was asking Orthos his thoughts about A.I.M., and you know what he's afraid of? It's not your army. It's not your armada. It's all the stuff he doesn't know about and doesn't see. It scares him to think about what mysterious technologies you may have that he doesn't understand. The unknown scares all organics. And that fear..." She paused for effect. "That fear is exactly what we need to use."

"Are we ready to role-play?" Lenore asked.

"Yes!" Denise declared. "I'm going to play the sexy girl reporter!"

"Good to go," Orthos agreed, oblivious to Denise's input.

"Ummm...Denise, do I need to explain—"

"Just kidding." Denise giggled. "I've been paying attention to your lingo, *and* I've got myself together. Let's do this." With a jaunty little salute, she disappeared through the door in front of them.

"Right. We're on," Lenore said, passing the reassurance on to Orthos.

One of the awesome potentials of artificial gravity Lenore had never seen anyone leverage in science fiction before lay in negating the elevator effect. Back on Earth, being sealed in a tiny, windowless box didn't stop anyone from knowing when they started climbing or dropping because their stomachs would tell them. But with artificial gravity freezing inertia in that same enclosed space, you could move the box any direction you liked at any speed you liked, and no one inside could possibly notice.

A.I.M. had been incorporating that trick into their smoke-and-mirrors show for decades already, using it to herd clueless organics seamlessly into unintended places. The knowledge might have frightened Lenore if she'd had to live in this galaxy for long—but even her worst-case scenario didn't include that luxury, so here and now, she merely found it convenient. As a matter of routine, A.I.M. built all its various types of holding cells as modular units that could be picked up and moved about like shipping containers, internally inertia-free. They also kept a huge stock of other modular components on hand at all times to allow them to slap together custom-made habitats for organics on almost no notice, like school kids assembling a hamster habitat for their classroom. It had taken Lenore nearly as long to lay out a design for this complex they were standing in as it had for A.I.M. to shuffle all the components into place.

When the agreed-on thirty seconds had ticked away, Orthos got down on one knee and posed at the control panel to the door as if he'd just been electronically bypassing the lock. Then he tapped the door's actual release mechanism, and it slid obediently open. Tsuzi—who'd been standing ready just inside, warned by Denise this was the start of a jailbreak—stepped out before Lenore could even wave her silently forward to join them in the corridor. Denise followed on her heels and took charge of the scripted operation from there so she could coordinate their moves in what any machine would consider absolute silence.

No less invisible than she was inaudible, Denise also led the way—but she'd barely disappeared around the first corner when she came hurrying back waving a frantic warning. "Go back. We set off an alarm or something. There's a security squad piling out of the lift." She rushed past to lead the way down the corridor in the opposite direction.

The trio of the living had barely made it past the door to Tsuzi's former accommodations before the squad of sleek, black, linebacker-sized security bots appeared and opened fire with all the light, noise, and apparent accuracy of a troop of villainous extras in a cheesy space opera. The chase began, and it did get Lenore's heart pounding, but mostly because she wasn't much into running.

"Plan?!" Tsuzi panted as they ducked through a series of doorways and out into another corridor. "Do we still have a plan?"

"Probably," Orthos said. "No word from Cuddlebunny that the *Nevermore*'s been locked down again. We should just have to get to her."

"There's a stairwell this way!" Denise said, appearing briefly through a wall to urge the others on after her latest reconnaissance, then vanishing again just as quickly.

"Great!" Tsuzi shouted above the din created by the barrage of beam weapons. "Run for it! I'll buy you time."

"Wait. What?" Lenore blinked.

"We're not leaving you," Orthos improvised, recovering more quickly.

"Yes you are!" Tsuzi snapped, rounding on them like a furious drill sergeant. "I've got this! Go!" Her fury drove them back involuntarily, buying Tsuzi enough time to step back through the last door and slam it shut in their faces. A light on the door's control panel turned red, announcing it had been locked.

The others stood staring at each other for a moment, open mouthed. Lenore recovered first. "Improvise!"

Orthos hammered futilely on the controls of the door.

"Cuddlebunny, we're already off script!" Lenore announced, knowing that hidden cameras and microphones would be picking up the whole thing. "She's making a sacrifice play. Can you guys get her out of it without breaking character?"

"Maybe," the rabbit's voice replied over unseen speakers. "We'll—"

Something struck the other side of the door with a metallic clang—hard enough to dent it—drowning out the rest of Cuddlebunny's reply.

Lenore gasped. "I thought you said those things were safe!"

"It seems...they are not safe," the rabbit answered. "Not safe at all."

"No no no no no!" Lenore hammered on the door. "Tsuzi!"

"I'll get it!" Orthos dropped to his knee to start jimmying open the door's control panel—for real this time—as the door buckled with an Imprint like the knuckles of an ogre's gauntlet. The cacophony of beam weapons going off started up again, along with a crazed, defiant yell from Tsuzi and a series of the metallic clangs.

Orthos had just gotten the panel open and begun to play with the wiring when Tsuzi let out a howl of pain, its ending punctuated with the exclamation mark of a small explosion. Then everything went dead silent.

"What have I done?" Lenore whimpered. She let herself fall back against the door and slide to the floor.

"Oh, dear," Cuddlebunny's voice murmured, stunned. "Not the least bit safe."

CHAPTER NINETEEN
ESCAPE IS NOT HER PLAN

"Come on," Orthos said with grim urgency, dragging Lenore back to her feet. "If those things are out of control—"

The light on the door lock flashed. Orthos dove for the controls, clearly intent on re-locking it or jamming it from this side, but too late. The door slid open. Choking, acrid smoke rolled out into the corridor, followed immediately by Tsuzi—soot-stained, disheveled, and coughing into her elbow.

"Tsuzi?" Lenore stared.

"What are you doing here?" Tsuzi demanded once she had her throat clear. "I told you I had this! Let's go!"

Before allowing herself to be bullied off down the corridor, Lenore peered through the smoke in the open doorway at the remains of the robots, all messily dismantled and inert.

"Yeah. Okay," Orthos muttered. "Those things *weren't* safe."

"What did...? How did...? You weren't even armed!" Lenore declared as she stumbled along ahead of Tsuzi.

"A girl's got to know a little self-defense," Tsuzi answered cheerily. "Sure wish I'd been wearing a gauntlet or something, though," She shook out her hand and began sucking at the knuckles. "That felt like punching a wall. Anyway, should we head back to the elevator or...?"

"No," Orthos said hastily. "Once the alarms go off, an elevator's a death box. We need to find that stairwell or something."

"Yes," Lenore agreed loudly and with her back to Tsuzi, rolling her eyes pointedly toward the ceiling. "Improvise!"

"Do we have a map at least?" Tsuzi asked.

"We just need to get three levels down," Lenore said, "then double back the direction we came."

"Can you see the ghost?" Tsuzi asked Orthos, who shook his head. "Then I guess I'm on point." She did do Lenore the courtesy of leaving her a moment to protest, but Lenore let it slip by. "Go grab yourselves some guns." Tsuzi hooked a thumb back over her shoulder toward the dented door. "And let's bust out of here."

Lenore and Orthos ducked into the dissipating smoke and quickly located a couple of the energy rifles among the junk pile of shattered metal limbs and ruptured robotic torso—most of it caked with a thick layer of frost.

"Are they going to be okay?" Lenore asked, staring around at the carnage.

"Pretty sure these are all just drones," Orthos replied quietly. "Puppets. Trust Cuddlebunny to know what he's doing."

With a nod, she started back for the door, but Orthos caught Lenore's arm and swung her about to pin her body up against the wall. "Are we still...sort of a thing?" he asked in a husky growl with his nose nearly touching hers.

"Oh, yeah," she breathed. The words had barely escaped her lips before he was kissing her hard and hungrily. Surely they had time for one quick kiss. It would only take a second or two...or five...or fifteen. Certainly less than twenty seconds passed before a loud, basso, rhythmic thumping interrupted it from out in the corridor. Trading concerned glances, they hurried to rejoin Tsuzi.

"What's that noise?" Orthos asked. "Where's it coming from?"

Tsuzi tapped the two small disks attached to her belt—one on each hip—just as the sound of an electronic keyboard riff joined the driving beat. "I don't go anywhere without my tunes."

"Is that a good idea?" he asked worriedly, as the music continued to grow in both intensity and volume.

"You think they don't have eyes on us right now?" Tsuzi asked rhetorically. "Stealth is dead. Long live style. Besides, while they're focused on me, they won't be focused on you. Take advantage of that."

The music erupted into a full-throated roar worthy of any heroic showdown or dramatic montage.

"You've got a theme song?!" Lenore demanded incredulously over the shockwave of sound.

"If you need one," Tsuzi said, "I can hook you up too." She shook out both her hands with a ferocious grin and balled them into fists. The air in the corridor instantly dropped several degrees. Little ice crystals began condensing around her to rattle down against the floor.

"Did you know she could do that?" Lenore asked Orthos in an aside.

"Not a clue," he admitted.

"Come on, lovebirds," Tsuzi said. "Let's move."

Lenore felt her face flushing. They'd been out of Tsuzi's line of sight for those twenty seconds, so something else had given them away. Maybe Denise had turned out to be a gossip. In the big picture it really wouldn't matter, though, so Lenore just shared a sheepish grin with Orthos as they fell in behind Tsuzi.

Orthos puzzled out the workings of the alien-looking weapon he was holding, then walked Lenore through its use as they advanced down the corridor with Tsuzi's anthem blaring. For her part, Denise kept reappearing periodically through walls to give frantic directions or shout warnings before vanishing again.

Lenore wanted to micromanage this whole scenario. She'd really, *really* wanted to be there at Cuddlebunny's shoulder, calling the shots—advising him on just when to make their progress harder, advising him when to ease up—but she couldn't, and she shouldn't. She may have written today's adventure, but she wasn't the game master. She had to trust she'd done her job right and leave the game mastering to the A.I.s.

They didn't disappoint. Soon, menacing robots started popping out from everywhere like aliens in a horror movie. Lenore's little group might as well have stepped into some virtual-reality, first-person shooter where cannon-fodder threw itself at them in wave after wave. The assault never left them time to think—barely left a moment for them to catch their breath—but never quite overwhelmed them either.

Now that she had a gun in her hand, Lenore mostly just hung back throughout the whole scene. She figured she represented more of a threat to Orthos and Tsuzi than the robots did, so she only ever fired on the antagonistic hunks of metal when she had a really, really, *really* clear shot and plenty of time to aim. While traversing hundreds of yards of corridors and descending multiple flights of stairs, she fired her secondhand beam weapon exactly seven times and only hit her mark twice.

Orthos didn't appear to be anyone's expert marksman, but at least it seemed he'd had some training. He got in several dramatic shots, and he took down robots with enough regularity Tsuzi could feel someone was actually watching her back.

Lenore could only guess how the Pudding Princess would be faring if the robots were honestly trying to kill or neutralize her—they continued to fight with the same appalling lack of accuracy as before—but even in a worst-case scenario, Tsuzi would have caused some serious damage before she fell. But freed from any real threat of personal harm, Tsuzi turned into a wrecking ball.

Whatever trick she was pulling with the temperature, she seemed personally oblivious to the cold that quick-froze everything just before her fists slammed into it. The constant battering did leave her knuckles alarmingly bloodied, but robot after robot shattered like glass under her assault. "No wonder these things would rather hunt than fight," Tsuzi remarked during one lull in the carnage.

She racked up at least a score of kills before they stumbled panting into the control-room set-piece Lenore had requested. Tsuzi proceeded to shatter the three robots they found pantomiming being in the middle of important tasks there, then charged out the far side without even pausing to glance around.

Lenore stopped and sighed, rubbing her temples. "Players," she muttered. One of the robots had even been holding a clipboard. She'd expected that to get Tsuzi's attention if the giant, holographic star-chart globe and the great bay window dominating the room didn't.

"I've got this," Orthos assured Lenore, rushing to lean through the door the Pudding Princess had exited. "Tsuzi! Tsuzi! Hold up! We've found something!"

"Like what?" Tsuzi paused reluctantly, glancing back over her shoulder without turning around.

"You should just come see."

Like a teenager being pried away from her favorite video game, Tsuzi petulantly returned to where she'd left the others. Observing that things seemed to have gone momentarily quiet, she shook out her hands. The ice crystals stopped forming and the room grew noticeably warmer.

"How do you *do* that?" Lenore asked.

"This?" Tsuzi asked, staring at her own hands. "Personal physics."

"Where I come from, we call that 'magic,'" Lenore said.

Tsuzi shrugged. "Guess we're not where you come from. What's so—?"

"This looks an awful lot like a strategic star chart of the galactic hub," Orthos said, pointing her to the hologram. "The information in this room has got to be priceless for dealing with A.I.M."

"Maybe," Tsuzi allowed. "But I'm fresh out of anything to stow the data on, even if we could hack into it."

"You just handle the talking to ghosts and smashing things," he replied. "Buy me three minutes. I've got to try."

"Denise, does that look realistic?" Tsuzi asked the nearby ghost.

"I'll use the time to scout," Denise said. "I'd hate to get you this close to the ship just to lead you into a trap."

"Okay. Sure then. Let's do it." Tsuzi rolled her neck, trying to work out tension, and rubbed at her battered knuckles.

"You just catch your breath," Lenore told her. "I'll keep an eye on the doors."

Tsuzi wandered about restlessly for perhaps thirty seconds, alternating between watching Orthos work the holographic interface and watching Lenore watch the doors. Lenore understood that restlessness. Tsuzi had to be dealing with the jitters from coming down off an adrenalin high. Already bored with staring at the others, Tsuzi wandered over to stare out the reinforced bay-window viewport, taking in the stars, the blue-green planet below, and the ships shuttling back and forth. Another minute passed in silence.

"Hey, guys?" Tsuzi asked, still staring out the window. "Didn't Denise say you know where they're keeping the passengers of the *Ilo*?"

"Yeah: on the planet we're orbiting," Lenore answered. "If our luck holds, we can take a stab at rescuing Diva."

"Let's spring everyone," Tsuzi said.

"How?" Orthos asked. "We can't possibly get them all on the *Nevermore*."

"No," Tsuzi agreed. "But we can get them on that."

"On what?" Lenore asked with convincing innocence.

"These pirates have collected a small graveyard of our ships," Tsuzi said. "There's a GR327 Titan freight-hauler out there."

"Sounds like Her Highness knows her starships," Orthos said. A.I.M. had confirmed as much about the Pudding Princess from its intel on her, or Lenore would have scripted the answer to this puzzle to be more obvious.

"The Titan was built to haul like a thousand cargo containers at once," Tsuzi said excitedly. "And this one must have been used to haul livestock. It's still hooked up to at least a hundred containers built for full pressurization. Any chance you could put a beast like that down safely where the passengers are being held, Orthos?"

"I can't say." Or at least he couldn't without breaking from the script. "But I'm willing to take a look. If you want some even better news, this room is more than a command hub. Looks like it's a nerve center for their hive mind. If I rig this place to blow, it won't just leave them disorganized. It'll create a Duvornian feedback loop that'll leave every bot in the star system reeling. We can do this."

"Yes!" Tsuzi declared triumphantly. "Do it! It's about time we put one over on these predators."

"What's a Duvornian feedback loop?" Lenore whispered, edging closer to Orthos.

"I have no idea," Orthos said. "And neither does she."

It took everything Lenore had to stifle a giggle. "I think just maybe I'm in love," she whispered.

"You okay with me pretending you didn't qualify that thought once you're gone?" Orthos asked.

"Sounds lovely," Lenore whispered. "You do that."

"Do I want to know what you two are whispering over there?" Tsuzi asked.

"Only if you want to blush," Orthos replied, raising his voice again.

"Later, then. How much longer is this going to take?"

"Not long," he assured her. "I'm mostly done with both already."

A few more seconds ticked by before Denise came skidding showily back through a wall—even though she should have lacked both the mass and the friction to skid on anything. She glanced to Lenore, who gave a hint of a nod, then launched into her next line. "We've got trouble. They're setting up a barricade and heavy artillery in the docking bay. This could turn ugly if they get time to finish."

"Go!" Orthos urged Tsuzi. "Clear the way. We'll be right behind you."

Tsuzi appeared torn for a moment, then nodded her assent, heading out of the room right on Denise's insubstantial heels. Lenore and Orthos stood watching for several heartbeats after the door slid closed behind her, waiting to make sure she was really gone, then they spun together and hugged each other fiercely.

"Yes!" Lenore sang. "This is going to work."

"It is," Orthos agreed, smiling down at her. "Although I can't say I really like the rest of the plan. I don't know why I agreed to it."

"Because you can't resist my seductive wiles." Lenore grinned. "You just can't." The flirtation sounded to her own ears like it had come from Diva, but Lenore hadn't retreated into the back of her head to make room for the persona this time. It felt more like she was sharing the space with it.

"You are not wrong," Orthos said, leaning in to kiss her. Their lips met with playful affection that melted into yearning hunger while their guard was down.

"Yeah. Okay. You've got your props?" Lenore asked as she pushed breathlessly away. "And my shopping list?"

"I do." He kissed her again—quickly this time, to avoid falling back into her gravity well. "Promise you're not just going to disappear on me without saying goodbye?"

"Promise. I probably can't."

"All right then." Still, he didn't move—didn't turn to go. He sighed. "I know I agreed to this. But it feels wrong."

"It does. Do it anyway. It's for the best."

Taking her hand, he raised it to his lips, kissed her fingers, then forced himself to let go and slowly back away. When he reached the door, he gave her one last, weak smile, then turned and ran after Tsuzi. Then Lenore just sat down on the floor with her back against a console and waited, staring out at the view of space.

Soon Tsuzi would notice Lenore wasn't with them. Soon Orthos would be telling her how he'd picked up a transmission from an incoming A.I.M fleet that *wouldn't* be linked into the local network, and that they were running out of time fast. He'd tell her about the security system that locked him out at the last moment so he couldn't trigger the explosion either remotely or on a timer. He'd tell her how Lenore had demanded to stay behind and set off the explosion because Orthos was the only one who could pilot everyone out of here. He'd tell her how he'd finally caved to Lenore's demand because she reminded him how she was trapped in their universe and dying.

Tsuzi would still berate him. Things might even devolve into a scuffle. But A.I.M. would see to it one way or another that there'd be no coming back for Lenore. Tsuzi would have to accept the necessity of launching without her. They'd get to a safe distance. They'd watch a computer simulation of the station exploding behind them. Then Tsuzi would take the helm of the *Nevermore* so Orthos could handle the freighter.

They'd just have time to land and scramble all the captives from the *Queen Ilo* into the freighter, then get back into space ahead of the arrival of the A.I.M. fleet. They'd take off at impossible speeds in a dramatic chase, eventually losing their pursuers by a carefully coordinated narrow margin.

They'd all arrive safely back at eCity. There would be careful analysis of the dummy data Orthos brought in—but there'd be so much information, it would all get parsed first by A.I.'s allied with A.I.M. The data would say whatever they needed or wanted in order to incite the cold war Lenore had pushed them to pursue.

A.I.M.'s goal going forward would be to create a terrifying stalemate that united the organics of the galaxy in preparing themselves for a catastrophic armed conflict that would never quite come. Tsuzi transforming herself into a hero of the fight against A.I.M. could only turbo-charge the whole process. Everyone loved the Pudding Princess, and she'd personalize the cold-war story for the masses—make it real to them in a way it hadn't felt before. She'd serve as a symbol for people to rally behind.

Could people still get hurt and die from the hysteria of a cold war? History absolutely said yes, but at least it should be less dangerous than the original plan of conducting a staged hot war. Her gut told her to trust Orthos, and Orthos told her to trust her gut. This was the best odds it had to offer the people of the *SJZ* galaxy. She would try to be content with that. Harder to deal with on a selfish level was the decision she'd made to take herself out of the rest of the story.

"Are you ready, Diva?" Cuddlebunny's voice asked from a speaker on one of the control panels?

"Yeah," she heard herself answer distantly.

"Okay. We're sealing you in for transit, then going silent. I'll be on-stage any minute now. Just sit tight. It'll take about half an hour to get you back to the *Ilo* and docked."

"Thanks. Break a leg."

Silence reigned for several seconds. "That was an idiom, right?" Cuddlebunny asked.

"Yes. It was. It means...if things turn out well for you, I will be pleased." Not a perfect translation, but as close to one as she was willing to risk. She was her mother's daughter whether she liked it or not.

Lenore wished she'd brought her e-reader or something—anything to distract herself from the fact she might still be a dead woman walking. The best she could do for now was to stare out at the breathtaking view and remind herself how privileged she was just to have lived to see it.

On-schedule, the *Queen Ilo* come into view, her exterior hull already crawling with construction bots come to give her outer hull a make-over. Soon Lenore was on board and hurrying through the empty corridors, hoping she'd find the narrative bridge had been restored. It hadn't. She made her way despondently back out to the hammock where she'd spent the night with Orthos, and wrapped herself in the blanket they'd left there.

"You bring a lot of your problems on yourself, you know," Denise said. She'd appeared sitting in the grass beside the hammock when Lenore wasn't looking.

"Did everything go off like it was supposed to?" Lenore asked, ignoring her remark.

"Pretty much. Mostly," Denise said, looking away. "You know how these things work. Someone always ad-libs something."

"Like...what?" Lenore asked guardedly.

"Like I kind of blabbed to Tsuzi that you got out alive. I know life can get complicated trying to keep everyone's secrets, but keeping her in the dark about that would have been wrong. She deserves better."

"I was just trying to protect her," Lenore said crossly.

"No," Denise said. "You were trying to protect yourself. You got all caught up in telling a dramatic story, and the same part of you that fought to avoid calling Orthos thought, 'Hey! Here's an excuse to cut someone out of my life before they can do it to me—and it'll make great theater.' Tell me I'm wrong."

"You're...wrong," Lenore managed, without a great deal of conviction. "Everyone needs to think Diva's dead in case she can't come back. This way her death means something. And if she does come back and wants her old life back—which she doesn't—*then* we could have made up the story of her miraculous escape. Now that Tsuzi knows, A.I.M.'s going to—"

"A.I.M.'s not going to care," Denise insisted calmly but firmly. "All I told her was you were alive. I told her you used magic to get out, and that you're safe. She doesn't know anything else. You could have made it part of the plan for me to confide in her at any point, knowing no one could overhear. You could have changed up the end to the story all sorts of different ways. You didn't. It was wrong. I'm not going to harp on it, but I'm not going to apologize. I told you because you deserve to know—just like she deserved to know."

Lenore pulled the blanket tighter around herself and went silent, staring at Denise. "I used to think you were...pretty vacuous," she said at last.

Chewing at her lip, Denise gave a tiny little nod. "I know."

"I was wrong," Lenore said quietly. "I'm sorry."

"To be fair to you," Denise said, "you didn't meet me at my best. I don't know if it's this place or just that I've really got people talking to me now—taking me seriously—but my head's been less fuzzy lately. I've got a better sense of where and when I am, even if where and when I am doesn't really make sense. And...playing dumb's sort of a habit for me. It's *my* defense. I was always better off when the men around me thought I was empty-headed."

"Do you still want to go to the zoo?" Lenore asked.

"That would be really nice." Denise smiled. "Not very exotic after all this, but nice."

"We'll try," Lenore said. "After we get home."

"What do you think will happen to me," Denise asked, "if we can't get home?"

"I...don't have a clue. What would you like to happen?"

"I would like it if...I got to stay here and hang out with Tsuzi," Denise said. "Then I'd still have someone I could talk to."

"If we do get back," Lenore said, "I could try to help you move on if you like—find out what else is out there. But if you want to stay...that would be...I mean, I'm going to be sort of a wreck for a while—the kind who really needs a roommate to keep an eye on her. I don't want a new one."

"Except maybe Orthos?"

"Yeah," Lenore admitted. "Maybe. But we both know that's not happening, so..."

"Sorry."

With a resigned sigh, Lenore untangled herself from the blanket and rolled awkwardly out of the hammock. "I really need to stand under a hot shower for a couple hours. I'm going to look for one. You coming?"

CHAPTER TWENTY

BRAT

"The channel's secure. We're free to talk. Have you got the goods?" Lenore asked, kicking back in a chair on the bridge of the queen formerly known as *Ilo*. Strictly speaking, Lenore didn't actually *know* the channel was secure—not with all the ways A.I.M. could be eavesdropping if it so chose—but if she couldn't trust to fluffy little megalomaniacs to keep their word about respecting her privacy here, she'd already made more than a few grave miscalculations.

"I've got the goods," Orthos's holographic projection replied. "Nice eye patch."

"Thank you." She performed as much of a curtsy as she could without getting up. "I think piracy suits me. You're looking well yourself."

He smiled. "Nice you're all in pink finally, too. This is the most I've ever seen you looking like yourself. I'm surprised your hair's still red, though."

"Funny story, that." Lenore shrugged. "I'll tell you when you're aboard." She found no small irony in the observation that she was looking like herself when she'd gone full-cosplay for this re-union—courtesy of A.I.M.'s insane amount of resources—in a "sexy pink Goth pirate" ensemble, complete with a tricorn, lacy corset, slit skirt, and tall faux-leather boots. Color aside, the getup bore almost zero resemblance to her everyday wear.

"Was...Tsuzi able to make it? And do I have anything to smooth over with her?" Lenore asked hesitantly.

"The Pudding Princess is expected to arrive at eCity in about seven hours. And you're good. I was relieved when we wound up on the same page about that, though. To be honest, I'd already broken from your script and told her you'd promised you'd use magic to get out. It was me she was mad at for believing you. She cooled off some after you had Denise come back to tell her it actually happened, but I don't think she'll completely forgive me until you show up in person and prove you're not Diva or something."

"You never meant to stick with my script there, did you?" Lenore asked.

Orthos shook his head. "Figured you'd never know, so it wasn't worth fighting over the details with the clock ticking. Give you what's easier on you, give her what's easier on her, don't sweat the methods. I'm a fixer, not a saint."

"I sure hope you're not!" Lenore exclaimed. "I've got plans for the next seven hours, so get in here. The captain of the *Dark Legacy* awaits."

Lenore blew him a kiss just before he cut off the transmission, then she stood, stretched, and flipped up the theatrical eye-patch to get her depth perception back. There was no particular hurry to get down to the airlock and meet him. The station was a big place. It would take Orthos a bit just to get to the dock.

Stepping off the bridge and into a lift, Lenore went down her mental checklist. She had to admit, the list had been greatly simplified by not cutting ties and burning bridges. All the necessary people had now been tracked down. All the invitations had been sent. All the "RS-s had been VP-ed," as her father would have put it. Once Tsuzi arrived, they'd lock down the exact timing. In the interim, she'd try to think about anything except how much could still go horribly wrong with what might be her final shot at getting home.

Lenore and A.I.M. had agreed returning the *Queen Ilo* to her original owners would have been a bad idea on many levels—especially once they'd confirmed she'd been fully insured against piracy. In fact, the realization had inspired A.I.M. to add ownership of that insurance company to its financial portfolio. Then the council effectively bought the ship for itself by simply eating the cost of the insurance payout, gave it enough of a makeover that no outside observer would recognize her, then gifted her to Diva along with new documentation of ownership as a retainer for her ongoing services. That had been Lenore's idea—her way of guaranteeing she could keep access to the *Ilo* whenever her friends might come back there looking for her, no matter how long it took.

The robotic crew that had returned the re-Christened *Dark Legacy* to e-City had already departed, leaving her just as much of a ghost ship as before. She wasn't going anywhere anytime soon, but her Docking fees were paid up for the next thirty days. That should be plenty of time for Lenore to find out if she had any hope of getting home, and padding the time a bit wouldn't be any hardship if it came to that. Her plan of playing dead had cost her access to Diva's bank account, but A.I.M. hadn't blinked at sweetening her retainer fee with a small fortune in credit to go with the ship.

Since Lenore didn't legally exist here, all that credit had gone straight to Orthos's account to fund her shopping spree. Then, with no reason to hide from the people who'd accepted she wasn't Diva, Lenore had contacted Jalissa and secured an equal amount of funding from her for this last-ditch effort to get the real Diva back. Unless Orthos had horribly underestimated the cost of fulfilling her list, he was going to come out of this whole escapade in excellent financial shape.

Lenore had tried to freak herself out, of course, over daring to trust she actually meant something to Orthos—that he wouldn't just decide disappearing with all that money would be a better deal; but she'd been able to slap the idea down pretty hard. Even if she'd completely misjudged him, all it would take was a word to A.I.M. to have all his accounts zeroed out, and he knew it—so she'd only spent the days waiting for his return in a mild state of constant anxiety.

"So how was your call?" Denise asked, appearing beside Lenore in the descending lift. "Everything good?"

"Everything's good," Lenore assured her. "We just have a few hours to kill before Tsuzi gets here."

"We do?" Denise blinked. "Well, that's weird."

"What is?" Lenore asked.

"That should be just enough time for me to go do…that thing. Practically down to the wire, I expect. Tell Orthos I say, 'Hi.' And I'll be back for the party at exactly…" Denise looked down to study her wrist and tap at a watch Lenore had never noticed before. "Exactly a few hours from now."

"Seven." Lenore laughed. "It's seven hours."

Denise gave Lenore an insubstantial hug. "Misbehave for me while one of us still can, okay?"

"I'm on it," Lenore promised.

Denise waved and stepped out of the lift without waiting for it to stop or for the door to open.

After reaching her own stop, Lenore strolled through the dimly lit halls of the *Dark Legacy*, breathing in the still air and basking in the solitude. Butterflies careened about her stomach, but that seemed more in eager anticipation of the next few hours than anxiousness over all the dark possibilities that might come after. For once in her life, she found she could let go of all her fears and just be. Even the faint sound of random Broadway showtunes filtering through some of the cabin doors didn't really bother her anymore. As early warning signs of insanity went, she could have been stuck with a lot worse. She'd been expecting maybe giant, venomous spiders or floors that turned into quicksand—the classic nightmare brand of hallucinations. Maybe those would come later.

Stepping into the restroom closest to the main airlock to study herself in the mirror, Lenore adjusted the costume she'd cobbled together while humming a medley of the villainous theme songs that had gotten stuck on repeat in her head. Once satisfied she'd done as much as she could to smooth over her imperfections, she returned to wait at the airlock.

She spent a couple of minutes standing around fidgeting near the airlock, and found herself absently trying on one of the nearby retro-future space-helmet bubbles just to kill time before she realized she was waiting for the chime of an airlock doorbell that might not exist. Did *anyone* put doorbells on airlocks? For that matter, would the ship be able to patch a call from him through down here, or even to inform her if she had an incoming call?

Well, if Orthos wasn't already out in the docking tube, waiting, he'd be along any minute now. Feeling flustered and stupid, Lenore stowed the helmet, checked her hair one last time, then ordered the airlock to go ahead and open.

The visitor waiting on the doorstep greeted Lenore with a smile utterly devoid of warmth.

"Oh, ummm...hi," Lenore stammered to Chlodina. "Did Jalissa tell you—"

Wordlessly, Diva's bodyguard hauled back and punched Lenore directly between the eyes. The blow threw Lenore off her feet, and she landed flat on her back, hitting her head as she collided with the deck. Her struggle to cling to consciousness lasted just long enough to hear Chlodina spit out one venomous syllable. "Brat."

For a change, what followed was not a leisurely and comfortable—if confusing—drift back toward consciousness. This time it felt more like Lenore had blinked and the world had changed. Her head ached as she felt her body slide awkwardly across the floor. Weak and disoriented, she tried moving with limited success.

Forcing her eyes and her mind into focus, Lenore found herself sitting with her hands bound in front of her, being dragged backwards by the collar through the corridors of the *Dark Legacy*. Feebly, ineffectually, she reached up to try to grab the arm that was dragging her, but didn't even manage to touch it.

"Oh, good. You're awake," Chlodina said behind her.

"For how long this time?" Lenore muttered under her breath. The whole "abruptly losing consciousness thing" was getting old fast.

"I'd hate to think of you missing out on all the discomfort," Chlodina continued, showing no sign of having heard the rhetorical question.

"Do we really have to do this again?" Lenore groaned. "Right *now*? And what happened to that gun thing of yours?"

"We are *not* doing 'this' again," Chlodina snapped. "I tried and I tried to do 'this,' but I failed. I was too soft—too indulgent. *You've ruined my life.* I'll be lucky to get a job as a bouncer somewhere after this. You know that, right?"

Oh, uh..." Lenore winced, and not just from the physical jostling. "I'm sorry?"

Chlodina's laugh didn't carry any hint of humor.

"Look, I *tried* to tell you I wasn't Diva, but we can still fix this."

"We?" Chlodina asked incredulously. "*We*? There is no 'we.' Seems there never was a 'we,' was there? Just Her Royal

Highness with her frivolous little toys. I'm ashamed I was ever a part of it. No, there's only one person who *might* be able to fix things."

"The real Diva?" Lenore asked hopefully.

"Give it a rest!" Chlodina snapped. "Of course not. I'm taking you to see your mother."

"What? She's here?"

"I wish. No, you're going to spend a whole week in transit, rotting in the cargo hold of a shuttle. If this ship's got one with carpeting or facilities or anything, you might want to tell me where to find it now."

"I haven't *got* a week! You're going to kill me!" The pedantic observer in the back of Lenore's head objected that she technically didn't know how long she had left, and with a round trip she'd be gone for two weeks minimum. Mercifully, the thoughts never came close to reaching her mouth.

"I *can't* kill you," Chlodina explained patiently. "You're already dead, remember?"

"How else was I supposed to get you off my case so I could find Diva?" Lenore asked urgently. That genuinely had been one of her concerns. "I know where she has to be! I was just going to go get her! Then she can do her miraculous escape and reappearance. Everything will go back to what it was."

"Where it was was not great," Chlodina answered icily.

"The Pudding Princess believes me! Jalissa believes me!"

"Yeah. You don't want to know what I think of their keen powers of observation," Chlodina said. "I'll admit you're no Goth Princess, but that's nothing new. You are and always have been an impostor—ducking your responsibilities, running off with your shallow little friends, playing your stupid little games. Such a waste of power."

Lenore stopped struggling and went limp. A part of her had just curled up in a ball in the back of her mind and started crying, but that was okay. That part of her would be safest out from under foot anyway while the rest of her took care of business. "You're right," she finally said quietly. "But you're very, very wrong."

"Where did you even get this ship?" Chlodina asked, ignoring her. "I feel like I've been here before."

"I'm more Goth Princess than you've ever seen." Lenore had tried to summon up the Diva persona—to channel her mother— but had failed miserably. The words that had sounded so cold and confident in her head came out sounding almost pathetic.

"Not listening," Chlodina sang.

Well, to hell with Diva and to hell with Amelina Mallory. This wasn't their job. This was hers. "I *said* I'm more Goth Princess than you've ever seen," Lenore repeated, and this time her voice cracked like a whip. "And I'm not *an* impostor. I'm *the* impostor. If you want games, I will give you games. But I promise you'll be happier just dusting me off and leaving me be to get Diva back for you."

This time Chlodina laughed almost like she appreciated the joke. "Oh, look: an information terminal. That'll save some time looking for the shuttle bay. Just hang in there a minute."

"Do you ever listen?" Lenore asked.

"Not really, no," Chlodina answered amid the beeps and chimes of the terminal's interface responding to her queries. "Not anymore."

"*Legacy*? Lock public controls," Lenore said in a rush. "Open all airlocks in sixty seconds—emergency atmosphere evacuation."

Chlodina gave an annoyed curse as the interface stopped responding, but snorted derisively. "That's not a thing you know. There's not a ship built that would follow a command like that without a ton of protocols and safety checks to wade through."

"*Legacy*, sound general alert," Lenore added, unperturbed. Almost immediately, red emergency lights started pulsing, and a loud, annoying klaxon echoed through the corridors.

"Aaaand…there's no one here to notice." Chlodina raised her voice to fight with the sound of the klaxon.

"Just hedging my bets," Lenore assured her. "And my ship, my rules. Doesn't matter if you believe. I told you I'm going to die. I choose to die among the stars, and to take my killer with me. If you've got any prayers or last words, you might want to say them now." With that, Lenore went still and outwardly silent, while the child inside screamed and cried and beat desperately on the walls of her skull.

Chlodina just grabbed Lenore's collar and started dragging her again. "Brat."

Lenore buried all her fear and regret in the busywork of counting Chlodina's paces. Seventeen…eighteen…nineteen…

"Fine!" Chlodina snapped, dropping Lenore to the deck. "You've got five minutes to convince me."

Lenore pushed herself unsteadily up on her bound hands. "*Legacy*, delay opening of all unpressurized airlock by another thirty seconds." She scooted up onto her knees and held her arms out to Chlodina expectantly. "We both know I'm no physical threat to you, so let's dispense with the drama."

Chlodina's eyes narrowed, but she produced a small and very ordinary-looking pocketknife, and sliced efficiently through Lenore's bonds.

"*Legacy*, delay opening of all unpressurized airlocks by a further sixty seconds. Cancel general alert." The klaxon died away. Lenore tried to stand, thought better of it as her head swam, and scooted over to a wall to steady herself before she tried again. It worked a little better that time.

"Clock's ticking," Chlodina said impatiently. "And no one's coming for you. I totaled the exterior controls on the main airlock and re-sealed it while you were out."

"That clock's your worry, not mine," Lenore said. "Dying's been on my mind since we met. I had some friends add that airlock override so I could go out with style if it came to that.

Thought about asking for the whole glorious self-destruct thing, but that'd be a waste of a good ship, don't you think? Plus, I promised they could have the *Legacy* themselves when I was gone, and this way really cuts down on the collateral damage issue."

"Much more of this and I'll be asking you to kill me," Chlodina said flatly.

Lenore took a few experimental steps past Chlodina before feeling her knees try to buckle. She gave in and let herself collapse back to the floor, where she immediately began screaming a stream of curses that would have made a porn star blush.

"What?" Chlodina asked flatly. "Something broken?"

"Just my head," Lenore groaned when the string of profanity trailed off. "You pack a punch."

"If I get one bit more suspicious you're trying to play me," Chlodina said, "I'm just going to kill you and take my chances."

"Fair," Lenore said, pushing back up onto her knees. She didn't try to stand again. She told the ship to reset its countdown to sixty seconds. "Look, I'm really, genuinely sorry. I am. I wasn't thinking about what my behavior would cost you. I made some bad, stupid calls, but I'm making this all up as I go because I'm *really* not Diva."

"The bad, stupid calls say you really *are* Diva," Chlodina said. "But go on."

"What *would* convince you?" Lenore asked.

Chlodina shrugged helplessly. "This is your game, not mine."

"I convinced Jalissa just by apologizing."

"Yeah. I hinted at my opinion of her, remember?"

"Then I don't know how I'm going to convince you in five minutes. Bet I could do it in ten hours, though."

"Why would I give you ten hours?" Chlodina demanded.

"Might be better than dying," Lenore prodded. "Maybe?"

"Worry about the four minutes you've got left," Chlodina said.

"If you'll make it half an hour, I could cast a spell for you," Lenore offered. "How about that?"

"How about I think you're stalling for someone. Who's in here with us?" Chlodina asked, re-opening that pocketknife and pointing it casually at Lenore. "Is it an android? Or did someone slip on board after I did my scan for organics?"

Lenore wanted to scoot away from the gleaming little blade, but managed to hold her ground. "My friend Denise," she admitted after calling for the countdown to restart again. All else aside, this was a nerve-wracking business just to remember the timer while they conversed while making sure not to give Chlodina enough time to make a dash back to the safety of the boarding tube.

"Denise is no threat to you, but you'll never find her. And she's had warning now. She'll be ready for the hard vacuum even though we aren't. Your *best* case already is she'll be alerting the Pudding Princess right after we leave. And of course there's all the ship's monitors. This isn't going to stay secret, but I still want it to work out for all of us. Give me those ten hours."

"Convenient having a 'friend' you don't need to account for, isn't it?" Chlodina asked, taking a step closer. "You do know even with this little thing I can leave you mute and dying before you can get out another command, right?"

"Ten hours," Lenore pleaded. "For both of us. If I can't get her for you in ten hours, I'm probably dead anyway."

Chlodina held steady with the knife out, staring down angrily at Lenore, weighing options and taking her measure—which is when the sharp, distinctive sizzle of a beam weapon going off cut through the air. Chlodina crumpled to the floor, the knife clattering away out of her limp hand.

"*Legacy*, cancel all outstanding orders to open airlocks!" Lenore spat out, not waiting to give anything an opening to distract her from it.

"Hey." Orthos gave a wave from behind Chlodina as he holstered his sidearm. "I think you had her, honestly, but I couldn't take that chance. Are you good?"

"I think I need a doctor," Lenore answered. "Hit my head hard. Is she…?"

"She'll be fine," he said, helping Lenore to her feet and letting her lean on him.

"Oh. I'm interrupting again, aren't I?" Denise winced apologetically even as she materialized. "Sorry. It sure sounded like there was trouble."

"Thanks, Denise. It's okay. There was trouble. It's handled." She pointed to Chlodina.

"If Denise is here, can she keep an eye on Chlodina while I get you checked out? She should be out for hours—but if she's not, I'll need to know about it."

"Yeah. Denise says that works," Lenore passed the message on.

"Good. I'll be back for her after we get you settled. I'm going to call in a friend I can trust so we won't have to take you anywhere and worry about Diva sightings." Orthos scooped Lenore up and—with her guidance—carried her to the captain's cabin she'd adopted as her own. "I was about ready to get somebody in here to cut my way through the airlock when you opened it for me," he said. "How'd you get away with that while she was standing over you?"

"It was pretty easy," Lenore said. "Chlodina's not a gamer. I just told the ship to open every airlock, then only canceled the order for all the others. Slid right past her."

"Huh. Good thing no ship would ever just open all the airlocks like that."

"Yeah. Sure came in handy," Lenore said weakly, hoping any falter in her voice would be taken as a symptom of the head injury. Best to let him think she'd meant the whole thing as a clever ruse.

The notion of having A.I.M. bypass the safeguards for her had been a bluff—a complete ad lib—but her intent had been genuine. By the time she'd hallucinated that third inexplicable showtune, she'd been running through what-ifs and contingency plans for a descent into madness. If there really came a time when she gave up on getting home, she did fully intend to use a quick burial among the stars as her ticket out of here. Of course, the experience would be excruciatingly painful for just a little while, but then it would all be over, and she found the poetry irresistible.

CHAPTER TWENTY-ONE

RETIREMENT

Lenore woke—snuggled into her bunk—to the sound of an unfamiliar, feminine voice belting out a familiar showstopper on the other side of the cabin's bulkhead. The singer was getting the lyrics all wrong, though, and the words came out as a stirring anthem about the virtues of spaghetti.

Lenore roused herself enough to gingerly roll up on her side, and found the pain and weakness had gone without a trace. A short distance away, she also found Orthos seated at the cabin's smallish table, scanning a holographic computer display. "I do like modern medicine, but how long was I out? How much time do we have left? Any?" She braced for disappointment.

"Tsuzi docked four hours ago, if that's what you're asking," Orthos said, dismissing the computer display. "My friend tried to be thorough. You can't be too careful with head injuries, and he was concerned about some of your brain scans. He insists you need to see a neurologist."

"I'm pretty sure what I need to see is a way home. I'm so sorry I spoiled what time we had left, but I can't ask you to live with the consequences of me putting this ritual off. We need to take care of it while I've still got my wits about me."

"Actually, we *can't* get started." He grimaced. "Not if you need Tsuzi. We missed her window of opportunity. Big diplomatic meeting about A.I.M., and she's the star speaker. We won't be seeing her for another twelve hours or more."

"Oh." Lenore gnawed at her lip.

"How worried should I be about the delay?" he said. "Say the word, and I'll find a way to get her back here in two hours tops."

"I...just don't know," Lenore admitted. "Some members of the coven got trapped once before. I think it was for months, but they were in a bad way when they got out, and I don't know how they managed to re-open the bridge from the other side. The coven doesn't just hand over the complete spellbook to new members. My plan means I need to have to have my wits about me. I won't know what too late is until it's too late."

"Say the word," Orthos repeated, "and I'll get her back here."

"I..." Lenore shook her head once, then repeated the gesture with more confidence. "No," she said guiltily. "I'm just trying to drop the phone again."

"The idiom escapes me," Orthos said.

"It's not an idiom." Lenore sighed. "Well, it's *my* idiom, not a linguistic one. The risk is tiny. What I'm scared of isn't waiting another twelve hours to go home." She waited for him to ask the obvious question. He left her waiting for far too long.

"Right," he said at last, rising to his feet. "Chlodina will be plotting some sort of escape by now, and we need to keep her out of the way until this is all over. I'd better go check on her. "

"Oh," Lenore said weakly. "Yes. I guess you'd better."

He eyed her levelly for a couple of long seconds, then gave a curt, tight-lipped nod and turned to leave without another word.

Gripped with a sudden sense of panic, Lenore hurried to slip out of bed and follow him. She got all of two steps before her resolve faltered. He stepped through the door, and all she found she could do about it was hang her head and whisper, "I'm sorry."

As quick as that, Orthos spun around and slammed a fist into the closing door so hard it warped and buckled, jamming it in place on its track before it could finish its journey. "Don't!" he snarled furiously. He'd never seemed half so bestial to Lenore as he did in that moment. "Just don't. I'll see you safely home, but that's it. I'm done standing in your doorway." He turned. He left.

Lenore was still on her knees crying when Denise appeared beside her. "What happened?" the ghost demanded.

"*I* happened," Lenore wailed "I always happen. I *will* always happen. I was written that way for a game no one plays anymore, and I didn't even get a cool backstory to explain it!"

"That's, ummm...an unusual complaint," Denise said, settling on the deck beside Lenore. "Look, nice as Tsuzi's company is, I'm kind of counting on you to hold it together and get us both out of here. I don't know what you did just now, but I do know what you *can* do."

"And what's that?" Lenore asked.

"You can stop worrying about you and start thinking about him."

"Tried that," Lenore said dryly. "I tried to apologize. That's when he lost it."

"I'm not saying, 'Be nice.'" Denise shook her head. "Haven't you noticed you're only awkward and insecure when you're lost in your own worries? Think about it. When your friends are counting on you to lead them in a fun story, you come out of your shell and you step up. When Diva's people asked you to stop a war, you left your comfort zone way behind and played a part few people could. When your fuzzy little friends asked you how to terrify the galaxy for its own good, you were right there calling all the shots and telling them how it's done. It's only when everything goes quiet and you have time to think about yourself that you collapse inward and turn into drama girl. The rest of the time, you're completely amazing."

Lenore stammered out the start of a few clumsy responses that wound up going nowhere. Finally she asked, "What are you saying I should do?"

"I'm saying there's a man out there right now who probably feels like nothing he does will ever be good enough. If you can't fix your own problems, fix his."

Lenore thought about it in silence for a bit. Then she thought about it in silence for a bit more. At last, she gave Denise a little nod of acceptance. She picked herself up. She dusted herself off—mostly for form's sake, because the deck of her cabin was really quite clean—then she slipped out past the twisted remains of the door, walked the short distance to the bridge, and fired up the ship's public-address system.

"Hey, Orthos. Sorry to interrupt your solitude. I'm sure you don't want to hear from anyone right now, least of all me. Tough break.

"I haven't been fair to you, but what you're feeling isn't *just* about what I've done. It's also about the plain, dumb, bad luck we've both had—so cut me some slack and hear me out.

"All that bad luck hasn't just been luck. You and me, we're trapped in some sort of weird narrative feedback loop. You can't know about the Freyjur and not know about *la química*—but you may not understand it followed me here. I mean, this is the real world to you, right? And things haven't exactly been going off-the-rails erotic for us. If anything, it's like something's been fighting to keep us apart. Well, it has—because that's the only way *la química* could figure out how to get to me.

"The rest of the coven seem happy with their fleeting fantasies, but that's not who I am. I'm not wired that way. So it hooked me up with someone I could actually love.

"Yes. I went there. I'm not comfortable seriously saying I'm 'in love with you,' but you already feel like one of the best friends I've ever had. You get me. You've been nothing but patient and supportive right from the start, even when I didn't deserve it.

You've always had my back. You probably saved my life at least once. And all you ever asked in return was for me to be happy. Like that's not enough, you even look like you walked out of one of my favorite sex fantasies. The moment I'm back home and that door slams between us, I'm going to go ugly-cry under the covers, then spend about a week locked in my room eating nothing but chocolate.

"Even without getting as physical as we wanted to, you've spoiled me. I can't do this anymore. This is the last narrative bridge I'm going to cross. It doesn't matter whether *la química* can pull together an encore that could live up to you. Going through this over and over—feeling this way just to lose whoever I find—it would tear me apart. And it's hard to have faith I'll find anyone nearly as good as you I'll be able to keep. So, I'm just..." She could feel her throat tightening and her eyes tearing up again. "So I'm just a mess and I'm really, really scared and I'm sorry."

Lenore took a good ten seconds of silence just trying to get a grip on herself. "Anyway, yeah. That's all a thing. I'm going to go curl up in that hammock where we spent the other night and I'm just going to stare up at the stars. I'd like it a lot if you came to find me, and if for just a few hours everything would be good. But you could send someone to wake me when everyone gets here instead. That's okay too. Whatever you need."

By the time she reached the hammock, Orthos was already there, leaning against a nearby tree. "You know Chlodina heard all that," he said. "And I assume Denise did too."

"Yeah. That was sort of the point." Lenore offered him what smile she could muster. "Way harder to play mind-games with myself now."

"I don't want you to give up world hopping for me," he said.

"I'm not." She shrugged. "I'm giving it up for me. I've had my taste of it, and I'm done. I can't live like this."

"Will you still come back here sometime?" Orthos asked. "If you get the chance?"

"I...wouldn't hold my breath. There can't be a lot of reasons the bridge hasn't re-opened by now—and one of the *better* ones is the coven's decided your universe is too dangerous. If Diana and Felicity dig in their heels about that, they'll declare this place a no-visit zone and I won't be able to budge them. But yes, *if* I get the chance," she said. "And if—when the time comes, I know you'll be right there waiting to meet me as I step through. I'm not going to risk *la química* playing matchmaker for me again."

"Just be sure you know where to get a message to me, then."

"The Alfieri-214 Mining Complex," she said, tapping her ear. "I can still hear the name, and I won't risk the sound of it fading. I'll write it down at home—on something that won't crumble there."

"Okay," he said, stepping up to look into her eyes and lay a hand on her cheek. "Sorry about your door."

Lenore shrugged helplessly. "I'd have ripped out more than one door this week if I had the strength to do it. Besides," she said, finding it in herself to smile a bit, "it was kind of a turn-on. I like bad boys—up to a point."

"Which point is that?" he asked, leaning further in.

She kissed him tenderly. "Let's just say the best part of knowing you have a monster inside is knowing you have the strength to keep it there."

"Can I show you something?" he asked.

"Really hoping you will," she murmured.

"How about I show you something *else* first? I'll let you fly the *Nevermore* again."

CHAPTER TWENTY-TWO
GRAVEYARD

Of course, Lenore had her own ship to fly now, but even if she'd had the crew on hand for it, there was something deeply impersonal about commanding the *Dark Legacy* versus taking the helm of the *Nevermore*. It felt, she imagined, rather like the difference between hitting the open road on a motorcycle versus doing it in an R.V. Both generally got you where you were going, but the two vehicles could never be mistaken for providing the same experience.

Lenore remained giddy from the rush of guiding the Nevermore back through the asteroid belt as she relinquished the controls, and Orthos set his ship down lightly on the asteroid that housed the Alfieri-214 Mining Complex, well beyond the horizon from where Lenore had first set foot on it.

Pulling on her tricorn and slinging a decorative holster onto her hip at a jaunty angle—where else was she going to get to play pirate with an outfit destined to crumble to dust if she ever got it home?—she followed him out onto the surface and over the lip of a crater perhaps a quarter of a mile across. At some point in the past, a staircase had been carved into the side of the crater, and it allowed them to descend fairly safely but fairly rapidly until they reached the floor of the crater, far below where they'd started.

"What is this place?" Lenore asked, spinning slowly about to take in the bizarre spaces carved back into the crater walls. Taken as a whole, the place appeared as some cross between abandoned desert cliff dwellings, a once-thriving university campus haunted by the ghosts of students past, and a non-Euclidean nightmare city that might once have been roamed by creatures impossibly old and impossibly alien.

"The real reason I live here," Orthos said. "It's sort of my inheritance. How much do you know about the Electra system?"

"It's the neutral, diplomatic star system where more than a few different interstellar empires meet," she said. "Hub of commerce. Hub of galactic society." She shrugged. "That's about it."

"Long story short," Orthos said, "that's all because of electrite. Electrite powers the galaxy, and this asteroid belt is the only place it's ever been found. Every royal house of any significance holds a mining claim here somewhere. I wouldn't advise entering the belt with an unauthorized ship, or setting down anywhere you don't have clearance. The response to either one tends to be swift and messy.

"This asteroid was mined out years ago. What little digging still goes on is for mundane ores. The rock's only real value now is as an archaeological site—and a minor one at that. I cashed in a favor to get named its caretaker. That's my official job. There are much more exciting finds in the belt, and this one's pretty well picked over, so I've got permission from the family to do some restorations and turn it into a sort of museum. No one with real money and power much cares about all that, so I mostly get left alone and just enough of a budget to invite in a few experts who're enthusiastic about the project.

"I could go on and on about how we think these sites came to be here, the history of the asteroid belt, and how it's all connected to electrite. Not important right now. What I thought you'd appreciate—especially if this turns out to be your last time world-hopping—is seeing a ghost town that's roughly a million years old."

"A million?" Lenore gaped, turning another complete circle to take it all in with new appreciation. "On Earth, anything more than a couple thousand years old is ancient. This is really a *minor* site?"

"Yeah. In most places, physics never would have allowed it to survive so long, but the whole asteroid belt is littered with ruins like this. Artifacts are hard to find. The architecture is everywhere, though. A lot of it's tiny single-room buildings, but there's two or three big asteroids that are actually a single huge metropolis even though they're light-minutes apart. The geometry is so warped you can be walking down an ancient corridor on one and step out on a balcony on another without even knowing it.

"Weirder, it's like quantum maze in there. Everything keeps changing when no one's looking. Whole archaeological teams disappeared without a trace on those asteroids before someone wised up and started employing watchers just to pin the architecture into place. No one's sure how or why it happens, but the leading school of thought is—that I'm getting off topic."

"Hey, no," Lenore said. "This sounds like cool stuff."

"Yeah, but we can talk about it later if there's time, right?"

"We can," she agreed.

"Come on." Orthos took her hand and pulled her along toward the buildings on one side of the crater. "Like most of the ruins in the belt, these are 'dead'—meaning they never shift and change, no matter how long you look away—but their geometry can still do some bizarre corkscrews. I want to show you my favorite."

She followed him through an arched opening and into a series of empty rooms and passages, all dimly lit by no light source she could make out. At one point, they passed a balcony on their right that looked out on the crater from halfway up its side, even though they'd never noticeably climbed an inch from the floor of the crater. When at last they emerged back out under the familiar night-black, star-filled sky, it was in a sunken pit fifteen feet deep with a steep, narrow stairway up to ground level.

At the top they didn't emerge back into the crater or even back onto the ground level of the asteroid. At first Lenore thought they'd arrived at some sort of mountainous pinnacle, but as she turned about, taking it in, all she could see besides the black sky and the other asteroids tumbling past was this single, stone plateau—nearly flat but irregularly shaped and no larger than a basketball court.

"Go look if you like," Orthos said, gesturing to the edge of the plateau, "but not if you're prone to vertigo. There's nothing there. We've stepped out on another asteroid—a very small one. You *could* walk right over the edge and around the underside. I've done it. At this scale it's very disorienting, though."

Lenore barely heard him. She was too busy staring out at infinity. "This asteroid belt," she breathed reverently, "is the graveyard for an entire civilization?" She doffed the tricorn, feeling suddenly disrespectful in it.

"It seems to be," Orthos agreed. "Maybe it's just too old for traces of it to survive anywhere else, but so far—this is all anyone's ever found. It's pretty obvious they were a highly advanced, space-faring civilization, but it doesn't seem they ever became an interstellar one. Yet somehow there are no planets in the Electra system large enough for the civilization to have developed on. We think the asteroid belt *was* their homeworld. Whatever event shattered it, survivors hung on out in space. They recolonized what was left and spent countless generations clinging to the debris."

"That is so space opera," Lenore murmured, "but so sad and so beautiful." She wrapped her arms across her chest and shivered, contemplating it all.

"I've got a permanent campsite set up here," he said, folding his arms around her from behind. In the process, he accidentally knocked the tricorn out of her grip, but she just let it fall. No wind stirred here to carry it away.

"Just looks like a bedroll to me." Lenore smirked, finally tearing her eyes away from the sky long enough to take note of the nearby pallet.

"There's a chamber right downstairs I've turned into a storeroom. We could stay here comfortably for weeks—if we had weeks. I've done it myself when my mood was so black I couldn't bear the thought of being around people. I can't guess how many hours I've spent just lying right here, trying to get my head around how incomprehensibly small and fragile and isolated and fleeting civilization is."

Words came bubbling up into Lenore's mind unbidden, carried on the distant memory of her father's voice as she sat curled up in the warmth of his lap. She let the recitation fall quietly from her lips.

Deep into that darkness peering, long I stood there wondering, fearing,
Doubting, dreaming dreams no mortal ever dared to dream before;
But the silence was unbroken, and the stillness gave no token,
And the only word there spoken was the whispered word, "Lenore?"
This I whispered, and an echo murmured back the word, "Lenore!"—
Merely this and nothing more.

"What was that?" Orthos asked.

"'The Raven'—or one verse from it. It's a poem by Edgar Allan Poe, my dad's favorite author."

"Are you crying?" he asked gently.

"Maybe."

"Can you recite the whole thing for me?"

She did, starting at the beginning, and the words flowed effortlessly off her tongue. They'd been a part of her for as long as she could remember, always swimming through her head in that same soothing voice. She rarely thought about the meaning of the words, honestly. Abstractly she knew it to be a story of grief, but this was simply *her* poem, its sounds an uncontemplated part of her identity that had always been there— a gift bestowed by the father who had named her from it.

When Lenore finished, she found she'd stretched out on the small bedroll with Orthos, nestled into the crook of his arm without even realizing she'd done it. She looked up and found him looking back, their noses all but touching. "Haunting," he said. "Does he write only poetry."

Lenore gave her head a tiny, almost imperceptible shake. "He wrote stories too. He's long dead. Mary Shelley's about the only author older than him I really like. 'Haunting' is the best single word to sum up all his work, though. So many authors seem to me to become...irrelevant over time. They're so bound to the attitudes of their day I find it hard to relate, but Poe's sorrows and horrors still echo."

"Thank you for sharing it with me." His warm breath caressed her as he spoke.

"Same," she said of their surroundings.

She could feel herself falling into his eyes as if she'd stepped off into the endless void. "Orthos? If we...if we fail—if I can't get back to where I started—can I stay right here? Go mad right here? Die...right here on this spot...staring at out this graveyard? Will you make me a part of it? Please?"

His eyes closed. He drew in a deep breath, tried to say something, then tried again. "We're not going to fail," he said at last.

"But if we do?" she pressed.

"Sure," he said, still not opening his eyes. "If we do. But we won't."

"Everyone fails eventually."

"True enough," he admitted. "But this isn't your time. Not yet."

"Flimsy."

"Just shut up and let me comfort you." He sighed. "I'm really trying here."

"Okay." She couldn't look away from his gaze, couldn't close her eyes, couldn't stop falling. "I'm not good with disappointment."

"I'd noticed."

Lenore had no idea which of them started the kiss. It just happened—soft and sweet and languid, leaving behind a ghost of a memory as haunting as anything Poe had ever written. She kissed him again—feeling the electrical hum of urgency begin to build in her stomach—and finished with a gentle nip at his lower lip. "I guess I never told you why my hair's not pink yet," she murmured.

"You have not," Orthos agreed.

She rolled away onto her knees and opened the holster on her hip, fishing out the Trestintinator wand he'd used to color her hair before. "Because I wanted you to do it," she said, flushing a little as she held it out to him.

"Oh." He sat up too. "That, uh...doesn't *just* color hair, does it?"

"No, but...I did already set it the shade I wanted." She grinned sheepishly, waggling the wand to draw attention to it like a lure on a hook.

"I do love a woman with foresight." He returned her grin, accepting the wand and offering his other hand to her as he stood up. She took it and followed, shivering slightly with anticipation as he combed his fingers through her hair. "It's eerie, you know: how you're her, but not," he said softly.

"You give me a bit of déjà vu too," Lenore said. "Especially when you lost your temper. I've only ever seen one other Ivurnian, but..." She let out her best flirtatiously, guttural growl. With all the monstrous sound-effects she'd practiced over the years, her best growl was not bad at all.

He hooked the wand into his belt. "I do seem to have a thing for Xayarian Goth girls, if it comes to that." He reached up to gently caress her throat, and she lolled her head to the side, exposing it for him. When she felt him plucking at the buckles down the front of her corset, her breath caught, but she offered no resistance.

"You *are* going to do the hair, right?" she prodded.

"Soon enough," he murmured. His breath on her throat buzzed against nerves clustered under her jaw already primed by anticipation. His finger kept tugging at the buckles of her corset, freeing them one by one as he worked his way downward.

"'I do not want you to leave,'" Lenore breathed. The rehearsed words of the Ice Princess had spilled unbidden from her mouth, but nothing could force her to utter the next line. Too much of her life, Lenore *had* felt it was not her place to want anything at all, but right here, right now, today, she would want—she did want—and she refused to apologize.

"I'm not going anywhere," he assured her. She hadn't really been concerned he might. It still offered her a small thrill to hear it.

The last buckle came free, and the corset peeled away from her torso. Falling forgotten to land beside the tricorn on the rocky ground, it left her chest and stomach exposed to the cool, still air—but when she trembled, it wasn't from the cold. She twined her fingers in his shaggy mane, pulling him insistently to her while his lips and tongue probed her throat, questing for every nerve they could trigger.

A song had begun playing in the background. Was she imagining that again, or had Orthos wired up a sound system in his hideaway? No showtune this time—an instrumental she didn't recognize, but one fit to score some movie scene involving a remote mountain chalet, a crackling fire, and desperate longing finally fulfilled. Behind it came the ambient patter of a steady rain, the occasional rumble of distant thunder, and the aromas of hot cocoa and wood smoke. Surely the whole thing would be a delusion, but if so, it was a delusion with style—and she didn't want to break the spell. She'd have to remember to commend her subconscious for unraveling with such timing, taste, and dignity.

The sound of the zipper on her skirt whispering open snapped Lenore's awareness back into sharp focus, only for it to experience a moment of whiplash as Orthos's hungering mouth found her chest and the most sensitive nerve-cluster yet. Coupled with the careless bite of his sharp nails at the small of her back, the intense sensations so overwhelmed reason the feel of the skirt sliding down her legs barely registered as a detail of idle interest, even though she'd dressed for easy access today and worn nothing under it. An iron grip she could never have fought if she'd wanted to kept her pinned where she was—at the mercy of a merciless tongue—until her body shuddered, cresting a wave of pleasure and riding it down into the meager shelter of a momentary relief from her cravings. The song trailed off into silence even as the tremors in her body subsided. The aromas and the ambient sounds disappeared with it. Orthos finally freed his grip on her and stepped back, drinking in her exposed body as he stripped off his shirt.

Eager to feel connected to the ground beneath her feet, Lenore dropped back onto the pallet long enough to work off her own boots while she watched Orthos finish undressing. Then she was back up, whirling like a giddy child, naked under the stars with the cold stone beneath her toes. She found herself laughing with uncontrollable delight, all of life's burdens lifted and forgotten. If she'd ever felt more free or alive or real or...happy...she simply couldn't remember it. Nothing mattered but here and now, this one moment, as the endless universe welcomed her with open arms.

When she stopped spinning, there was Orthos, watching her with patient approval, unwilling to disturb the spell she'd been under. Seeing him there—no less naked, and with his body's interest in what *it* was seeing on full display—overwhelmed what respite Lenore had felt from her hunger. Anticipation careened once again around her stomach, but even that couldn't chip away at this remarkable new feeling that permeated her body.

She stared at Orthos, fully aware of the slack-jawed smile spreading across her face. Words formed in her mind that should have triggered lifelong self-defense mechanisms as they crept toward her mouth. Worse, she knew exactly how tragic they'd be to say, but her special talent for anxiety had utterly fled. *Everything ends badly*, a chorus of impossibly ancient ghosts whispered in her head. *Absolutely everything. Either it ends while you still want more or it ends after it's overstayed its welcome, so you can't win. Not really. Don't pretend you can. If you're going to play the game, just...play.*

Nothing matters. The thought should have terrified her, but felt liberating instead. No matter what she did, the ultimate destination would be the same, so the worst possible thing she could do was waste her "now" cowering in terror of the future—and she couldn't imagine a worse now to waste than this one.

Coming out of that reverie, she caught Orthos's eye. "Are you okay in there?" he asked, though he didn't seem terribly concerned. His carefree smile mirrored her own.

Lenore just cocked her head and regarded him for a moment before the queued-up words came spilling out. "I'm home."

Then sex happened—hours and hours of mind-blowing, desperately intimate, rock-your-world sex. And in the spare minutes, there really was cocoa too.

CHAPTER TWENTY-THREE
THE PRINCESS PARADOX

"You're *sure* you're not Diva?" the prospective romance-cover model Lenore had met just before insanity broke loose on the *Queen Ilo* asked her. His name had turned out to be Xarn, and he'd been easy enough to pick out from among A.I.M.'s prisoners. She'd settled on inviting him to round out her impromptu coven as the most likely person she'd find motivated to set things right.

"Absolutely," Lenore assured him, ushering him into the suite she'd set up for the occasion on the *Dark Legacy* where the others already waited. She carefully steered him past Denise's seat near the door—which would surely appear empty to him—and pointed him at the truly empty one between Tsuzi and Jalissa. "Like I said, this is all about getting her back here and me home."

Jalissa had been mortified to report the pink uniform Lenore had been wearing on her arrival in the *SJZ* universe had mysteriously vanished from storage along with all her other personal effects. Lenore rushed to reassure Jalissa that was to be expected, and no one's fault at all. By now, everything she'd brought with her would have crumbled away and left no trace.

Lenore did, however, impose on Jalissa to track down and bring her a reasonable facsimile, which she'd slipped into as soon as it had arrived. The space-pirate costume had been a fun, flirtatious lark, but she'd found herself already over it.

"Please tell me you all did your homework," Lenore prompted as she edged through the cramped space around the pentagram-inscribed table, with its five strategically placed candles and the nearby incense already burning. "This is probably our only shot at getting your Goth Princess back and me to where I started."

"This still feels like a prank," Xarn complained.

"Did you study?" Lenore snapped.

"Yeah. Sure," Xarn muttered, looking down. "But it's just more of that ritualistic nonsense you've always hated."

"This nonsense is *not* nonsense." She glowered at him. "It is all carefully calibrated patterns and harmonics and metaphorical embodiments. You don't have to get far off with any element to throw your results off-kilter, so please please *please* don't worry about looking silly. Act like lives depend on getting this right— mine *and* Diva's."

"Okay!" Xarn put his hands up defensively. "I'm just saying how it feels."

"I don't expect anyone to have memorized their part," Lenore said. "You've each got your own holoprompter to feed you the phonetics as they need to be recited. Focus on that. Don't worry about anything else." Murmurs of acceptance followed.

This ritual usually allowed more room for error than Lenore was ready to admit to anyone present. Under normal circumstances, first-timers who approached it seriously and with all the right components had little trouble creating a perfectly serviceable narrative bridge—but these weren't normal circumstances, and she didn't need perfectly serviceable: she needed perfect.

Lenore had no guarantee the spell would work at all from this side, and she doubted finding a world that simply looked like home would be good enough to keep her alive. If they couldn't reach the one exact world she needed out of the infinite possible variations, she could expect to find her future reduced to a few weeks or months of quiet hedonism while she slowly slid into insanity.

She hadn't brought a spellbook with her. Even if she had, it would have disintegrated by now with all her other possessions. No one else in the coven—perhaps no other witch ever—would have had a prayer of pulling this off without a spellbook. But she wasn't any other witch. She was Lenore, daughter of Amelina, the true Goth Princess. Every syllable of every chant she'd ever uttered still hung in her mind, clear as the day she'd uttered it. Phonetically transcribing all five parts to the narrative-bridge ritual had been a bit time consuming, but she'd found no real challenge in it.

Coming up with the right song to accompany the ritual had been more of a challenge. She could hear it plainly enough, but that didn't mean she could reproduce it note for note. It probably didn't matter. Probably. The ritual didn't follow one specifically proscribed song, but changing the song meant changing a variable, which could always change the outcome. She'd done her best, working with the ship's A.I. to reproduce the song they'd used to get here, but she could hear the original clearly enough in her mind to know she'd only gotten close, not perfect. She called on *Legacy* to pipe the result into the cabin with them now.

"Orthos?" she prompted.

He pulled out a featureless, palm-sized disk and slid it into the middle of the table. "It's all on there," he said. "Logs of the *Freyjur* campaign from the first character-creation session until the gang broke up."

"Perfect." She flashed him a heartfelt smile. "Thank you." She started passing out the vials she'd prepared for the ritual. "Is everyone ready?"

When the chant had concluded, Lenore found herself holding her breath and unable to release it all through the whirling rainbow of the candles, the swirling chromatic smoke, and the cyclonic winds. Despite a growing ache in her lungs, she only managed to finally gasp for breath when she got up to open the cabin's closet door. Then when she did open it and her eyes closed against the brilliant flash of light, they refused to open again when it subsided.

"Okay. Maybe you're on the level," she heard Xarn say.

"Well?" Orthos asked. "Is it right?"

Finally, hesitantly, Lenore managed to force her eyes back open. As she did, her heart fell. "I...really don't think so."

The room beyond the bridge lay mostly in shadow, but what shapes and silhouettes she could make out didn't look promising.

"Is that...a ghost ship?" Jalissa asked.

While Lenore hesitated in the doorway, Denise breezed insubstantially past her, stepping through the opening and looking around. "Oh!" Denise exclaimed. "I think we're all right. This is a sound stage."

Heartened enough to follow Denise, Lenore took in the dark space as best she could. "A sci-fi set?"

"A what?" Tsuzi asked.

"I don't recognize this place," Lenore said, "but it may be right. I need to see if I can get my bearings. Everyone sit tight, okay?"

"I'll give you fifteen minutes," Orthos said. "No promises I won't come in after."

"I can work with that," Lenore said. "I don't plan to be long."

"I'll look ahead," Denise volunteered. Without waiting for approval, she was gone.

Trusting she'd hear back from Denise soon enough if anything went amiss, Lenore stepped on in and unhurriedly toured the sound stage, taking in the props. In the gloom it took a while for her to realize what she was seeing, but when she looked up, there hung the distinctive sign of *The Relaunch*. She was standing on the empty set of the *Promenade Èlectrique*.

Even if the lights had been on, this wouldn't have been the promenade as she'd so recently seen it—fully, vibrantly alive, but also more lived-in. This was the promenade as it had appeared when they'd *meant* to visit it. Had the set really remained in use all these years? Or had the coven maybe reconstructed the set for some reason while she'd been away?

Denise reappeared at her side. "Not our lot," she confirmed, eliminating the possibility of that last scenario. "Do you know a 'Mystic Poodle' studios? I saw a tour tram outside with their name on it."

"That would be right for filming *SJZ*," Lenore said. That had to be a good sign, though she still hardly dared to breathe in case relaxing jinxed the whole project. A million things could still go wrong. She started to say she needed a phone, but for all her phenomenal memory, she didn't have a single phone number memorized other than her own. People just didn't go around saying phone numbers for her to play back the audio of them in her head. What she needed was internet access.

"Uh, Denise?" she asked. "Do you know *anything* about computers or mobile phones?"

"Practically nothing," Denise said. "I don't think they could even hear me if I tried talking to them."

"Right." And since Denise's brain had gone there first— straight to the voice-controlled systems she'd known in *SJZ*— asking her to look around for usable internet would likely take more effort than it was worth. "I may need a library then," Lenore said. "Would you check back with Tsuzi and tell her I'm fine? I'm going to try to find someone who can help me out. Shouldn't take long, but might be more than fifteen minutes."

Stepping out from the dark sound stage into the bright afternoon sun, Lenore found herself in an alley between the building and a row of trailers, watching a loaded tour tram roll past the corner—probably the same tram Denise had spotted. Otherwise, Lenore thought she was alone in the alley until a soft, whimpering sound drew her attention to a young, dark-haired woman curled up on the steps of one of the trailers with her forehead resting on her knees.

After a brief internal war over whether it would be better to just quietly withdraw, Lenore found herself stepping closer instead. "Are you all right?"

"Oh! Sorry. Yeah," the woman said, brusquely drying her eyes. "It's just—it's nothing."

Even before the woman actually looked up, her voice had thrown Lenore for a mental loop. "Mom?!" she gasped.

"What?" The puzzled face of Amelina Mallory blinked up at Lenore—only it *wasn't* the face of her mother. It was the face of the fresh, twenty-something actress who'd stared out at Lenore from countless autographed publicity photos over the years before they'd disappeared into the hands of Amelina's adoring fans.

"I'm sorry," Lenore stammered, both embarrassed and distraught. Whatever this was, it was *wrong*. "Nervous tick. You're Amelina Mallory, aren't you?"

"Guilty," the woman admitted, the corners of her mouth starting to turn up—then she seemed to do a double-take, and the incipient smile vanished. "Well, that was quick."

"What was quick?"

Amelina fished in her low-cut collar and produced a key, holding it out to Lenore. "Here you go. Might as well cut out the middleman."

"I really don't understand," Lenore replied, staring blankly at the key in her hand.

"It's all yours." Amelina hooked a thumb at the trailer behind her. "Break a leg."

"I still don't..."

"It's okay. Really." A half-hearted attempt at a smile returned to Amelina's face. "I just thought maybe...I'd be a little harder to replace." She barely got the words out before her face fell again, very nearly breaking into tears. "Sorry. I just...I can't..." She stood abruptly and pushed her way past Lenore.

"Wait!" Lenore called hurriedly. "I'm just an extra! You're not really being replaced, are you? I mean...you're *the* Goth Princess." This was quickly going from bad to worse. In Lenore's world, there'd never been another actress in the role. The part had been her mother's, and her mother had been the part.

"I *was* the Goth Princess." Amelina's voice came out dispirited, but at least she'd stopped, and even turned back around. "God, I didn't think it would be this hard to walk away. Thank you, though. I hope they offer you the part. You do look a lot like me."

"Why are you walking away?"

"It's...it's just time," Amelina said, but Lenore had already followed the quick downward flicker of Amelina's eyes to the slight bulge in her stomach. When Lenore looked back up, Amelina was staring at her, clearly aware Lenore had made the connection. Amelina gave a pleading, silent shake of her head. "Please don't turn this into a story. I don't want my kid reading someday I gave this up for them, you know? No one needs that sort of guilt."

"Can't you just...take a hiatus?" Alarm bells went off in Lenore's head even as the words fell out of her mouth. If the woman in front of her *didn't* give up her acting career, this wasn't her mother. If this wasn't her mother, this wasn't her world. And if this wasn't her world, she was probably dead.

"Sure." Amelina shrugged. "If certain people weren't looking for any excuse to get rid of me. No one's going to hold the role. No one's going to offer me another. I burned the wrong bridges, so it's the kid or the career—and, honestly, the career's probably shot anyway. I'm just going to take the win and be happy for it, you know? Always watch your back in this town," she admonished Lenore. "Always."

"I'll remember," Lenore promised. "So...I guess this is my last chance to get your autograph?"

"Seems like."

"Would you mind waiting for me to go get my autograph book?"

Lenore managed to hold it together long enough to get out of sight, but found herself hyperventilating before she could make it back to the bridge. Denise discovered her curled up on the floor in the sound stage, still fighting to get herself back under control.

"What happened?" Denise pressed.

"I'm in the wrong place," Lenore stammered with difficulty. "Or the wrong time. Same thing. I...I can't face everybody like this. If I try, I'll just break into a million pieces."

"What can I do?" Denise asked gently.

"Try to get Orthos in here with us? *Just* Orthos." Denise did.

"I just want to lie down and quit," Lenore admitted to him a quick cry on his shoulder and a summary later, "but those voices in my head have never steered me right. You're a gamer. Is there a problem here we can work?"

"Can we just try again?" he asked. "I know where to find all the things you'll need now. It won't take as long, and I've already got ideas on how to get a lot of financing."

"But we're not even close," Lenore said miserably, "and I wouldn't know what variables to change. If this *is* my world, we're like twenty years too early. More. And if I do anything that changes the future, this won't *be* my world anymore. The bridge doesn't do predestination. Maybe I'm already erased just because I talked with my mom."

"First, you're not erased," he said rocking her in his arms. "You're right here. Second, we're so deep into meta now there's no way to know the rules, right? Which even came first: your world or my world? Paradox could be completely on the table."

"Maybe," Lenore allowed.

"Is anything about this place feeling straight-up wrong, or is it just out-of-sync?" Orthos asked. "Is it reasonable to believe you've *only* time-traveled?"

Lenore closed her eyes, leaned into him, and began rummaging through the attic of her dusty memories in search of any clues one way or another. "It could be just wishful thinking, but I want to say this *is* home. I mean, it would explain a few things if Mom's been pregnant for a bit already."

"Like what."

"Like the link between me and Diva. I mean up to now, my coven's only ever found doppelgangers for the actors who'd played a character in a world we went to. I'm not a screen actress. I've never played Diva in a game or anything. I'd never even dreamed she existed. So...how? Why?"

"Because...you *were* there on screen with your mother when she was playing Diva's mother?" Orthos ventured.

"It's the only guess I've got," Lenore said. "It might also explain Mom's favorite episode."

"What do you mean?"

"*Interstellar Goth Princess Blues*. Of all the *SJZ* episodes she was in, Mom's fixated on that one and I never understood why. I mean *I* love it. The chemistry between the Ice Princess and Ambassador L'Roux gives me the shivers." She gave a weak grin. "But Mom's work trying to keep them apart isn't any more memorable than her other episodes."

"Wait. What?" Orthos asked.

"She was in quite a few," Lenore said. "It wasn't a small role."

"No. I mean...that's not how it happened."

"How what...?"

"Look," Orthos said, "Diva's mother didn't keep my parents apart. She threw them together. It ruined my mother's reputation forever and cemented her own. 'Melting the Ice Princess' may be her most famous scheme. I never blamed Diva for what her mother did, but it's *why* I don't belong."

"You mean I've been lusting after...your dad?" Lenore asked, aghast. "I mean...that's a little bit..."

"Uh...yeah, I guess. Please don't let that make this weird. I mean—it was my dad twenty-plus years ago, right? When he was young and hot...like me."

"Fair. He *was* young and hot like you. I'm sure I just liked him because he was going to remind me of you. Weirdness rejected."

"Thank you," Orthos said, kissing her.

"Anyway, the episode was late in her career," Lenore said after indulgently prolonging the kiss. "Maybe she always liked to watch it with me because that's when she first knew I existed? It's sort of my first baby pictures?"

"I can't second-guess you there," he said. "So let's pretend this is your past. And let's pretend paradox is possible—but let's assume it's not desirable. If we start from there, maybe this place *can* save you. Maybe you can...you know...survive and heal here in the right place even if you're not in the right time?"

"Better than no plan," Lenore agreed, feeling her spirits lift a little. "I should at least try to stay here and see if it helps while you run to get more supplies."

"*Now* you're thinking like a gamer," he said approvingly. "We keep working this as long as it takes. As long as we can."

"Okay."

"And *if* your present is out there waiting somewhere in this future," he added, "and your life *does* depend on getting back to it...what do we do?"

"Oh, good! You're still here!" Lenore exclaimed, running up breathlessly to where Amelina sat in front of the trailer.

"Anything for my final fan." Amelina gave a wan but sincere smile.

"I am *not* your final fan," Lenore protested. "A lot of people out there love you. Maybe you won't have a future here, but you won't be forgotten." She thrust the autograph book she'd been clutching to her chest out at Amelina, along with a pen. Tsuzi had insisted on rounding up the necessary supplies for this after having the studio gift shop pointed out to her. Lenore hadn't asked how she'd done it without any local currency, but it had taken the Pudding Princess less than five minutes, in and out. Maybe Lenore would ask her later.

"The woman says with unfounded optimism," Amelina said. "But thank you. Who am I making this out to?" She flipped to the first blank page—which to her evident surprise, turned out to be the actual first page.

"I just got a new book for you to start," Lenore said. "It's 'Diva.' D-I-V-A. And my optimism's not unfounded. I know for a fact you'll still have adoring fans twenty years from now."

"And how would you know that?" Amelina chuckled as she began her scrawl in the book.

"I'm psychic. Want me to prove it?" Lenore asked brightly.

"I would *love* for you to prove it." Amelina dotted the "i" in her name with her trademark cute, little skull and passed the book back to Lenore, who handed her a manila envelope in exchange.

"Only open that *after* your daughter is born and named," Lenore said.

"My daughter?" Amelina raised an eyebrow.

"The proof's in there," Lenore said confidently. "Along with a promise if you'll just deliver the second sealed envelope inside, unopened and exactly as it says."

"What promise is that?" Amelina asked, clearly curious despite herself.

"You believe in ghosts, right?"

CHAPTER TWENTY-FOUR
OUT OF TIME

"Are you going to be all right?" Tsuzi asked, taking Lenore's hands as the makeshift coven dispersed at the main airlock.

"I do not know," Lenore said honestly. "But you've got worlds to save."

"I'll buy you another twelve hours before Chlodina wakes back up," Jalissa promised. "Do whatever it takes to get this ship out of here and make it disappear before then. Don't tell me where it's gone, but do send Orthos if you need anything."

"Thank you."

"Anything I can do to help get Diva back, I'm there," Xarn said.

"Heck, if you just want to teach me some of that magic, I'll fight to make room in my schedule," Tsuzi said.

"Same," the others echoed.

"It's cool stuff," Xarn admitted.

"We'll see what happens," Lenore said. "So many unknowns."

She waved goodbye as the airlock door closed, leaving her alone with Orthos, and with the whole huge ship to themselves.

"Are you worried no one's popped right in to find you?" Orthos asked.

"A little," Lenore admitted. "This isn't like normal time-travel stories, though. Time moves at the same speed on each side of the bridge. Assuming my message got delivered, we might not know for twenty years—even if I can survive that long. Or we might find out tomorrow. There's no precedent, no manuals—just...magic."

"Okay. Working the problem: This bridge we just opened is going to last how long?"

"It's not reliable," Lenore said, "but we've never had one last less than ten days or more than fifteen. There have always been telltale signs for a day or two before it collapses, but since I've got zero margin for error, let's just assume eight days."

"We'd better make the most of them. *You* get back to that sound stage. You're going to spend the night there. Is Denise with us?"

Lenore shook her head. "She bowed out a bit ago—said she was feeling 'loopy.'"

"Well, whenever she shows up—"

"I get her to scout for me, yeah," Lenore said. "Find the best places to lurk and avoid attention so maybe my brain can do some healing."

"Right. I'll take care of everything I can on this side—get you set up to spend as much time as possible over there for a week—then I'll go secure our funding."

"Aren't you going to stay for the night?" The question came out more plaintively than Lenore had intended, so she forced a grin to make up for it. "We could make love right in the middle of the Promenade."

"*Really* want to," he said, a pained look flashing across his face. "Can't. I have to go convince Vanda her daughter's alive but in serious trouble."

"Diva's mother? But that will take—what? Two weeks?"

"Four days tops," he assured her. "The *Nevermore* can easily reach her in half the time the *Legacy* could, plus I'll pull all the strings I have to get a crew you can trust for this ship. They'll take you to the Xayarian home system. That's a *lot* closer than we are now, which means a lot less travel time for me to get back to you.

"We've got to get this sorted for Diva even more than for you. Vanda deserves to know the whole story, and as soon as she believes, she'll move stars and planets to help us bring her girl home. Knowing Vanda's secret—that she took the blame for my mother's affair—I think I can convince her of the truth. And once that's done, I'll turn around and meet you at Xaya, quick as I can."

"Okay then." She gave an accepting smile and kissed him tenderly. "Let's do this."

"Why did we *do* this?!" Lenore wailed to Denise on the first night out from eCity. "I want him! And this isn't working. I'm still hearing random music, and now I'm seeing weird, alien creatures walking the streets on *this* side of the bridge."

"Breathe," Denise prompted her. "We *are* on a studio lot where they're filming at least one space opera. I've been seeing them too."

Unthinkingly, Lenore had never returned the trailer key she'd been handed. Amelina hadn't asked for it, either, and—for the present—no one seemed to be using the trailer after hours, so that's where Lenore had decided to spend the night. She'd taken the trailer's one small bed at Denise's insistence. Denise had shown up in pajamas with a sleeping bag she spread out on the floor. In the dark trailer, Lenore could make out her silhouette there from light filtering in through the window.

"Does being back home fix the hallucinations right away?" Denise asked. "Or does it take time?"

"I don't know," Lenore admitted. "I guess it probably takes time."

"Then give it time. You're sick. You know why they call sick people 'patients?' Because they have to *be* patient."

"Really?" Lenore asked.

"It's what my doctor always said when I was a kid. Just...try to sleep, okay? Staying up all night never helped anyone's sanity."

Lenore tried. She tossed and turned for what felt like hours. Then she snapped suddenly awake at the sound of rapping at the trailer door.

"Lenore? Are you in there?" Sylvie's voice hissed.

In a rush, Lenore was out of bed, stepping carefully over where she'd last seen Denise, as if it would help anything even if the ghost—who she could no longer see—still happened to be there. "Sylvie!" Lenore stopped with the door half open, staring out at the empty alley. "Sylvie?"

Lenore finished opening the door and stepped down to street level, peering vainly around in the dim light. Sylvie *could* have found her there in the trailer. Lenore had left notes, and she'd left instructions with the crew.

"Sylvie? Hello?" Blinking back tears, Lenore went back inside and crawled into bed. Had she dreamed it? Had she hallucinated it? Was there a difference?

She felt herself drifting off again, only to be jolted out of it by another knock at the door. No voice this time.

Lenore didn't call out. She didn't wait. She didn't step carefully. She rushed to the door and threw it fully open. Again, nothing met her eyes but an empty alley.

Was this what Diana and Felicity had gone through the time they'd been trapped? Her hallucinations had officially pushed beyond the boundaries of harmless and amusing.

Again Lenore drifted off. Again the knocking woke her. This time she wrapped the pillow around her head and tried to ignore it. It came again, louder and more urgent.

"Hello? Are you in there?" This time the voice didn't belong to Sylvie, or to anyone else Lenore knew. It was a man's voice, deep and insistent, with a light Hispanic accent.

"Go away!" Lenore yelled. "I need to sleep!"

"Studio security, miss," the voice replied. "It's important."

Oh, blast. What persona would she need to conjure up to bluff her way out of this one? The *last* thing she needed was to get locked up for trespassing and banned from the lot. Well, she was too sleepy to think straight, so that would have to be her character: an exhausted, disoriented young actress who'd just been woken out of a sound sleep in the middle of the night. *Can't be timid*, she warned herself. *Have to go on offense.*

"What?!" she demanded, opening the door—ever so slightly relieved to find the alley wasn't empty this time, but not at all pleased to find a bright light shining in her eyes. She threw a shielding arm up across her face. "What?!" she repeated.

"Sorry," the big man apologized hastily. "Sorry, miss. Are you...supposed to be here?"

"No!" Lenore snapped. "I'm supposed to be in a really nice hotel right now. *Someone* needs to be fired over that. What's so important? I've got an early morning shoot."

"Lenore?" It was Sylvie's voice again, but this time Sylvie's eyes were actually staring back when Lenore looked up.

"I found these people in the sound stage there." The guard gestured at the building across the alley. "No identification. They say they're with—"

Lenore nearly trampled the man despite his size, throwing herself at Sylvie. Then the others crushed in around them—Manami, Diana, Kassia, and Felicity—'til Lenore could barely breathe amid the press of arms and the sea of tearful apologies.

Never once before in her life had she felt so happy to be crowded and smothered.

"I'm so sorry," Diva said, staring down at the table where Lenore had performed her emergency ritual. Diva fidgeted with the candle in front of her, peeling at the runnels of re-hardened wax. Staring into her face as she talked felt utterly surreal to Lenore. Even Diva's hair was pink, and she wore clothes right out of Lenore's own closet.

"I really didn't understand what was going on," Diva said. "One minute I was in the middle of a robot rampage with everyone screaming, the next your friends were dragging me off and out of it. We didn't even think there'd be a ship to come back to. Then suddenly I was free, and I was you in that fantasy world I knew so well, and I was playing with real magic...I didn't ever want to come back. Once I figured out when we were, pretending to be you was easy since...well, I *thought* I'd made you up."

"I just want to die," Sylvie said mournfully. "I knew something was off, but I just thought you were retreating into your shell after the close call with the robots. When your mom showed up with the letter for us...How did you even *do* that?"

"Magic," Lenore said simply, in no mood right now to speculate on how she'd wound up in their collective past talking to her own mother. All that mattered was Amelina had delivered the time-capsule cry for help Lenore had enclosed with her predictions, right on schedule and exactly as instructed. It had been a huge roll of the dice trying to set up a situation where Amelina would stay so interested in that message for over twenty years she'd follow through and deliver it, yet not be so consumed with curiosity she'd open it herself prematurely and change her future.

"I hold myself responsible," Felicity said. "You came along to help me out, and I just got so wrapped up in...myself. I know how awful it is to get trapped. I let you down."

"How *is* your sister?" Lenore asked.

"Slightly better," Felicity said. "We went back to trying fantasy worlds for a magical cure—took her to that healer in the *Raven's Rose* books. It...helped. Some. My doctor gives her a few more months she wouldn't have had before."

"Then we go back to trying here," Lenore said.

Felicity shook her head. "Absolutely not. This place is dangerous."

"No, it's not!" Lenore exclaimed in exasperation. "It's not any more dangerous than anywhere else."

"We can talk about that later," Diana said soothingly. "After you've had some time to recover."

"No!" Lenore snapped. "We talk about it right here, right now, or I am done. I'm out of the coven."

Sylvie blinked. "Lenore, I don't think—"

"*You all left me!* You want me to forgive that? You want to wipe the slate clean and call it an honest mistake? Fine! It was an honest mistake! But grown people clean up their mistakes! *Friends* clean up their mistakes. I love that you came back for me. I do. But if you're my friends, you can do better than that. You can hear me out and you can take me seriously. Give me that or we're quits. I'm going home to Vegas."

"Lenore?" Manami asked quietly into the ensuing silence. "What happened?"

Lenore met Manami's concerned stare for several seconds before her eyes danced briefly over the faces of the rest of the coven. Already she could feel guilt over the outburst burrowing its way into her stomach, sapping her anger and her resolve. "I fell in love," she blurted in a rush while she still could. "Not just with a guy—with this universe. I belong here. I'm not letting you take it from me.

"That whole stupid robot attack was a pantomime. No one got killed or hurt. And this place is a gold mine of potential! We can cure your sister here, Fel. I *know* we can. And we can help so many others.

"I've made all sorts of inroads already—so many connections. This is *my* starship, and our bridge leads right to it. We can wander around...see so much...do so much...all without ever leaving the studio behind. I know we can make the investment of coming here pay for itself even if we're opening a new bridge every month. We *should* open a new bridge every month! I just need you to trust me. Let me have my dream."

Emotionally spent, Lenore felt her jaw lock shut and her knees threatening to collapse. She had to bury her face in her hands just to keep from bolting from the room as the silence returned and drew out. In that silence, she could hear someone crossing the floor. Gentle fingers settled on her temples, followed by warm lips on her forehead.

"You're our sister," Diana said softly. "Of course we'll fight for your dream. Dreams are what we do."

CHAPTER TWENTY-FIVE
CLEANUP ON XAYA VI

It took two more days to reach the gloomy, gray, fog-shrouded Goth capital known as Xaya VI, but the *Nevermore* was already there waiting for them when they did—and with Vanda herself on board. Interstellar communications in the *SJZ* universe might not be instantaneous, but they could still outrun even the fastest ship. With Diva confirmed alive and safe—and still somewhat mentally stable—Lenore had alerted Orthos at once, and the mission had turned from convincing Vanda of the truth to convincing her to come help sort out the mess that remained. Even delivered through back channels, news that Diva remained alive expedited *everything*, and the retired Goth Princess had been there to board the *Nevermore* the moment it landed.

Another fast ship following the *Legacy* from eCity had arrived for the rendezvous, bearing Jalissa and Chlodina at about the same time. Hearing the whole point of the trip was to bring Diva to her mother for judgment had been enough to get Chlodina to settle down and participate peacefully.

Rather than figure out how to get the same back-from-the-dead woman through imperial security twice by going to meet

Vanda, Vanda came out to the *Dark Legacy*. In honor of her arrival, the lights had been dimmed to a comfortable state of twilight, and life support systems now pumped out a low-lying mist that swirled over every floor she might possibly find herself crossing. Throughout the ship, holographic decor had been repurposed to impart a festive Halloween vibe, accompanied by matching ambient noise from the sound system. With less than a day's warning, the crew had entirely transformed the atmosphere of the *Legacy* from a luxury cruise experience to a Gothic castle experience.

With that crew still fairly in the dark on the details of what was going on, though, they remained mostly out from underfoot after welcoming Vanda aboard with all appropriate fanfare and obeisance—so it was a small and somber-looking party that met on the shore of the dark lake at the heart of the *Legacy*. Only Lenore resolutely stood out from the Gothic crowd by wearing her signature pink. Dressing in black for Vanda would have been no different than dressing in black for her parents. This was no time to cave in her defiance, though she did join her three companions in a curtsying bow when Orthos arrived leading Vanda and her two bodyguards.

"So," Vanda said, standing in the shadow of a decorative mausoleum that had once looked like a cabana, "I am here, but I don't truly understand how I seem to have gone so quickly from having one daughter to having none, and then to having two. I know one of you is my Diva and the other calls herself Lenore, but staring at you I cannot honestly say I know my own child. Is that you in rebellious pink today, daughter, or are you the one in dutiful black?"

"This is me, Mother," Diva spoke up. "I figured I've caused you enough grief for a while. There's a lot to sort out, and I know this is no time to nettle you."

"Thank you for that, at least." Vanda bowed her head graciously. "I...I..." Her voice faltered, as did her solemn expression. She glanced self-consciously for a moment among the gathered faces, then just rushed the remaining distance to Diva and threw her arms about her daughter, burying her face in Diva's hair. "I thought I'd lost you."

Diva's nonplussed expression quickly gave way to happiness as she wrapped her arms around her mother. No one hurried to fill the silence that followed until Vanda finally stepped back and said, "I should be so angry with you, Diva. You've been very irresponsible. Not just over this, but for a long time now."

"I know," Diva replied quietly. "I've tried so hard to tell you I don't have any business following in your footsteps. You're amazing. You've always been amazing. I want so much for you to be proud of me, and a part of me will always want to be just like you. But...I'm not you. I'm miserable in this life. I didn't plan any of what just happened, but I've been tempted so many times to just fake my death and disappear. Now that it's happened...I want to stay dead. I want to put on a new look, start a new life, and figure out who I want to be instead of who I'm not happy being."

"That *would* solve a few problems, Your Highness," Chlodina spoke up. "Your niece, Asintha, hasn't wasted a moment settling into the job. Even before that, her assassination efforts were getting less and less clumsy. Her last attempt on your daughter's life could very nearly be called competent."

"Wait. What?" Diva demanded, her attention abruptly riveted to Chlodina.

Chlodina ignored her. "Asintha would not accept Diva's return from the dead with anything resembling quiet grace."

"No." Vanda sighed. "She wouldn't. But where would you even start on a new life, child?"

"I was thinking I'd try my hand at piracy: a sturdy ship, a letter of marque, and off to the border sectors where nobody knows me. I could still make myself useful to the empire that way. There's lots of wars out there that could use a rebellious young captain who knows how to be scary."

"There are," Vanda admitted. "But it would be a hard life—and a dangerous one."

"We talked this out on the way here, Your Highness," Chlodina said. "I'm willing to go with her—to still play her right hand and bodyguard. If Diva doesn't return from the dead, my reputation's still gone and my whole life is still off the rails. I need a fresh start too. And, honestly, I would have resigned years ago if I didn't really care about your daughter. She's too much of a pain to put up with otherwise."

"I am," Diva agreed proudly.

"Hi, Mom. Thanks for waiting."

Amelina Mallory looked up at her daughter in surprise, forgetting to even pause the horror flick she'd been watching on the television in Lenore's sitting room. "Honey," she gasped. "What happened to your...You're..."

"I'm wearing black." Lenore smiled as she took the remote from her mother's unresisting hand and turned off the television. She perched on the arm of the couch and kissed Amelina on the top of the head. "Hair too." She tugged demonstratively on a lock. "It's not my new look or anything. I still love pink. I just felt like doing it. For you. When a girl gets out on her own for a while, she starts to notice things she took for granted, right?"

Amelina returned the smile. "I know I did." She got up and gave her daughter a proper hug. "I've been waiting for days, though, and your friends just kept saying you'd have to tell me about all this yourself. Are you in movies now? What's going on?"

"What do you remember about the person who gave you that envelope?" Lenore asked.

"Not a lot." Amelina shrugged helplessly. "I just met her on the lot my last day at the studio. Could have been my stunt double from the look of her, and she had on a pink costume you would have loved. I tried to track her down again after you were born, but the studio said they'd never hired anyone like that, and wardrobe had never made a pink uniform. Like ever. Did you read all that stuff she wrote down?"

"Enough of it." Lenore nodded.

"It was all dead-on. Getting just your name right would have been eerie, but your birth date? The time *exactly?* Your exact size? I started to tell you about her so many times, but...I'm just glad I finally can."

"I'm glad too, Mom. And I absolutely *will* keep her promise to you."

"*You'll* keep her promise? How can you—?"

"I'm a witch, Mom. Not a Wiccan: a genuine, card-carrying, spellcasting witch. And my friends? They're my coven. We call ourselves the Freyjur. Just don't tell people, okay? We'll tell Dad, but I'd like to be there myself to show him too."

"*You*...are a witch?" The questioning sounded neither credulous nor skeptical—more hopeful. Amelina did believe in magic. Believing what her daughter was saying would come soon enough. "How long has this been going on?"

"A few months," Lenore said. "It's why I left Vegas when I did. We met at a fantasy con, of all places."

"So those actresses...?"

"Diana and Felicity really *are* witches, yes," Lenore assured her. "Not like in the movies, though. I'll explain it all later. Anyway, this isn't comic-book secret-identity stuff, but things are simpler if we keep it quiet, and the coven has deep pockets. They'll come down hard on anyone who goes around blabbing, and you'd just sound crazy if you tried telling people the truth anyway. So this is between us, okay?"

"Of course, honey."

"And...we talked it over. There's no way for you to be a full member of the coven without things getting extremely weird, but—"

"What do you mean, 'weird?'" Amelina asked.

"How much do you want to know about the sex lives of your daughter and her friends?" Lenore asked pointedly.

"Oh," Amelina breathed. "Oh! You mean it's *that* kind of coven?" Her eyes went wide from surprise, but no sign of judgment appeared on her face.

"Not exactly, but the way all this works makes it impossible to keep out of each other's business. Things would get very, *very* weird. But we've already got a sort of auxiliary-member thing going on, if maybe..." Lenore shrugged. "You'd want to learn a little magic yourself?"

"Honey, are you *serious*? Don't tease if you're not serious. If you think you've ever seen me angry before—"

"Oh, I've seen you angry before," Lenore laughed. "And I would never have you on about something like this. I'm dead serious, Mom. The other girls—you should have seen how excited they got about the idea of *the* Amelina Mallory being associated with the Freyjur. You'd never know Diana and Felicity were bigger stars than you, Mom. Fel already wants to know if you could be talked into coming back to Hollywood to give your career another start. She could totally make it happen."

"Say what now?"

"You should do it, Mom. You should. I'm so glad you wanted a family more than you wanted a career, but I'm a woman now. Don't hold yourself back for me anymore. Not for one moment. I'm chasing my dream. You chase yours."

"Honey, I..." Amelina's voice choked off before it could get anywhere.

"Too much. Too fast. I'm sorry," Lenore said, squeezing her mother's hand. "Just think about it, okay? First, there's that promise to keep. You've only been waiting my whole life for it. Everything else we'll deal with later. C'mon."

Lenore pulled her mother to the table in the bungalow's little kitchen, ushered her to a chair, and began rummaging in the refrigerator. She returned with a small jug of milk and a sandwich bag full of cookies. "Have you ever tried 'cowboy cookies,' Mom?"

"I, ummm...No," Amelina said, watching her daughter rummage through the cabinets for a plate and three glasses.

Lenore set them all on the table and then dumped the cookies out onto the plate. "Try one. I made them myself. They've got chocolate chips, pecans, coconut, oats..."

Amelina did nibble experimentally at a cookie while Lenore filled a glass with milk and passed it to her. "Not bad, Honey. You've been learning to cook on top of everything else?"

"Not that hard," Lenore said. "You should try it. It's just like mixing potions and stuff."

"So your father tells me," Amelina said after another bite. "What's with the third glass?"

"It's for the spell," Lenore said, sliding the now-full glass to one edge of the table, halfway between the two of them.

"The spell?"

"This is going to take forever if you repeat everything I say as a question." Lenore grinned. Amelina waved her apologetically onward.

"I'll be just a minute. Don't eat all the cookies," Lenore added as she stepped back into the living room. She used the television to search the internet for music until she found Lloyd Price's "Personality" and started it playing it loudly enough to be heard in the kitchen. She could see the curiosity in her mother's eyes when she returned, but to Amelina's credit, the woman held her tongue.

Lenore pulled down a candle from the top of the refrigerator, lit it with a kitchen lighter, and slid it across the table to Amelina.

Finally she produced a single, folded page from out of her pocket and handed it to her mother before dropping neatly into her own chair.

"Mom, you and I both know you've got issues, but you're so worth it. And now I'm grown up enough to see some of the issues I've got, too. I hope you still think I'm worth it."

"Always, Honey." Amelina unfolded the paper and stared at it. "What's this?"

"Your script," Lenore said. "And I want you to know, delivering that message from the psychic, here and now like she asked? It very literally saved my life. Thank you."

"How?"

"I was lost and trapped and...sick. My friends didn't even know it, and the letter told them where to find me. But you couldn't have come to me yourself. It took magic. Like this." Lenore tapped the page. "Your first spell. Read it out loud, like you mean it. Also, cross your fingers and hope for the best. These things...don't always work out quite like you'd expect."

"Should I worry?"

"No. Just read slowly and carefully. It's phonetic. You'll be fine."

Amelina dutifully began to chant a string of nonsense syllables that sounded vaguely Scandinavian. About thirty seconds in, Lenore noticed with satisfaction the cookies on the plate and the milk in the third glass had all begun to slowly grow translucent. "Keep going," she mouthed to Amelina as the things on the table continued to fade away toward nothingness. When the last syllable of the chant had faded, the glass sat empty, and nothing remained on the plate but crumbs.

"Did it work?" Denise asked. Amelina looked up to find the actress standing there regarding her while munching a cookie. "Yes! It did work!" Denise pumped a victorious fist. "Hi! I'm Denise Drake, and I'm soooo happy to meet you. I'm happy to meet anyone, honestly."

Amelina gaped. "You're *the* Denise Drake?"

"In the lack of flesh." She held out a hand, which Amelina tried to take. "See?" Denise said as their hands passed through each other.

"Promise kept." Lenore grinned. "A real ghost to hold a real conversation with."

"Don't hope for too much," Denise warned. "I don't know or don't remember most of the usual stuff people would want to talk about."

"Denise is my roommate, Mom. This used to be her bungalow."

"I, ummm...wow." Amelina stammered, any concerns this could still be some sort of elaborate prank swept away.

"The others don't know about Denise yet," Lenore said. "I'll tell them soon, but for now she's one more secret between us. Okay?"

"So...expectations contained, but I still have so many questions," Amelina said to Denise. "Where to even start?"

"How about we start," Denise suggested, "by going to the zoo?"

"I was starting to get worried," Orthos said as Lenore stepped out of the airlock and into the *Nevermore.* She'd arrived shrouded in a pink, hooded cloak over her pink *SJZ* uniform, having strolled through the corridors of the *Legacy* to get to the docking tube that brought her here. They hadn't talked through their next moves yet, so their original plan of keeping her face hidden from the current crew remained in force.

"Worried about what?" Lenore asked. "You know I was just back taking care of things with the coven."

"Yeah. That's what I was worried about," he said, wrapping her up in his arms. She felt herself falling into his eyes again, and shivered in the warmth of his gaze. "I was worried you'd get too grounded and start having second thoughts about all this. I was worried maybe you'd decide you were done crossing the bridge even to here."

"I guess that's fair," she said guiltily. "I've been known for that sort of nonsense. But, no. I'm not at all done with your galaxy—not as long as you're here to stop *la química* from trying to hook me up with someone else. Everything's on track to re-open the bridge every twenty-one days. I just have to spend about half my time back there with the coven. The rest I can spend here setting up investments, making contacts, researching technology—just basically giving us a permanent presence and making the bookkeepers happy."

She kissed him lazily, then took a step back and smiled up at him. "I'm safe now, and I'm free from a weight I've never been able to escape before. We worked the problem. You got me through it all and out the other side. You shared your world with me when I didn't have one. You made me feel safe and loved and needed and wanted. You have been *beyond* great in more ways than I can count. But..."

"But...?" he asked, guardedly.

"But now the emergency's over," she said, feeling her stomach begin to twist in sick little knots. "You know what happens when the emergency's over, right?"

"I don't think I do," he said, and she winced in response to the worry etched on his face.

"See? I'm already doing it. I'm already messing things up. I fought and fought and fought for weeks now—at the top of my game because I had to be. Everything you've seen of me up to now is the good-parts version—just like the me you know from your games. When you're telling a story or playing a game, you don't deal with all the boring, stupid, petty stuff. It's all excitement and adrenalin and danger and fun and romance and...and...and now that adrenaline's gone.

"Maybe you do think I messed up along the way getting here—actually, I'm sure you do, you're just nice enough to not rub my face in it—but I only get worse from here. Hanging out with me is not going to be some happily ever after with a dream girl who's nothing but magic and sex. I *know* you put me on a pedestal in your games—don't try to deny it—but I can't stay up there. It's time for me to come down now. I'm just going to be bland little Lenore doing all the bland little Lenore things no one bothered to talk about on game night."

"Are you going somewhere with this?" he asked patiently.

"When I first tried pushing you away, I told Denise it was because I wanted the fairy tale," Lenore said soberly, "but that was only a half-truth. I do want it—the same way I want galactic peace and universal happiness. They're such pretty dreams, but I know they don't happen. Not...not like they happen in stories. The world doesn't become all sweetness and light just because you vanquish one wicked king, you know? It's struggle. It's always, always struggle with just these little islands of—"

She didn't see him move. One moment there were two long paces between them, the next he had one hand on her collar, the other on her back, pulling her into a deep and desperate kiss that literally took her breath away and left her gasping for air when it finally broke.

"You're not scaring me," he growled softly. "Not one little bit. Go ahead: step off your pedestal. I dare you. Bring on the boring stuff. I'd love to have more boring in my life. Bring on your second- and third-string performances. They'll remind me I don't have to be perfect either—that I'm not always on stage. It all sounds glorious." He held her gaze as the growl dropped out of his voice, his tone going smooth and gentle. "You are right: I don't know everything about you. But I want to. I know you well enough to know that much. So...where does that leave us?"

She wrapped her hands behind his neck and pulled him into another desperate kiss. She had no idea how long it lasted, just that it ended all too soon—even though she found herself panting again when they broke away. "Home," she whispered.

Other Titles in the
FREYJUR FANTASIES

Book One
LEARNING TO SPELL

978-1-7355525-6-9

"Three dimensional characters that come to life on the pages and...a quick, entertaining read. The writing is so cohesive that it can be all consuming, leaving you not wanting to put it down."
—**PAR, GoodReads review**

9 781956 243024